Praise for the Peggy Lee Garden Mysteries

Perfect Poison

"A fabulous whodunit that will keep readers guessing and happily turning pages to the unexpected end. Peggy Lee is a most entertaining sleuth and her Southern gentility is like a breath of fresh air . . . A keeper!" —*Fresh Fiction*

"Another homerun for Jim and Joyce Lavene. A top-of-the-notch, over the fence mystery read with beloved characters, a fast paced storyline, and a wallop of an ending."
—*Midwest Book Review*

"Joyce and Jim Lavene provide a fascinating whodunit with unusual but plausible twists and plenty of red herrings."
—*Genre Go Round Reviews*

"You will enjoy this to no end. Highly recommended."
—*Mystery Scene Magazine*

"Joyce and Jim Lavene have done it again! This book is filled with plot twists and surprises as the story unfolds, taking us right alongside Peggy as she sifts through the clues to unravel the mystery." —*The Muse Book Reviews*

"A story that would be a perfect combination for plant lovers and mystery buffs." —*Mystery Morgue*

continued . . .

Poisoned Petals

"Joyce and Jim Lavene are a fabulous team who create poignant, entertaining mysteries. The investigation is cleverly plotted and potted . . . A delightful botany mystery."
—*The Best Reviews*

"*Poisoned Petals* blends a love of gardening with a well-plotted murder mystery. It's an enjoyable and cozy read, perfectly suited for lounging in the garden on a summer day."
—*The Muse Book Reviews*

Fruit of the Poisoned Tree

"I cannot recommend this work highly enough. It has everything: mystery, wonderful characters, sinister plot, humor, and even romance."
—*Midwest Book Review*

"All the characters are well drawn and cleverly individualized. The botanical information never gets in the way of the story, and the plot is just complex enough to keep the reader in suspense."
—ReviewingTheEvidence.com

"I love the world of Dr. Peggy Lee! The Lavenes have a wonderful way of drawing their readers into the world of well-rounded and sympathetic characters . . . Well crafted with a satisfying end that will leave readers wanting more!"
—*Fresh Fiction*

"The authors do a wonderful job of crafting a mystery that is organic to both Peggy's area of expertise and her personal involvement. Information about plants and gardening is woven seamlessly into the narrative . . . I'm looking forward to much more in this series."
—*The Romance Readers Connection*

Pretty Poison

"A fun and informative reading experience . . . With a touch of romance added to this delightful mystery, one can only hope many more Peggy Lee mysteries will be hitting shelves soon!" —*Roundtable Reviews*

"A fantastic amateur sleuth mystery . . . Will appeal to men and women of all ages . . . A great tale." —*The Best Reviews*

"Peggy is a great character . . . For anyone with even a modicum of interest in gardening, this book is a lot of fun. There are even gardening tips included." —*The Romance Readers Connection*

"The perfect book if you're looking for a great suspense . . . *Pretty Poison* is the first in the Peggy Lee Garden Mystery series, and I can't wait for the next!" —*Romance Junkies*

"Joyce and Jim Lavene have crafted an outstanding whodunit in *Pretty Poison*, with plenty of twists and turns that will keep the reader entranced to the final page. Peggy Lee is a likable, believable sleuth and the supporting characters add spice, intrigue, and humor to the story." —*Fresh Fiction*

"Complete with gardening tips, this is a smartly penned, charming cozy, the first book in a new series. The mystery is intricate and well plotted. Green thumbs and nongardeners alike will enjoy this book." —*Romantic Times*

A CORPSE ❧ FOR YEW

Joyce & Jim Lavene

BERKLEY PRIME CRIME, NEW YORK

THE BERKLEY PUBLISHING GROUP
Published by the Penguin Group
Penguin Group (USA) Inc.
375 Hudson Street, New York, New York 10014, USA
Penguin Group (Canada), 90 Eglinton Avenue East, Suite 700, Toronto, Ontario M4P 2Y3, Canada
(a division of Pearson Penguin Canada Inc.)
Penguin Books Ltd., 80 Strand, London WC2R 0RL, England
Penguin Group Ireland, 25 St. Stephen's Green, Dublin 2, Ireland (a division of Penguin Books Ltd.)
Penguin Group (Australia), 250 Camberwell Road, Camberwell, Victoria 3124, Australia
(a division of Pearson Australia Group Pty. Ltd.)
Penguin Books India Pvt. Ltd., 11 Community Centre, Panchsheel Park, New Delhi—110 017, India
Penguin Group (NZ), 67 Apollo Drive, Rosedale, North Shore 0632, New Zealand
(a division of Pearson New Zealand Ltd.)
Penguin Books (South Africa) (Pty.) Ltd., 24 Sturdee Avenue, Rosebank, Johannesburg 2196,
South Africa

Penguin Books Ltd., Registered Offices: 80 Strand, London WC2R 0RL, England

This is a work of fiction. Names, characters, places, and incidents either are the product of the authors'
imagination or are used fictitiously, and any resemblance to actual persons, living or dead, business
establishments, events, or locales is entirely coincidental. The publisher does not have any control
over and does not assume any responsibility for author or third-party websites or their content.

A CORPSE FOR YEW

A Berkley Prime Crime Book / published by arrangement with authors

PRINTING HISTORY
Berkley Prime Crime mass-market edition / May 2009

Copyright © 2009 by Joyce Lavene and Jim Lavene.
Excerpt from *Ghastly Glass* by Joyce and Jim Lavene copyright © 2009 by Joyce Lavene and Jim
Lavene.
Cover illustration by Dan Craig.
Cover design by Lesley Worrell.

ISBN: 978-0-425-22810-4

BERKLEY® PRIME CRIME
Berkley Prime Crime Books are published by The Berkley Publishing Group,
a division of Penguin Group (USA) Inc.,
375 Hudson Street, New York, New York 10014.
BERKLEY® PRIME CRIME and the PRIME CRIME logo are trademarks of Penguin Group
(USA) Inc.

PRINTED IN THE UNITED STATES OF AMERICA

10 9 8 7 6 5 4 3 2 1

For Pat Long,
publisher of the Weekly Post.
A great editor, gardener,
and friend.

1

Muscadine

Botanical: *Vitis rotundifolia*

These grapes are native to the southern United States. They were discovered by Sir Walter Raleigh, who wrote home of their abundance. The Algonquins called muscadine Ascopa, meaning "sweet berry tree." The Mother Vine is the oldest living vine known, dating from the time of Raleigh, and still grows on the coast of North Carolina. Some vines are male and some are female. Male vines provide pollen but do not produce grapes. Female vines produce flowers that catch the wind-driven pollen from the male vines, and produce fruit.

"YOU STOMPED ON THAT SKULL, Margaret. Mind your feet!"

Peggy Lee pulled her booted foot out of the knee-deep mud and debris. She still couldn't believe she'd agreed to accompany her mother on her outing with the Shamrock Historical Society. One of the first things her mother had done after moving to Charlotte last month was to entrench herself with the local history museum. Somehow, she'd managed to drag Peggy into the group as well.

It wasn't that she didn't enjoy and appreciate history, but plants were more her thing, and she wished she was home in her garden. She looked at some nice, fat cattails as they swayed gently in the afternoon breeze.

"We need you over *here*." Lilla Cranshaw Hughes beckoned her daughter, then lowered her voice. "Please stop daydreaming. You're making me look bad in front of Mrs. Waynewright. You know she won't tolerate *that*."

Peggy slogged away from her mother, her redhead's temper bubbling beneath her calm exterior. Just because her hair was mostly white now didn't mean she didn't get just as angry. *Especially* with her mother. Why she couldn't be more like her pleasant, even-tempered father, she'd never understand. And why her mother always brought out the worst in *her* was a lifelong mystery.

One thing was for sure: She had to find a polite, well-mannered way to get herself out of the historical group with its petty jealousies and problems. She had more important things to do. She had a life her mother's intrusion had disrupted. She was probably needed at the Potting Shed, her garden shop in Center City. But her cell phone, miserable, traitorous wretch that it was, hadn't rung in over an hour. Next time, she'd tell her assistant, Selena, to call her.

Peggy rehearsed over and over what she was going to say to get herself away from her mother for at least an hour. She decided she'd lie, if needed, and tell her that Selena had called, and she had to leave right away. She'd have to call someone to come and get her, since she'd made the mistake of coming out with the group in the museum van. But she wasn't above that, or lying, to get out of this mess, although a fifty-plus daughter shouldn't have to lie to her mother anymore.

"Grab this bucket, Margaret." Lilla shoved a yellow plastic container toward her daughter. "You can at least do *that*. Jonathon will take care of handling the bones and such that we find. You probably aren't trained for that, are you?"

Peggy snatched the yellow container. She wouldn't have

said if she'd trained twenty years for the job. "No, Mom. I'm a forensic botanist. We look at living matter on bones only if we have to. And I hate to tell you this, but Selena just called from the Potting Shed. I have to go back. Something's wrong with a shipment, and she needs me."

It wasn't *too* big a lie, really, Peggy soothed her conscience. Selena *was* having problems with her boyfriend. She pushed aside a low-hanging muscadine vine as she inched through the heavy mud. A trickle of the spring-fed creek still ran under the mud, keeping it moist, making walking through the stuff even more difficult.

"They'll get along without you," her mother said. "We need you here. Have you ever seen such a mess?"

Peggy looked around. The worst drought North Carolina had ever seen had brought lake levels down so low that piers stood five feet above dirt where water had once been. Boats were dry-docked. People who lived in expensive lake houses tried to decide if they should get out before it got worse.

Already many cities in the Piedmont, including Charlotte, were down to less than a three-months' supply of water. The governor and city officials had declared states of emergency, restricting people to lower water consumption and raising the price of the water they used. The governor had challenged the populace to emulate his twenty-six-second showers in the face of the calamity.

Brown grass and dirty cars had become badges of heroism in the area as people did without, trying to wait out the drought. Those with green lawns who secretly watered at night paid the price with stiff penalties such as having their water service interrupted. Stores were emptied of low-flow showerheads, and residents put bricks in their toilet tanks to use less water per flush.

The local wildlife and fish were suffering as well, as the lakes and other water resources dried up in the baking-hot fall sun. Sweltering temperatures added to the problem, causing evaporation and massive fish kills. Deer migrated into the city to find shelter when the leaves fell from the dry trees, and frogs and other amphibians retreated into an early hibernation away from the parched topsoil.

But Peggy thought the strangest thing she'd seen was Lake Whitley. The hundred-acre lake, created by damming Little Whitley Creek, had completely dried up. Besides the expected pieces of old boats and lost fishing poles where the bottom of the lake had been, there were almost a hundred graves.

"It's amazing, isn't it?" Jonathon Underwood was standing beside Peggy as the ladies of the group—Jonathon was the only man present—argued over who was going to take photos of the find. "Who would've thought we'd ever see this village again?"

"Or these graves." Peggy looked up at him. Jonathon was well over six feet. She moved her foot away from a chest cavity separated from the head and arms. "Why didn't they move the graves before they dammed the creek?"

"They did move some of them, actually," he told her. "These were the ones left behind. The state charged the relatives of the dead with collecting them and making sure they were moved to higher ground. These people didn't have any family left to take care of them. Most of the graves are from the early 1800s. As you can imagine, many of their relatives had moved away from the village or died by the early 1900s, when this happened."

Peggy had met Jonathon only that morning when they all set out together for the dry lake. He was a sober, serious man with gentle brown eyes and a boyish mop of brown hair. He was the director of the Mecklenburg County History Museum, and was far more patient with her mother and the other ladies than she'd ever be. "Did you know this was under the lake all these years?"

"Oh, yes. There are maps of the village. You can see over there where the town hall stood." He pointed to what was left of the structure, little more than four partial stone walls. "And over there is where the school was. Whitley Village was one of the first towns in this area to have its own academy. Teachers came here from across the state to train in their profession, then went on to other schools."

There was even less of the impressive academy left. The gray stones were nearly buried in the mud and debris that had covered them for more than a century. "If this place was so important, why did they cover it up? Why not move it?"

"People were eager for the wealth that electricity would bring to the area." Jonathon shrugged his shoulders beneath a green T-shirt. "In comparison, history and schooling didn't mean very much."

"So now you reap what you can find out here." Peggy looked at the scattered bones and upended wooden coffins that filled the mud around them. "What will happen to the bones?"

"Your mother and the other ladies will make sure they get a proper burial. Mrs. Waynewright is cataloging the bones as we take them out." He waved to the senior member of the historical society, cheerfully referred to by the other members as the Iron Matron. She didn't wave back. She was seated on the heavy moss that covered the sides of the lake, a large ledger in her lap. "Most of the graves that were moved earlier are located in a cemetery over there in the woods. These new remains will be added to that cemetery." Jonathon looked at Peggy across the top of his wire-rimmed glasses. "Did I hear you say you're trained as a forensic botanist?"

"Yes, she is." Lilla stepped into the conversation. "She taught botany at Queens University for many years. Her specialty is botanical poisons. Now she helps the police and the sheriff's office investigate crimes. Except when she's running that little garden shop of hers."

"You're very accomplished." Jonathon grinned. "I took

the six-week course in Raleigh and sometimes work with the police as a forensic historian."

"Really?" Peggy's mother slipped her hand through his arm. "You're very accomplished as well, Jonathon. Just what does a forensic historian do?"

"Well, it's similar to being a forensic botanist," he explained. "I help discover and sort historical evidence the police can use from a crime scene. I imagine I get a lot fewer calls than Dr. Lee. There aren't many crimes that involve historical artifacts."

"Please, call her Peggy." Lilla smiled and patted his arm. "She's a very good cook, too. And she lives in an estate on Queens Road. It's not actually hers. It belongs to her late husband's family, but she can live there as long as she likes. Where do you live, Jonathon?"

Peggy felt the slight bubbling of her temper turn into a full boil. *What was she doing?* It was obvious. Only her mother would think of setting her up with a man she'd barely met!

Her phone actually started ringing in the pocket of her jeans. *Finally!* Grateful for the reprieve, Peggy passed the yellow bucket to her mother and pushed through the bone-littered mud to a rock, where she sat down. "Please tell me something horrible has happened and I have to come home."

"Sounds like you're having a good time with your mother." Steve's voice was edged with humor that Peggy didn't share.

"That's easy for you to say," she told her lover. (She refused to think of him as her boyfriend. It was undignified.) "I'm standing knee-deep in mud full of human bones while the Shamrock Historical Society tries to sort skulls from femurs. How's your day going?"

"As well as can be expected with a malignant mole on a Yorkie and bad canines on a collie. It'd be going a lot better if we'd slept in the same bed last night. My house is empty without you."

Her heart softened toward his bad attempt at humor. "I'm sorry. I wish I could just come out and tell them. But I can't."

"But you're working up to it."

She acknowledged his hopeful tone, imagining his face as he spoke, thinking how much she loved looking into his eyes. Peggy pulled herself back before she began acting even more like a love-struck teenager and reminded herself that her hyperjudgmental mother was standing less than ten feet away.

"I am," she promised. It was a lie, but she didn't think he could tell the difference from her voice.

"Because this can go on only so long," he continued.

"Are you threatening to break up with me because I can't tell my parents we're sleeping together?" She laughed, the humor of the situation hitting her funny bone. "If so, maybe we could sneak out tonight. You could pick me up at the end of the block and we could go to Lovers' Lane."

"I'm glad this is making you laugh. I hope you're laughing when I announce our engagement to your family next Tuesday night at dinner."

She sobered at once. "You wouldn't! You know how my family feels about proper mourning. They'd be very upset." She was putting it mildly. As her mother had just reminded her that morning, no Cranshaw woman had ever mourned her husband for less than five years. It just wasn't done.

"Give me an option or I pop the question."

"Give me a little more time."

"Peggy, it's been a month already. I'm too old to sneak around somebody's parents. Let's think of some way to take care of the problem."

"I will. I promise." She hoped she sounded more sincere than she felt. She might be fifty-three years old, a botanist, and a mother herself, but when it came to confronting her parents with unpleasant news, it was like she was still seventeen.

"What do you mean you're in mud filled with human bones?" Steve asked, as though suddenly realizing what she'd said.

"I'll tell you when I see you." She saw Jonathon and her mother headed her way. "I'll talk to you later. Love you." Peggy closed her cell phone like a naughty schoolgirl and looked up at them with a smile.

"I hope everything's all right." Jonathon looked worried. "I appreciate your help today, Peggy. I know you have a lot to do without helping us find what's left of Whitley Village."

"I was explaining about the Potting Shed and everything else you do." Lilla smiled in a way that let her daughter know she was working on her behalf. "Jonathon has five cats."

"Really? That's interesting." Peggy knew her mother was probably telling Jonathon her whole life story, from winning 4-H ribbons to opening her store. She couldn't convince her that she and Steve had a serious relationship. Lilla was always looking for new suitors for her daughter. It might not be right to get married again just yet, but her mother was looking toward the future.

"Yes." Jonathon took his wallet out of the back pocket of his khaki cargo shorts. "They're my pride and joy."

"Margaret named her dog Shakespeare. I'm not really sure why." Lilla turned to Peggy. "Weren't you thinking about changing his name to something more doglike?"

"No. I wasn't." Peggy smiled at Jonathon to keep from strangling her mother. It had always been this way between them. She'd vaguely thought this historical thing might bring them closer together, now that Lilla was living a few miles away. But she was beginning to think it might drive another wedge between them. Sometimes she wondered how this woman could be her mother.

"I think Shakespeare is a fine name." Jonathon put away his cat pictures. "I enjoy plays and poetry, too."

Peggy didn't know what to say. She didn't want to encourage him along the romantic path her mother had no doubt sent him. He was probably half her age. She could just imagine her words: *She's alone like you, Jonathon. I'm sure the two of you would have so much in common.*

It ended up that she didn't have to say anything. Geneva Curtis screamed and fell backward into the mud. "Everybody come here! You won't believe this!"

Mrs. Waynewright got to her feet quickly, quite spry for her age, to see what was happening while the rest of the group slogged toward Geneva, who was trying to get out of the gooey mess she'd fallen into. They gathered around her, grasping her arms, the thick mud creating suction that popped as it released her. She would've fallen forward if it wasn't for Annabelle Ainsley and Lilla holding her up.

"What is it, Geneva?" The president, Dorothy Myrick, looked around where they were standing, her fists on her ample hips. "Please don't tell me you saw a snake again."

"I didn't see a snake this time," Geneva assured her in a loud voice. "Although a water moccasin is nothing to fool around with."

"There are no water moccasins in this area," Mrs. Waynewright yelled from the shore. "That was probably just a plain old water snake. I'm sure it was more frightened of you than you were of it."

"I doubt it." Geneva's thick black curls shook as she disagreed. "But that's not why I screamed. Take a look over there."

"That's the old post office." Jonathon looked at his map of the village. "One of the few relics we have from Whitley is the post office sign."

"That may be. But there's something in there." Geneva's dark eyes were large and frightened on her chocolate brown face.

Jonathon picked up a sturdy piece of wood from the mud while the women began to fall in line behind him. Peggy couldn't imagine that anything out there could be that ferocious. She fell into step beside him.

"We've had a lot of problems out here with theft," he confided as they advanced on the deteriorating post office. "None of us realized there is a market for human bones. We could afford to hire someone to protect the site only at night. He leaves at first light and goes to his 'real' job. The first week we lost ten skulls and various other bones."

"I've read about that," Peggy said. "Some of the market is for trinkets and the rest is medicinal. People believe powdered human bones are good for them."

"Yes." He glanced at her, then looked away. "Good for male stamina, I understand. You know?"

She smiled as she saw his face turn bright red. He obviously hadn't thought about his explanation before he got started. "It seems odd the black market could reach a little area like Charlotte, but I suppose someone could consider this to be a wealth of material."

"It was right over there." Geneva pointed to the eastern side of the stone walls that marked the abandoned post office. "I was poking around in the mud with a stick, and I saw it."

"Don't leave us in suspense." Dorothy adjusted the colorful scarf that covered her gray-streaked brown hair. "What did you see?"

"I'm not sure."

There was a collective sigh from the rest of the women. Geneva was the youngest of the group, probably in her late forties, and frequently indulged in flights of fancy that included seeing ghosts in cemeteries and imagining the shuffling of leaves as woodland creatures about to pounce on them.

"This is a wild-goose chase," Annabelle mumbled, her round face florid from the sun beneath curly white hair. "We're not going to get anything done if we keep jumping every time Geneva sees or hears a booger."

"There really was something," Geneva defended. "Wait till you see."

Geneva's friend and mentor, Grace Kallahan, pushed through the mud to reach her side. The large black woman, who had been a psychiatric nurse, looked around the group as though daring anyone to say another word. "Don't pay no never mind to them, honey. You saw something that wasn't normal. It won't hurt us to take a look."

Lilla nudged Peggy. "It's always like this. We go out to put shaving cream on tombstones so we can read them, and someone forgets the shaving cream. This is the most unorganized group I've ever been in. It's a good thing I moved here. I think they really need me."

"I'm sure that's true," Peggy agreed. "They seem a little scattered."

"And that's why I wanted you to be a part of the group, too. You're organized and you could get us into all kinds of places. You're a descendant of a Revolutionary War hero, too. Captain Jeremiah Cranshaw would be proud of you joining us."

"Thanks." Peggy had heard about her famous great-great-great-granduncle who'd died in the battle of King's Mountain since she was a baby. It was a great source of pride to her mother's side of the family.

"Is this where you saw it?" Jonathon had reached the side of the post office.

"This is it." Geneva pointed to the mud. "See? There's my stick."

"What I'm curious about is why you screamed and fell over *there*," Annabelle said. "This is a long way from where you were."

"The sheer horror of it hit me as I was making my way back," Geneva explained. "That's why I screamed and fell. It was like a delayed reaction, I guess."

"Very delayed," Annabelle agreed.

Each of the women picked up a stick to poke around in the mud. Grace dropped hers right away when she realized it was an arm bone. Jonathon walked slowly through the area, kicking his feet, hoping to find something.

Peggy stood to one side, watching the group search the thick, brown mud. There were too many of them to find anything. Whatever Geneva saw would no doubt be lost in the traffic. That's why police kept people out of crime scenes.

The dying October sunlight was drifting across the ghost of Lake Whitley. Another day in the search for what remained of the village was over. In all fairness, the group had collected a sizable number of bones and household artifacts that day. They were all piled on the shore near Mrs. Waynewright, who'd covered the find with tarps.

The group knew they were working against time and nature as the active Atlantic hurricane season advanced. One or two good storms could leave this area underwater again, with possibly another hundred-year wait until it was dry enough to salvage.

She glanced down at a spot where the sunlight was gilding across something white in the mud. Absently, she leaned down and touched it with her gloved hand. It was probably another shard of pottery.

What her fingers encountered was soft, pliable. She pushed at it, thinking it might be some form of plant life or even a dead fish. Instead, as she prodded it, the round white surface moved, revealing the face of a dead woman with bright red lips.

2

Weeping Willow

Botanical: *Salix babylonica*

China is the original home of the lovely weeping willow tree. It can grow to twenty-five feet tall and has rough bark. It will grow quickly in a season but does not like drought, though an otherwise dead tree can be brought back to life with a single cutting once the weather turns wet. The tree symbolizes renewal, growth, and vitality.

"CAN ANYONE ID THE DECEDENT?" Mosquitoes and flies buzzed Charlotte Police Detective Al McDonald. He ignored those he could, and swatted at the rest. He held his tattered notebook in one hand while he looked over what had become a crime scene.

He'd addressed the question to the entire group, but with no reply forthcoming, Peggy responded. "She was Lois Mullis. She was supposed to meet everyone out here, but when she didn't show up, they assumed her lumbago had kept her home."

Al glanced up from writing down the information. All eight of the Shamrock Historical Society members stared back at him. They were covered in mud and had various twigs, plants, and other debris on their clothes and in their hair. "Peggy, can I have a word with you?" He nodded at the rest of the group and walked a few yards away to wait for her.

"What do you think is wrong, Margaret?" her mother whispered, a worried line etched into her forehead. "You don't think he thinks any of us did this, do you?"

"At this point, he doesn't know what to think. John used to say you never knew what was happening for at least a day or two. Right now, Al doesn't even know what killed Mrs. Mullis. It may be natural causes. He has to ask these questions. It's part of his investigation."

Peggy knew the routine all too well after thirty years of marriage to a police officer, then homicide detective, for the Charlotte Police Department. John Lee seldom spoke in great detail about his investigations, but she had learned through the years to read between the lines and fill in what he didn't say. Most of the time, she was dead-on.

She was sure it had something to do with her own recent pursuit of criminal investigations. Her part in looking into those happenings was mostly guesswork until her newfound occupation working as a contract forensic botanist for the police. Now the cases she was involved with were more than secondhand information. And she loved it.

Cautioning her mother and the other society members to remain calm, Peggy left them standing by the large brown van with the shamrock logo on it and walked to where Al waited near a beautiful weeping willow tree. "What is it?"

"I feel like I'm questioning my mother's bridge club," he complained. "Where did you find these people?"

She explained about her mother's involvement with the group. "You must've forgotten to take your vitamins today if they're bothering you. Not that I think any of them was involved with what happened to Mrs. Mullis."

"Of course not. What a surprise! Peggy Lee, champion of the innocent, thinking these people could do no wrong."

She raised one cinnamon-colored brow above a bright green eye. "You *are* out of sorts, aren't you?"

Al nodded toward the body, which was being removed from the dry lake. "Do you know *who* Lois Mullis is?"

"Besides being treasurer of the Shamrock Historical Society? No, not really. I met her briefly at our swearing-in party a few weeks ago. She didn't seem like anyone out of the ordinary to me."

"You spend too much time in that garden shop, Peggy. Lois Mullis is the chief's aunt. She gives to every charity in Mecklenburg County, attends every ball, tournament, and society function we have. And she's dead on *my* beat in suspicious circumstances. That means triple paperwork, really bad headaches, and a lot of yelling and cursing. I don't need it. I'm tempted to retire right now."

"Like you could. Mary doesn't want you underfoot at home. And you live for this job. So get over it and figure out what happened."

He laughed, his large frame and broad, black face shaking. "Girl, you're a pistol! I suppose you talked to John like that, too, huh?"

"If he started feeling sorry for himself."

"All right." He pulled out his notebook again. "Who found the body?"

"I guess you could say it was a joint effort. Geneva saw something that made her scream, and we all walked back with her. I saw something white in the mud, and it was poor Lois, bless her heart."

"So you say Mrs. Mullis was supposed to be here today."

"She was. This is the core of the group. I think there's about ten of them altogether, but these seem to be the movers and shakers. Or in this case, bone finders."

"What the heck are they doing out here?" Al looked back at the ghoulish scene of the dry lake and swatted a mosquito on his face. "I mean, is it safe to be out here with all that stuff? Aren't there diseases?"

"Not after a hundred years, or so our local historian tells me. Maybe you know him, Jonathon Underwood? He's a contract forensic historian for the Charlotte-Mecklenburg Police. I guess we're kindred spirits."

"And all these little old ladies are out here digging up these old bones to add to their collection?"

"You could say that. But their collection is as prestigious as you just described Lois Mullis. All of them have relatives who are wrapped into the fabric of the history of this area. Every one of them can trace their roots back to the Revolutionary War and beyond."

"That's fine and good." Al accidentally marked his face with the pen in his hand. "That still doesn't account for us having a dead geriatric socialite out here in the mud."

"I realize that." She reached up and cleaned the pen smudge off his face. Al had been John's partner and an adopted member of their family for many years. "I wish I could say something else to help, but that's all I know. I think you'll find all of these women are as well connected as Lois. It's not going to be easy."

He took a deep breath. "Thanks for your help, Peggy. I'll just dig in like always. You remember how John used to call me the old hunting dog? That's what I am, I suppose."

They walked back to the group, who wore their anxiety on their sweaty faces. Jonathon stepped forward. "I think I should be the one responsible for Lois's death. I organized this trip and knew who was supposed to be here and who wasn't. I never dreamed she was here all the time and we didn't know it. Has someone called her family?"

As he asked the question, another police vehicle joined the twenty or so others already on the scene. But this one was more impressive: a shiny black SUV with a siren and the police chief insignia on the side. The driver swung wide to align the vehicle with the gray hearse, and the occupant of the backseat jumped out. Chief Arnold Mullis ran to the side of the stretcher bearing his aunt's body.

"Here comes trouble," Al muttered. "Excuse me. You folks wait right here. We'll need to talk to each of you about what happened."

Everyone waited until Al was gone, then they formed a circle around Peggy and threw questions at her the way children throw snowballs in the winter.

"This is terrible." Mrs. Waynewright's frown on her eighty-plus face expressed her displeasure. She was a sturdy woman with pale skin and thin, gray hair. "Does that man believe one of us hurt Lois? None of us even knew she was out here, did we?"

"And along those lines," Dorothy Myrick said, "where is Lois's car? She must've driven out here. If we'd seen her car, we would've known she was here."

"Of course!" Grace Kallahan slapped her hands together. "She was kidnapped. Someone probably pushed her into their car and drove her out here. Check the records on her ATM card. Those people always go after the ATM card."

"If they aren't after something else." Geneva lowered her voice dramatically, dark eyes saying what her words didn't.

All the women gasped in dismay, and their hands flew to their faces. "This can't be happening," Grace said. "Not to us. The Shamrock Historical Society has been together for more than fifty years, and *nothing* like this has ever happened to us before."

"We need a lawyer." Annabelle Ainsley's voice was decisive. "Dorothy, isn't your son-in-law the district attorney? He could represent us."

"Don't be stupid, Annabelle," Mrs. Waynewright cautioned. "The district attorney *prosecutes* people! He can't represent us if he's accusing us of a crime."

"Besides, my son-in-law is a corporate attorney, not the district attorney," Dorothy added.

Peggy had heard enough. "No one is being accused of anything yet. We don't know what happened to Lois. She may have had a heart attack and died out here before we arrived. The police are here to figure that out."

"Then where's her car?" Geneva demanded. "She didn't *walk* out here, not with her lumbago. If she drove out here, her car would be here now."

"She's right," Lilla hissed, caught up in the investigation. "We have to find Lois's car."

"But which one?" Grace asked. "Lois had that silver Mercedes, the one with the gray leather trim inside. But she also had that old brown Cadillac she liked so well. The one her husband gave her for her fiftieth birthday. You know the one I mean."

"Would she have driven either one of them out here?" Annabelle questioned. "Don't forget; she was a stickler on keeping her cars clean. Not an easy thing to do right now. Would she have brought either one of those vehicles down here, knowing how dirty they'd get?"

Mrs. Waynewright put her skeletal hand with its plethora of diamond rings on Annabelle's shoulder. "Look! Isn't that Arnie? That poor boy. They were very close, you know. Let's go over and say something to him. He needs all the support he can get right now."

"But the police officer said to stay here," Jonathon reminded them.

"We aren't suspects"—Geneva looked at Peggy—"right?"

Peggy shrugged. "Not as far as I know. They'll want to ask you some questions, so don't go too far."

The words were barely out of her mouth before all of the ladies swarmed to see Chief Mullis. "You think this will be all right?" Jonathon looked at her. "I mean, they have a valid point about Lois's car."

She agreed. "They do. There's no point in speculating

about it. We'll have to leave it to the police. At least for now."

TWO HOURS LATER, a rookie police officer who'd started on the force at the same time as Peggy's son, Paul, dropped her and her mother off at historic Brevard Court. College Street was crowded, but the squad car cut through the traffic like Moses parting the Red Sea.

"Thanks for the ride," Peggy said. "I'm glad things are going so well for you, Allan. I know your mother is very proud of you."

"She'd like it a lot better if I wasn't wearing this uniform," he confessed with a smile. "She wanted me to follow in the family footsteps, you know. Everyone *must* be a lawyer."

"And there's nothing wrong with that noble profession," Lilla added. "I don't understand why men want to play with guns and wear uniforms. Is it the shiny buttons?"

Allan laughed, his face lean and vital beneath his crew cut. "I don't know about other men. It might sound corny, but I wanted to make a difference. I wanted to be out there helping people who really need help."

"You sound like Paul," Peggy intervened. "I'm glad we had a chance to talk. I'll see you later."

Lilla got out on the crowded sidewalk that led to the wrought iron gate opening into Brevard Court. The shops in the courtyard were arranged carefully around the brick walkway that led into Latta Arcade, a turn-of-the-century cotton marketplace upgraded for shopping. The atmosphere between the arcade and the courtyard was relaxed, almost as though it still lingered in a bygone era. Traffic on College and Tryon streets disputed that claim, but even the hectic pace of the city couldn't budge the dose of Southern hospitality the area reflected.

Cheerful red begonias nodded in the warm breezes that swept through the courtyard. Peggy enjoyed seeing them there, survivors of the hot, dry summer. With the drought had come water restrictions, which precluded using any of the precious resource on something as trivial as plant life. She'd circumvented those rules by catching rainwater in barrels located outside her shop and using it to water what she could.

Summer was always hard on garden shops since it was an in-between season. Too late for spring planting; too early for fall bulbs. The drought had made a miserable season even worse as water restrictions forced Charlotte's residents to give up taking care of their plants. Fall wasn't looking much better. They were only a few weeks into autumn, but there was no relief in sight for the area's thirst. Barely two inches of rain had fallen here in the last few months.

"I'm going to call your father and have him come get me." Lilla took out her pink cell phone and pressed speed dial. "I know you'll want to stay here a while. I don't want to take you away from anything."

"Thanks." Peggy barely heard what she'd said. She was focused on getting to the Potting Shed. It had been a trying day since she'd joined the expedition to Lake Whitley at six-thirty this morning. It hadn't improved upon finding Lois's dead body. She just wanted some peace and quiet in her own world.

"I'm sorry I dragged you into all that," Lilla continued as she waited for Peggy's father to pick up the phone. "Who knew that would happen? I never dreamed I'd actually see a dead body that hadn't visited the funeral parlor yet."

Peggy stepped into the Potting Shed and took a deep breath of the sweet air. It was a mixture of plant life, mulch, and fertilizer. The scent teased her nose and was a balm to her troubled spirit.

There was no sign of the summer flood that had forced her to close the shop for a month of renovations. A pipe, probably as old as the shop, had burst, ruining the heart pine floors and damaging the walls and shelves. Good insurance and a lot of help had put it all back together even better than before.

The furniture she'd once carried samples of was gone, no longer part of her stock; she couldn't compete with the Smith and Hawken garden store that had moved in virtually across the street in the Wachovia Atrium. In its place was a large pond, the antithesis of the drought outside. Minicattails were in full bloom alongside heavenly white lotus flowers. They perfumed the shop with their magic.

This was all possible, despite the drought, because businesses were allowed an exemption from water restrictions. It was anyone's guess how long that would last. Everyone was nervous seeing the lake levels drop each day on television.

"So, how was the bone-gathering trip?" Selena Rogers, Peggy's head shop assistant asked from behind the counter. Selena was a striking girl with sun-burnished brown hair and brilliant blue eyes. She worked part-time for Peggy and was the backbone of the retail business. Selena was in her second year of college.

"It was unusual." Peggy didn't want to go into it any further.

"We found a dead body," Lilla blurted out.

Selena stared for a moment, then started laughing. "I'm sorry. Really. I couldn't help it. But it's getting where it's not an outing with Peggy if you don't find a dead body."

"What's so funny?" Sam Ollson came in from the back storage area and took off his gloves. "You guys have all the fun up here while I'm in back shoveling manure."

"I guess Jerry came through with that delivery." Peggy tried hard to change the subject. Selena was right. It was as though dead bodies were attracted to her. Of course, some of that was because of her work with the police. The few times she'd been involved in situations that required her to see a dead person had been out of her control.

"Oh, no"—Selena held up one hand—"you're not getting away that easy."

"She found another one." Sam shook his golden blond hair away from his face. "What happened this time?"

"I don't want to talk about it," Peggy said. "I came here to get away from it."

"Well, *I want* to talk about it." Her mother took a deep breath to do just that. "It was a terrible experience."

Selena grabbed a Coke from the minifridge and settled Lilla on a bench near the pond. "You poor thing. Sit here and tell us all about it."

"They just want to hear the lurid details, Mother," Peggy told her. "Please don't indulge them."

"Hey! We're like the Scoobies," Sam protested. "We've solved a few mysteries with you, Peggy. You can't just cut us off this time."

"There's nothing to cut off," Peggy said. "A poor old woman died in a bad situation. Case closed. Nothing to solve. Could we get back to work before I fire both of you?"

Sam smiled, deep blue eyes twinkling in a perpetually tanned face. He was a giant of a man with a large chest and muscled back from his years working as the head of landscaping for the Potting Shed. "You can't fire me, partner. We have a contract made unbreakable by my attorney-sister."

"You could fire *me*, I suppose." Selena scratched her head. "But I don't think it's very likely. So step aside if you don't want to share the gory details. Spill it, Mrs. H."

Lilla fanned herself with a large seed packet she'd taken from the shelf beside her. "I've never seen anything like it in my life. The poor woman was out in that mud for God knows how long. People poked her because they didn't know what she was. Who could deserve such a fate?"

Peggy excused herself from the drama. Sam and Selena moved closer to hear everything.

It wasn't that Peggy couldn't handle what she saw, and possibly had seen worse. It wasn't necessarily that she felt so bad for Lois. At the moment, she felt worse for herself. Maybe it was selfish, but it had just been that kind of day. Seeing the dead face in the mud amid the hundred-year-old bones of villagers made her feel old and tired. No doubt some time alone and a cup of peach tea would put things in proper perspective. But right now, Selena's laughter was more than she could handle.

She walked through the shop, checking on her plants. Some of them were growing on shelves under ultraviolet light beside their boxes and packages. There were also hydroponic pumpkins and cucumbers spiraling down from the ceiling with their roots above the tender, green vines. The sight of them never failed to impress a customer. She was thinking about adding a few flowering vines, but couldn't let herself use any more water for the shop than she was already using. She recycled and used whatever water would've been wasted, but she felt guilty using more than her share.

The bell on the courtyard door to the Potting Shed rang as it opened. She knew it had to be someone familiar, since the three by the pond never moved or stopped discussing Lois's death.

"Hi, Grandma!" Paul's voice rang through the shop. "Where's Mom?"

"She's back there sulking," Selena told him. "Did you hear she found another dead body?"

"I heard."

Peggy came from the back of the shop and smiled at her son. Paul was tall and lean like his father, John, who'd died while answering a domestic violence call more than two years ago. That was where their likeness ended for the most part. Paul had fiery red hair, like Peggy in her youth, and bright green eyes. He also had her temper, a fact that had put them at odds many times.

"There you are!" He hugged her. "Are you okay?"

"As good as can be expected." She wiped away a stray tear that had somehow formed on her freckled cheek.

"I heard what happened out there. Poor Mrs. Mullis. It had to be terrible for all of you. What were you doing out there, anyway?"

"I was helping your grandmother with her group project of collecting bones for the historical society."

"You didn't tell us that," Sam said. "That makes it even better."

While Lilla explained the importance of collecting the bones from the dry lake, Paul offered to take his mother home. "You look like you could use some time on your own."

She was surprised and pleased by his perception. This from her son whom she sometimes despaired of understanding. Was that how her mother felt about her?

Her cell phone rang, and when she answered, Geneva Curtis was on the other end. "Peggy? We need your help. Something's wrong with what happened to Lois. We don't think it was an accident. We're at her house. Can you come over?"

3

Zinnia

Botanical: *family Asteraceae*

These flowers, which have grown to be tremendously popular in the United States, are native to Mexico, where the Spaniards called them mal de ojos *(ugly to the eye). They were first cultivated in Austria in 1613. In the language of flowers, zinnia means thoughts of absent friends.*

"I THINK IT IS PERFECTLY right for me to come with you," Lilla said. "Even though I wasn't invited, I *was* the one who introduced you to the group in the first place."

"That's fine, Mother," Peggy said for the tenth time since they'd left the Potting Shed. She hadn't been happy about leaving the shop so soon, but her mother had convinced her that the ladies needed her. Unfortunately, there was no foot traffic coming through Latta Arcade. With a sigh, she agreed to close early so Selena could go home and study for a test while she went to meet with Geneva and the other ladies of the historical society.

Paul, who'd made the decision to ride along with them, drove them to their destination in his new Jeep. He was proud of his new toy, even though it went against his mother's beliefs in conservation. He didn't have a problem with the internal combustion engine, a fact his grandfather found perfectly fine.

"So, where are we going again?" Ranson Hughes, Peggy's father, asked from the backseat as he held on to the roll bar. He'd arrived at the Potting Shed to pick Lilla up just as they were leaving. "I thought we were going out to supper with Steve."

"That's next Tuesday, Dad," Peggy reminded him.

"I told you," Lilla began, "we have to go and see the historical group. Margaret found a dead body, and they think there's something at the dead woman's house she should see."

"Then why aren't we going in Paul's squad car?" Ranson laughed. "I think we should have our sirens blazing for this emergency!"

"Grandpa, I told you I can't chauffeur my family around in a car that belongs to the city," Paul said. "My boss wouldn't take kindly to that."

"It sounds to me like you need to have a man-to-man talk with your boss," Ranson replied. "He obviously undervalues you. You could go anywhere and get a job. You could go to Charleston!"

"Not now," Lilla whispered. "We just moved up here to see him and Margaret more often. What good would it do us if he moves back home?"

Peggy put her hand to her sunburned forehead. She was starting to get a headache. It was just the day for it. She wished she could be more concerned about what the Shamrock Historical Society had to say about Lois's death. But she was more worried about the lack of customers at the Potting Shed.

She couldn't afford a massive advertising campaign. The shop had received good coverage on its grand reopening, but that was two months ago and long forgotten. She'd tried to think of nonexpensive ways of getting the word out. But just as she came up with some clever idea, the new drought report was issued. How could anyone make money on something that depended on water right now?

Even worse, the few times before when traffic to the shop had been slow, Sam's part of the landscape business was booming. That was not the case this fall. Many of their regular clients were cutting back on the work they usually had done this time of year. Sam and Keeley Prinz, his helper in all things landscaping, were keeping up with their indoor plantscaping at apartments, offices, and some retail establishments. It just wasn't enough.

All this came on the heels of her decision to give up teaching at Queens University to work as a contract botanist for the police. It was interesting work and she enjoyed the challenge, but it came only from time to time. The shop had been doing so well, she'd felt justified in her decision. Now she was starting to regret it. That gnawing fear she'd felt when she'd first opened the business after John's death was returning.

She looked out at the passing scenery as they drove toward the Plaza-Midwood area of the city. The azaleas were brown and crisp next to wilting oaks drooping in the gas fumes and heat. There were no signs of the colorful flowers that had made the city famous. The drought had driven them all underground to wait for cool, damp weather. How could she expect anything less for her garden shop?

"Are you sure this is the right way?" Lilla scanned the same scenery. "I don't see anyplace that looks like somewhere Lois would've lived. Maybe we should go back to Myer's Park."

Ranson snorted. "You're such a snob! Just because you see some ethnic restaurants and some buildings that aren't exactly in the best of repair, you want to run back to your safe haven."

"I never said that," Lilla countered. "I only meant that I know Lois lived by a country club in a large estate house. I don't think we're going to find that over here."

"As a matter of fact, there are several large estates and the oldest country club in the city behind this façade," Paul told her. "Just wait, and you'll be surprised."

Peggy knew the area well. Several of her friends lived in the Plaza area. She was surprised to see how many people were watering their lawns, despite the drought. The precious crystal droplets shot up in the air across emerald green grass and wet the sidewalk. "They must not know there's a drought."

"They probably have wells like you." Paul smiled at her. "I know you don't water the grass, but it's really no different."

"I suppose you're right, but it seems so flagrant."

Her son laughed at her. "I can't believe you said that! You, who are beyond a doubt the most plant-loving person I know. I'd think you'd be happy to see a little green."

"I am. I just feel guilty with what little bit I do at the house. This makes me feel worse."

Paul was right about the area opening up into older estate houses set on large, manicured lots. The brick and stone fronts faced the street that led to the Charlotte Country Club, which people needed more than money to join. There were probably more historical pedigrees in that single organization than in the rest of the city.

Here the crape myrtles were green and healthy. The flowers on the taller bushes were pink, red, and white, as they should've been; only it was October and summer was gone. The hot weather had kept those plants blooming when they should have retreated before the autumn breezes.

"Oh, look at those zinnias!" Lilla said as they pulled into the Mullis's drive. "What a wonderful display. I wonder who does her gardening."

"That may be an imprudent question to ask at this time," Ranson chastened her. "The woman has been dead only a short while."

"She lived here by herself." Paul turned off the Jeep's

engine and leaned across the steering wheel to look up at the three-story house. "I know that only because I heard some of the guys talking. Chief Mullis was always worried about her being over here alone. His uncle died of a stroke a few years back. He was afraid his aunt would go the same way. Supposedly, she had a bad heart. I guess you never know."

They all looked up at the pink granite façade glittering in the light. The front windows were huge, bowing out from the castlelike walls. It was a house created to last many generations. No doubt there would be another family of Mullises who would move in now that Lois was gone.

Peggy admired the landscaping without shouting her appreciation. The colorful zinnias were only a small part of the whole picture. The design was tasteful, and put together so well that the eye easily followed the clean line from the taller plants and bushes to the shorter ones. The old oak trees that guarded the perimeter were trimmed and well cared for. It was a masterful blend of harmony and function. She wouldn't have minded if the sign in front said MAINTAINED BY THE POTTING SHED.

That was a reminder of another thorn in her side. Sam hadn't gone back to college this fall. Something had happened that made him want to give up becoming a doctor, much to his parents' consternation. She knew how they felt, since it had been only a short time since Paul had dropped out of college to become a police officer. She wasn't happy about it, since he'd shown such promise of becoming a great architect. And she'd been sure he'd done it only as a memorial to his father, John. Or worse, to try and find the man who'd killed him.

She and Paul had gotten through that. Now she felt guilty because Sam had wanted to run the landscaping business full-time. Only there wasn't enough business right now to make the living he'd envisioned. He'd changed the name for his part of the firm they'd both worked so hard at to TPS

'Scaping by Sam. She'd made him her full partner in a business that might be on the way out.

As they sat admiring the house and grounds, one of the four garage doors opened. All the members of the Shamrock Historical Society looked out at them like large owls blinking at the light. Paul got out of the car, and the garage door slammed shut.

"I think you might've scared them off." Peggy got out on her side. "They weren't expecting the police."

"Sorry. I didn't know they were doing something illegal."

"I don't think they are," she argued. "Maybe just a little off-color."

Lilla walked up to the garage door with Ranson and pounded on it. "It's all right. He's my grandson. He isn't here in his official capacity. He just didn't go home and change clothes yet."

"Don't say that, Grandma," Paul hissed. "If they broke into the house, we have a problem. Even though I'm not on duty, I can't look the other way. Especially since this house belongs to the chief's family. Don't promise something I can't hold to."

"Paul, would you please get back in the Jeep?" Peggy asked.

"Mom . . ."

"I promise if there are any desperate criminals in here, we'll let you take care of them. But I think you'll find these women are as well connected as Lois. You aren't going to want to arrest any of them."

"Especially since we have a key!" Geneva called from behind the garage door. "You tell him we have pepper spray, and we aren't afraid to use it."

Dorothy responded, "Don't be ridiculous! You don't use pepper spray on a police officer. Lois hasn't been dead long enough that she won't come and get you for the very idea.

Don't forget her family is five generations of law enforce-
ment."

"Then what are we going to do?" Annabelle asked. "The
fuzz is out there waiting for us."

"I'm feeling a little like Butch Cassidy right now," Grace
added. "Only I don't have a gun to shoot my way out of
this."

"Let's all calm down a minute," Peggy advised. "If you'll
open the door so we can talk, I promise Paul won't bother
you."

Slowly the garage door opened, and Geneva poked her
head under the bottom of it. "All right. We're coming out.
Or maybe you all should come inside. We don't want anyone to see us."

Peggy glanced at her mother and father. "Okay. We'll
come in there."

"I told you that you should've told her to come alone,"
Grace said.

"I would've, but it sounded too melodramatic. Besides,
it's just Lilla and her husband. They won't say anything."
Geneva glanced at the Jeep where Paul kept his distance.
"I'm not too sure about *him*."

"He's my son, despite the uniform," Peggy assured her.
"Besides, what are you so worried about? Did you break
into Lois's house?"

"No!" Mrs. Waynewright smoothed her avocado-colored
shirtwaist dress. "We wouldn't do a thing like that! We had
a key. Lois gave it to us in case she lost hers."

"And there was that time when we were meeting here
and she couldn't get here until after the meeting started,"
Annabelle recalled. "We let ourselves in that day, too. Her
housekeeper was off, and we just went in and got some
cheese and strawberries and went on."

Peggy was impatient with the group not getting to the
point. "And why are all of you here?"

"Because the police won't listen to us. They keep saying Lois probably had a heart attack or something out there at the lake. But how did she get there?" Dorothy drummed her fingers on the smooth silver finish of a late model Mercedes. "Both of her cars are still here. None of us took Lois there. She wasn't planning on meeting us out there, with her lumbago and all."

"But if she *had* gone out there," Geneva started, "she would've driven one of these vehicles. How hard is that to understand?"

"I'm sure the chief has taken that into consideration." Paul's voice was decisive in the closeness of the garage.

Geneva let out a startled yelp. "Who let him in here? Why are you here? You're supposed to be out *there!*"

"Look, I'm not here to arrest anyone or give you a hard time." Paul walked farther into the heart of the group. "I just thought maybe I could explain a few things about our procedures."

Peggy smiled as she recognized her son's carefully modulated crowd voice. No doubt it was the same voice he used when he stopped a speeder. It was strange hearing that tone, the same tone John had adopted so many times, coming out of his mouth.

"That's exactly why we asked Peggy to meet us here," Annabelle told him. "She's as near to the police as we need right now."

"Paul's right." Peggy backed him up. "He knows a lot more about this type of thing than I do." She wasn't sure if it was true, but she didn't want them to panic.

The members of the Shamrock Historical Society who weren't members of Peggy's family huddled together, speaking furiously with dozens of hand gestures before Geneva finally turned around and said, "Okay. He can stay."

"Thanks." Paul smiled at them. "Now why don't you tell me about the problem from the beginning?"

All the voices began at once. Paul stopped them, and

had Annabelle tell the story by herself. "We found Lois dead at Lake Whitley. *They* think she died from natural causes. But she wasn't supposed to be there. She couldn't make it because her back was acting up."

"Lumbago," Geneva interjected with a solemn nod of her head.

"So there we are, looking for bones and artifacts, and we find Lois. She's been dead awhile." Annabelle looked at Peggy. "Wouldn't you say so? I mean, I'm no expert but people don't turn that color right away when they die. My husband was dead awhile before he was that color."

"I agree with you." Peggy thought back to Lois's body. There were several unusual aspects to her death.

"Anyway, Lois went out there before us, even though we'd been out there since seven-thirty this morning. She went into the mud, where she had a heart attack and died. That's what the police want us to believe." Annabelle had a belligerent look on her round face. "Now we want to know, how did she get there? She didn't drive. Both her cars are still here."

"And if she didn't drive"—Geneva couldn't keep from butting in—"how did she get there? And how did her car get back here if she drove herself out there?"

Paul ran his hand across the back of his head. "Have you ladies considered that she might've taken a taxi or had a friend drop her off? I'm sure there's more to this than you know."

"I knew he was going to say that!" Dorothy pushed her blue scarf back on her head. "I knew it. I believe I told all of you what they'd say."

"Hush, Dorothy." Annabelle turned to face Paul. "Young man, I know you're trained to do what you do. But I was Lois's friend for fifty years. We grew up together. I'm telling you Lois would *never* take a cab. Not if her life depended on it."

"All right." Paul acknowledged her argument. "What

about a friend taking her there? Maybe she changed her mind at the last minute and didn't want to bother you. Isn't that possible?"

Mrs. Waynewright had drawn herself up to her full height of barely five feet, and looked as though she planned to give Paul her take on Lois's death. At his question, she fumbled for a handkerchief in her pocket, then conceded, "I suppose that could be what happened."

"If it is, we'll find out." Geneva patted Mrs. Waynewright's shoulder. "Right, Peggy?"

Peggy's head came up fast from her contemplation of the spotless garage floor. "What? I mean, I don't know what else I can do."

"Your mother's told us about your exploits," Dorothy explained. "Of course, a few of us remember reading about Mark Warner and poor Park Lamonte. You helped the police with both of those cases, bless their souls."

"I did," Peggy admitted. "But they were accidental. I work with the police now. I don't know if I can do something like that on the side."

"What you mean is that you *won't* help." Dorothy folded her large arms across her chest.

"Of course she will!" Lilla sailed into the fray and put her arm around her daughter. "Margaret will do everything she can to help us find out what happened to Lois."

"Mom . . ."

"Right, Margaret?"

Peggy heard her father stifling a laugh behind her. The women stared at her, tears in their eyes. Lilla stared, too, but with an earnest, pleading look that reminded her that her mother was desperately trying to fit into this new environment after spending her whole life in Charleston.

"All right." She gave in to the stares and the tears. She knew her mother was trying to impress her new friends. And unfortunately, Peggy could remember what it was like when she'd first moved here with John thirty years ago. "I'll do what I can."

"Thank you!" Geneva threw her arms around Peggy, followed by the rest of the society members until they resembled a Carolina Panthers' Sunday huddle at the stadium.

Paul shook his head with a look on his face that didn't bode well for her helping the group. Her father just seemed to find the whole thing hilarious. Peggy ignored them both, trying not to think about her failing garden shop and the fact that she might have to go back and beg for work at the university again.

"That's settled." Annabelle wiped the tears from her face, leaving a long, brown smudge on her cheek. "What do we do first?"

"I don't know right now," Peggy admitted. "I wasn't prepared for this. You'll have to give me some time to think about it."

"Let me give you my cell phone number." Grace wrote the number down on the inside of a matchbook she had in her purse. As she did, all the other women found something to write their cell phone numbers on as well. "You'll let us know when you have some idea of what to do."

"I will." Peggy shoved all the pieces of paper into the pocket of her jeans.

"If I could say one more thing"—Paul interrupted—"I think I can give you an idea of where to start."

The other women looked at him with skepticism and outright hostility, but Peggy was grateful for any help he could give her. "Where's that?"

"Since all of you knew Lois so well, maybe you'd be the best people to contact her friends and find out if someone gave her a ride to the lake. And if you can't find anyone who took her, that would give you something to go to the police with."

"What a good idea!" Peggy put her hand on her son's

shoulder. "That's *exactly* where we should start. Each of you come up with a list of friends and then cross-reference them. When you have a master list, you can divide it up and contact each person on it. Once we have that information, there may be no need to go any further. If you find someone who took her out there, that might be the end of it."

The women nodded slowly, taking it in. "We'll need your cell phone number, Peggy." Geneva rummaged in her huge purse until she found some paper. "That way we can call you when we find out."

"I have a few business cards with me." Peggy pulled them from her pocket. They were a little wrinkled and muddy, like her, but they'd do. "Call me as soon as you know something."

"What a wonderful idea, Paul!" Lilla commended her grandson. "What would we have done without your help?"

"Yes, Officer Lee." A stern male voice interrupted their soft and fuzzy moment. It was Chief Mullis. "And if I'm not interrupting, what the hell are all of you doing in Aunt Lois's house?"

4

Eucalyptus

Botanical: *Eucalyptus globulus* (also known as Tasmanian blue gum).

Eucalyptus can be a tall evergreen, although many plants never grow more than a few feet high. It is native to Australia and Tasmania. A volatile oil is distilled from the leaves of the plant and used medicinally, primarily for its pungent, anti-inflammatory effects. The plant is a wonderful gray green color that dries well and can be used in floral arrangements. It is believed to be a blessing, repelling evil spirits, when placed by a door.

THERE WAS A GREAT DEAL of foot shuffling, and many glances were thrown Peggy's way. She took a deep breath and prepared to defend their actions, but Paul jumped in an instant before she could speak. "I'm sorry, Chief. I thought it would be a good idea to hear what your aunt's friends had to say about her death."

"So you thought you'd break into her garage to listen?"

"We didn't break in," Geneva enlightened him. "Lois gave us a key."

Grace held up the key with an impertinent glare. "She trusted us. We were her friends."

Chief Mullis shrugged. "I'm sorry. I'm just surprised to find you here. I was afraid someone had broken into the house. I guess I thought it might help make sense of Aunt Lois's death if someone was here illegally."

"You don't think it was natural causes?" Dorothy asked.

"I don't know what to think yet. And neither do you. *Any of you*. It was a shock to find her that way. That doesn't mean she didn't have a heart attack." He smiled at the band of women. "I know she loved all of you. She loved your little historical society. We all want what's best for her now, so let the police do their job. They work very hard to come up with the right answers."

Geneva started to speak, but Mrs. Waynewright nudged her with her elbow. "That's just fine, Arnie. We'll all go home now. Thank you for tending to the situation."

The chief opened the garage door and shook his balding head. "Don't tell me all of you rode over in that Jeep? I can't believe you'd encourage that kind of behavior, Officer Lee. That vehicle was made to seat only five. It must have been well over capacity."

"Don't be silly!" Annabelle responded. "We parked our car down the street a little so it wouldn't be noticed while we were here. Peggy, Lilla and her husband, and this officer came when we called them."

"I don't know whether to be relieved or frightened that you'd think such a thing. You ladies have been watching too much TV." The chief smiled at them as they strolled out of the garage, but he held Paul back. "We need to have a word."

Lilla, Ranson, and Peggy got into the Jeep to wait. "Now he's going to lose his job," Lilla fretted. "I blame myself."

"I blame you, too," Peggy said. "I hope it won't be that bad."

Ranson added, "Paul's doing a fine job for the Charlotte Police. I'm sure they'll take that into consideration."

Paul's face was red when he finally emerged from the garage. He got in the Jeep, slammed the door, and started the engine without speaking. They were all the way to the street before Lilla finally blurted out, "I can't stand it anymore! What happened? Were you fired? Because if you were . . ."

"I wasn't fired," he replied through clenched teeth. "You could say the chief took me down a notch or two. If anything else like this happens surrounding Mrs. Mullis's death, it will be a lot worse."

Peggy sighed. She was almost too tired and dirty to care what happened next. She asked Paul to drop her off at home. The ride from the shop to her house on Queens Road was less and less appealing, especially considering it was rush hour. Charlotte drivers didn't like to share the road with bicyclists.

"Sure." Paul turned sharply on Kings Drive. "What's up with the Potting Shed? It seems really slow. Isn't this your busy season?"

"It should be," she agreed. "But this drought is really hurting business. I'm trying to come up with something clever to bring in customers."

"I suppose the problem is watering what you plant," Ranson said. "You just have to convince people to catch some rainwater for their plants."

Peggy nodded. "I know. But we have to have rain to catch."

"You'll think of something," Paul said. "You always do."

"Any good forensic work coming up?" Ranson almost rubbed his hands in anticipation. He loved being part of Peggy's "cases."

"Don't encourage her." Lilla dampened his spirits. "Why would you want our daughter out investigating dead people? Of all things for a woman to do!"

Peggy couldn't believe her ears. "Weren't you just begging me to help your friends find out what happened to Lois?"

Lilla rolled her eyes. "I wouldn't say *begging,* exactly. I was grateful you were willing to organize them. The poor old things don't know what to do. That's a different kettle of fish from you out there cutting open some stranger who died mysteriously."

Paul laughed. "Sounds the same to me."

"Well, I never!" Lilla refused to look at them as they pulled off Queens Road into Peggy's driveway.

Steve's green Saturn VUE, newly airbrushed with NEWSOME'S ANIMAL CLINIC, was parked close to the house. He was getting out of the SUV and waved to them as he came around to the back door.

"Steve must be here as much as he's home." Ranson chuckled. "I know it's not the cookin'. Must be somethin' else bringing him back."

Lilla perked up when she heard that. "I don't want to tell you how to live your life, Margaret, but people are going to talk if he's here all the time."

Paul laughed. "They must be talking a lot if that's the case. I've been here at midnight and six in the morning when Steve was already here. I think he has a crush on Mom."

"Look at that eucalyptus over there." Ranson tried to change the subject. "It won't take much more. I've never seen a time so dry. Looks like we need a rain dance or two around here."

"We could stop in for dinner," Lilla offered, already opening the door.

"Not tonight, Mom," Peggy said. "I'm taking a shower and going to bed. I might manage to eat some toast on the way. I don't think it's a good night for company."

"Maybe you should tell *him* that." Lilla nodded toward Steve as he approached the Jeep.

"Now, darlin'," Ranson whispered.

"Hey, are you guys getting out or just sitting here?" Steve asked as Paul rolled down his window.

"There appears to be a debate going on about that," Paul told him. "For me, it depends on what's for dinner. Mom says she's having toast and going to bed. Did you have something else in mind?"

Lilla sucked in her breath. "Paul! For goodness' sake! What kind of thing is that to ask?"

Steve laughed. "I wouldn't expect much more than that, Paul." He nodded to Ranson and Lilla. "Hi, there. If you'd like to come in, I'm sure I could scramble a few eggs."

"Presuming there *are* eggs," Peggy corrected him.

"He acts like he lives here," Lilla hissed at her husband in a way that made it clear to everyone what she thought of the idea. "Margaret, you'd better take care."

"I think you're right, Sweet Pea," Ranson told his daughter. "It doesn't seem like a good night to come in. Besides, we're having dinner next Tuesday, right? We'll see you later."

Lilla protested, but was overruled as Peggy got out of the Jeep and Paul started backing down the driveway. "I don't know what she expects from that man! She encourages him to take advantage of her at every turn. Why, if I didn't know better . . ."

Peggy waved as the Jeep sped away, mingling with the heavy traffic on Queens Road. It had been a good idea to let Paul drop her off here. She could barely make her tired body take her into the house. Her father was right about the eucalyptus she'd planted before the drought had reared its ugly head. It was looking pitiful. The twenty-five-room, turn-of-the-century house, built by John's great-grandfather, had a well that had been in place for years before city water had reached the property. But it was a huge yard, and it was hard to keep up by hand-watering everything from the well as much as it needed. The property had remained its original size despite the city building up around it. It was a blessing to have so much green space in the middle of the city, but right now it was also difficult to care for it.

Peggy and John had used the yard to grow experimental plants in the long, warm summers, and had even brought some of her botany students from Queens University there when she'd taught. John had enjoyed gardening, too. He'd planted pecan trees and an apple tree in the backyard between the old oaks. It would've been wonderful to think that Paul would live there someday, but John's nephew would inherit the property when Peggy gave it up.

The house was in trust for the oldest son in the Lee family. It had passed to John but wouldn't pass to Paul, since John's brother, Dalton, had a son older than Paul who was waiting for it. The trust was a good idea, though Peggy wished Paul would be the one to inherit. But maybe Paul's son would inherit one day. There was always that chance. She could only hope the next Lee to live there would enjoy the house and land as much as she had.

"From the look on your face, I'd say they're worth more than a penny," Steve said.

"What?"

"Your thoughts. You looked lost in them." He put his arm around her shoulders. "Is all this mud from this morning?"

"I'm afraid so. You don't want to know what kind of day this has been."

"Is that what you were thinking about?"

"No. I was thinking about the house and the land. Sometimes, I really hate that Paul won't inherit it. I know the trust keeps the land and house from being sold or broken up. But it would be nice to know he'd be here."

"I think you need something more than toast and a strong cup of peach tea." Steve started them walking toward the house.

"Is that your professional opinion?" She smiled up at him, realizing how lucky she was to have him in her life.

"I think you could say that. I am an animal doctor, and technically you're an animal." Excited barking echoed through the house as Peggy's Great Dane, Shakespeare, realized his family was finally home.

"I think he'll have to chase the squirrels in the backyard tonight." She yawned, opening the kitchen door. "I'm too tired to let him drag me down the street."

"You could go upstairs and take a shower, and I'll find something for us to eat," Steve offered.

"Am I that horrendous?"

In response, he put his arms around her and kissed her, mud and all. "Not *too* horrendous. I'll let Shakespeare out."

As they walked into the house, the 160-pound, fawn-colored Great Dane launched himself at them. Steve fended off most of the dog's excitement, but Peggy got her share of licking and jumping. Shakespeare was the first pet she'd ever had, and she was still getting used to living with him. It would've been hard not to love him with his energy and enthusiasm, but sometimes it was challenging living with him.

Peggy didn't argue with Steve taking care of dinner and the dog. It had been a terrible day. Being home in the big, old house helped a little. She checked the soil in the thirty-foot blue spruce that grew in the foyer. It was fine, and digging in the clean dirt was good for her spirits. By the time she walked up the spiral staircase to the second floor, she was humming.

The bedroom she sometimes shared with Steve was a mess. It wasn't that they were so messy, but Shakespeare had claimed this room as his own when she wasn't here. He loved to drag the dirty clothes out of the hamper and play with them around the room. She supposed she could close him out of the room during the day, but they'd made a truce that he could mess up this room and leave the others, especially the kitchen, alone.

Sometimes she thought about redecorating the bedroom and bathroom. They looked the same now as when John died. It was the same bed they'd shared. Once in a while, that bothered her. It didn't seem fair to Steve, and somehow seemed a little disrespectful of John's memory.

She couldn't remember how many times John had climbed out of bed in the morning and gone to look out the big front window at Queens Road to see how the traffic or weather was that day. He'd gotten out of their bed the night he was killed. They'd called him for a domestic dispute even though he was on Homicide. There had been an outbreak of the flu that had kept many officers out sick. The problem was only a block away, and Chief Mullis had asked John to check it out.

"I should be back quickly," he'd said as he dressed. "I'm sure they'll round up some officers to take over. They need someone there now."

Peggy had smiled and kissed him good-bye, then rolled over to go back to sleep. How many times had he been called out in the middle of the night during his years on the force? It wasn't that she never thought anything could happen to him. It was just a knowledge she constantly lived with, underlying their lives together yet rarely surfacing.

An hour later, Al, John's partner, had been at their house. Tears rolled down his dark face as he'd tried to explain what had happened to John. The wife had called in for help when her husband had threatened her. John had tried to reason with the husband, but he'd been shot, dying in Al's arms a few minutes later. The husband had escaped. He'd never been found.

She took a deep, shuddering breath and brought herself back to the present. She didn't want to forget John, would *never* forget him, but she also couldn't dwell in the past. Every time she looked at this room, it reminded her of that night. Something was going to have to change.

Not sure what she was going to do besides resolving to

do something, she pulled off her filthy clothes and jumped in the shower. The hot water and smooth lavender-scented soap made her feel better right away. She wasn't the kind of person who could ignore the past, but she'd made a new life for herself, and it was a good life. Steve was a wonderful man. The Potting Shed, begun from the tragedy of John's death and their dream of owning a garden shop, would survive. Her work with the police was still so new, she wasn't sure how to feel about that yet.

The phone was ringing and her computer was chiming with a message when she emerged from the shower. She ignored both, and wiped a towel across the mirror in the bathroom to clear the steam. Her hair, which had once been as red as Paul's, was now mostly white. It still seemed odd for it to be that color. She supposed that once the mind settled on the appearance of the body, it was hard for it to accept changes. Her face was pink and freckled, some from the hot water and some from the sun. Because of her work outside, she stayed tan most of the year. It worked well with the white hair, she thought, and emphasized her green eyes. There were a few more wrinkles on her face than she wanted to see, but that was the price one paid for getting older.

Steve knocked on the door. "Phone for you. It's Al."

Peggy thanked him and dried off quickly, adrenaline starting to pump through her body, chasing her exhaustion away. Maybe there was a case the police wanted her to look at. It would be unusual for Al to call her about work. Normally she heard from someone in the ME's office. She was probably getting excited about nothing. Mary might want to have her come to dinner one night.

She picked up the phone. "Hi, Al. What's up?"

"I know Ramsey usually contacts you about cases we need you on, but he's in St. Louis at a conference and Mai has her hands full taking his place. Could you come down and take a look at a few things on the Mullis case?"

"Lois?"

"Yeah. It seems it might not be as simple as we thought."

WITH A BRIEF EXPLANATION TO Steve, Peggy ate her scrambled eggs quickly and was ready to go.

"I'll let Shakespeare back in, then I'm going to check on my patients," Steve said. "I'll see you later."

She paused, putting on her light jacket. "Are you coming back?"

"Unless you're coming over there."

"It should be okay. After today, Mom should sleep well. Paul's on duty. It should just be us and the dog." Her heartbeat picked up a notch or two at the thought.

"Sounds good to me. I have some stale donuts I can bring over for breakfast." He slid his arms around her waist and kissed her. "We haven't had *breakfast* together for awhile."

"I don't think it's *breakfast* you're talking about." She smiled and kissed him back. "You never know, I might get ambitious and stop at Harris Teeter for cinnamon rolls on my way home."

"Don't you dare!" He drew back from her. "You get home as soon as you can. Stale donuts will be fine as long as we're eating them together."

She stared into his gold-flecked brown eyes, losing herself in his gaze. "Do you have a book with all the right phrases in it? How do you always know the right thing to say?"

"It comes from loving you," he said seriously, then grinned. "But you're welcome to search me if you think the phrase book is somewhere on my person. We could play good cop-bad cop."

"You mean good forensic botanist-bad veterinarian. Technically, I'm not a cop."

"Whatever works. Just get back here as soon as you can, and let's play."

They kissed again, and Peggy ran out the door. She gazed up at the stars and thanked them for letting her find Steve.

Fortunately, she'd plugged in her electric pickup even though she hadn't planned to use it that day. It was a wonderful invention that allowed her to drive a vehicle without feeling guilty. The only good thing she could see about the price of gas being so high was that the days of the internal combustion engine that had polluted the world were numbered. Being a botanist and a champion of all living things, she worried about conservation and cleaning up the world. Being a scientist, she knew the possibilities existed for better technology than the human race had accepted for too long.

The little red Ford Ranger she and some friends had modified hummed along the crowded city streets. She could remember a time when Queens Road was quiet after six p.m. Not anymore. Even after midnight, there were cars on the road. Traffic had increased along with Charlotte's population explosion. As with any growing thing, there were too many problems and too few answers for what had become her hometown. She'd been born and raised in Charleston, but she didn't think of it as home anymore. Charlotte was where her life and her loved ones were now. Morosely, she assumed it was where she would die.

But not just yet.

There were plenty of lights on at the building which housed the morgue and the ME's office. Plenty of squad cars, she noticed. It must be a busy night. She smiled at the guard and signed in at the door after she'd found a place to park. She hadn't realized that Paul's fiancée, Mai Sato, was in position to take over the office when Dr. Harold Ramsey, the county ME, was gone. It would be much easier working with Mai than with Harold.

At least she thought so until she saw Mai's bloodshot eyes and panicked face. "Peggy! Where have you been? I

had someone call you hours ago! I needed you right away.
Didn't it sound important enough for you to come over?"

Peggy took off her jacket and picked up her white lab
coat. "I'm sorry. I just got the message. What seems to be
the problem?"

Mai ran her hands through her long black hair until most
of it was sticking straight out from her head. "I have three
dead gang members and a man who was hit by lightning
last month whose son didn't think he had to do anything
with the body. And now this Mullis woman—the chief's
aunt, of all things—seems to be a suspicious death. Help!"

5

Passion Flower

Botanical: *Passiflora*

Passion flower, also known as maypop, is a woody vine with flowers, which reminded early pilgrims of the passion of Christ, which is how the plant received its name. Children play with it, creating a dancer from it with a little purple skirt and raised arms. The plant produces small berrylike fruit called granadilla or water lemon. The herb is approved by German Commission E for the treatment of insomnia and nervousness. Passion flower reduces spasms and depresses the central nervous system.

PEGGY MADE MAI A CUP of lemon balm and chamomile tea from the personal stash she kept in the break room. The kitchen area was a little too close to the refrigerated area where they kept the corpses for her taste, but things like that didn't seem to bother the other workers.

"It's been like a madhouse," Mai said as she sat down at the long plastic table. "I think Dr. Ramsey set this up to test me. He doesn't feel like I'm ready to be the medical examiner, even though I'm the assistant ME. He's never going to think I'm good enough or smart enough. Nothing I ever do is enough!"

Peggy looked up as she put a dollop of honey in each cup. "You need to calm down. I know you have a lot on your plate right now, but you can get through this."

Mai wrapped her slender hands around her cup of tea. "How? Nothing makes any sense. I look at the files and I can't see anything except Dr. Ramsey's evil face laughing because I can't handle the office while he's gone."

Peggy sipped her tea. The girl was clearly close to the edge. There had to be some way to bring her back. Mai was a brilliant young woman, not to mention (she hoped) the mother of her future grandchildren. If she couldn't cope with Dr. Ramsey, how would she cope with potty training a two-year-old?

"I don't even have any nails." Mai sighed as she looked at her hands. "I'm surprised I have any hair. I think I was pulling it out this morning."

"How long has Harold been gone?"

"Since this morning." Mai sipped her tea and looked at Peggy. "Pretty pathetic, huh? He's not even gone a whole day and I'm already falling apart. He's not due back from that conference for two more days. I might as well put on a toe tag and crawl into the freezer."

Police humor was something Peggy had grown to understand as she lived with John and listened to him and his friends. Morgue humor was something she hadn't yet learned to appreciate. She could handle being around the dead bodies, if she didn't think about it too much. Talking about them, making jokes about them, seemed beyond what her Southern upbringing would allow.

"You aren't finished yet," Peggy told Mai. Even if she wasn't dating Paul, Peggy would like her anyway. She was sweet and sassy, a nice combination for a young woman. "Just take a few deep breaths and finish your tea. Then we'll talk."

"What's there to talk about? I can't handle it. Dr. Ramsey was right." Mai slumped facedown on the table.

One of their coworkers came in with a pizza and nodded at Mai. "Is she faking it? That could be dangerous around here."

Mai groaned.

Peggy discarded her notions of tea and a friendly chat as the tech, Bosco, sat down and started munching his pizza. "Maybe a walk would do you more good."

"I can't." Mai's voice was muffled with her mouth on the plastic. "I have too much to do."

"It doesn't look to me like you're doing much of it right now." Peggy tugged on her sleeve. "Don't make me get a stretcher."

Mai knew Peggy's determination too well. To avoid being physically dragged from the office, she got to her feet and walked outside with her. "There! We're outside. Things don't look all that different to me."

"Let's walk. It'll do you good."

Still in their lab coats despite strict protocol to remove them before leaving the lab, they strolled down the sidewalk past a dry fountain with beds of half-dead petunias surrounding it. Peggy tried to divert Mai's attention by pointing to the crescent moon. Mai, however, couldn't get past the dead flowers.

"I don't know what I'm doing wrong," Mai lamented. "It's not like I don't know every protocol in the book, plus some. I know how to get the job done. It just seems to pile up on me. I guess I wasn't expecting so much to go wrong so quickly. Couldn't it have been peaceful while Ramsey was gone?"

"Let's see if we can develop a strategy to focus on one thing at a time." Peggy put her hands into her pockets. "Let's start with why you called me."

Mai's smooth, almond-colored brow furrowed. "It's that Mullis woman they found out at the dry lake."

"I found that Mullis woman. What seems to be the problem?"

"She wasn't exactly underwater, but there are all kinds of things in her orifices. I can't tell what they are. So I called you."

"You think they're plants?"

"Maybe. Definitely some twigs and other stuff I'm not familiar with." Mai shuddered. "Why do people feel the need to go out into nature in the first place?"

Peggy laughed. "Nature's not so bad if you keep it out of your orifices. So you want me to take a look at Mrs. Mullis and see if I can identify what you found."

"Exactly!" Mai turned to her. "Hey, this focus thing might be working. I can have George and Bosco work on the gang members. Pretty easy, since they still have the bullets in them. At least that makes sense to me. No twigs and worms and such."

"Do you think Mrs. Mullis died from something other than natural causes?"

"I don't think so. There were elevated BNP levels indicative of congestive heart failure. According to her records, she was on meds for heart problems. You know how it is, though. If this wasn't the chief's aunt and you hadn't found her in the mud, she wouldn't be here."

Peggy explained about Lois's cars still being in her garage and their belief that her death might not be so simple. "There might be something to it."

"Maybe. We'll see if you find anything suspicious. If not, she probably got a ride with a friend. It happens."

They walked back into the lab as the building lights came on outside. "Can that wait until morning?" Peggy asked.

"I don't see why not." Mai shrugged. "She's not going anywhere. The chief won't be satisfied with a quick job; he'll think we didn't take long enough. I'm going to set George and Bosco on those gang guys, and then I'm going home, too."

"Good for you! I'm sure we'll both be fresher in the morning."

Peggy thought about Lois as she waved to Mai and backed the truck out of the lab parking lot. It was sad in many ways that the world turned differently for people who were rich or well-connected. It was probably nothing more than a strange set of circumstances that surrounded Lois's death. And it was humorous in a grim sort of way that Mai found twigs and plant matter disgusting but blood and guts didn't make her blink. The world was a strange place.

Traffic was still heavy on the way back to Queens Road. If she ever got home again, she was taking all the phones off the hook, hiding the cell phones, and shutting down the computers. She just wanted a little quiet time with her favorite veterinarian.

She groaned when she saw her parents' car in the drive. What were they doing here at this time of night?

The answer was too apparent. It was like she was a teenager again and they were spying on her, trying to catch her doing something she wasn't supposed to be doing. It was ridiculous, she thought, parking her truck and plugging it in. She was too old and too tired for these games. She was going to march right in there and tell them she not only was dating Steve but sharing his bed as often as she could. He was right. They should've told them when they first met.

Loud laughter greeted her as she charged through the kitchen door. Shakespeare looked up at her, then hid his head under one paw, as though he knew what was coming.

Steve was sitting at the kitchen table, shaking the Yahtzee cup while her mother and father were challenging him to beat their high score. The words that burned on her tongue fizzled out as they all looked up at her.

"I'm glad you're back, Sweet Pea," her father said. "You're just in time to see us beat Steve at this game."

"It's late." She walked into the kitchen and closed the door behind her, weariness catching up and enveloping her. "I'm going up to bed. You can let yourselves out, if you don't mind."

"That's no way to treat your guest." Lilla glanced at Steve and smiled. "Of course we can see ourselves out, but you can hardly expect Steve to do the same."

"Maybe we should just leave now," Ranson said, "and let these youngsters have some time together."

Peggy was about to tell him that it didn't matter anymore that night when the cell phone she was supposed to turn off, rang. The number on the screen belonged to Geneva Curtis. She sighed as she answered it. There was no rest for the self-employed or the wicked, it seemed.

"We've talked to all of Lois's friends," Geneva said. "No one gave her a ride out to Lake Whitley this morning. There *is* something suspicious going on."

Peggy hardly knew where to start with that information. She explained that she'd be part of the investigation into Lois's death. "If I hear anything suspicious about her death, I'll let you know."

"Thanks. You're a lifesaver." Geneva whispered to someone else, then came back on the line. "We think Jonathon may have been responsible for what happened."

"What? Why would you think that?"

"Because she didn't want to ride out with us this morning."

"I thought that was because of her lumbago."

"I didn't want to say anything, but something happened between them at the last meeting. None of us were in the room at the time, but they acted strange and Lois wasn't herself. She didn't come to the first outing we had at the lake. Grace and I think that might be why."

"I don't know what to say. I'll check into Lois's death. If it was from natural causes, that will be the end of it. I think you're wrong about Jonathon. But we'll see."

"Thanks, Peggy. I knew you were the right one to talk to about it. Give my love to your mother. I'll talk to you later."

The whole time Peggy was on the phone, four pairs of eyes were glued to her. Shakespeare was the only one with good cause to wonder what she was doing; he hadn't been fed yet.

"Like I said"—she turned off her cell phone and put it in her pocket—"that's it for me today. I'm going to bed. I'll see all of you tomorrow."

Steve took the news well and gathered up the Yahtzee game. "I have an early day tomorrow, too. Go on up, and I'll feed Shakespeare for you."

"There's no need for that." Lilla might as well have fluffed out her maternal feathers as she flew to the kitchen cabinet. "Ranson and I will take care of that and lock up before we leave. Thanks for the game, Steve. We'll see you Tuesday night, right?"

Steve frowned but didn't say anything. "Right. Good night, everyone." He glanced at Peggy, then walked out the kitchen door.

"Shakespeare's food is in the pantry, Mom." Peggy tried to work herself up to telling her parents that Steve was where he belonged. "You know, we live in a different age than the two of you were raised in. Things have changed."

"You don't have to tell us," Ranson agreed. "Crazy things going on out there. But not all bad. There's cable TV and remote control."

"What are you trying to say?" Lilla asked.

Peggy stared at them. *Steve and I are living together—or trying to.* But those words wouldn't cross her lips. "Nothing. I'm tired. Good night. I'll set the alarm from upstairs."

There would be another time to explain how her life was at that point. It was possible she and Steve would get married in the future, not that she was ready for that yet. *Was he?* She walked slowly up the marble stairs to her bedroom, hearing the kitchen door close behind her parents.

PEGGY WOKE UP THE NEXT morning with a un-Shakespeare-like arm draped around her. Steve's face was close to hers, dark stubble peppering his chin and cheeks. She was more than glad to see him there, and moved closer to him.

"You're finally awake?" he muttered without opening his eyes as his arms tightened around her. "You were sleeping like the dead when I got back last night. You didn't even know I was here, did you?"

"No. But I'm really happy you are. I've missed you." She kissed him passionately and laughed as he opened his beautiful brown eyes. "I'm sorry I couldn't tell them last night and end this farce."

"That's okay." He smiled at her. "I can sneak in after they're gone. You know, double back after I pretend to go home, and make sure their car is gone before I sneak in through the basement. Lucky thing I know the alarm code."

"It's not as bad as all that," she protested weakly.

"Yes, it is. We have to tell them, Peggy."

"I know."

"Paul, too. I can't believe how many excuses I've had to come up with for being here early in the morning. I've dropped off your dry cleaning at six a.m., told him I was walking Shakespeare for you at ten at night, and I think he's already suspicious because I know how to work the dryer."

"Have I told you yet today how much I love and appreciate you?"

"I don't think you can get away with it that easy."

She kissed him again and snuggled closer. "How about this?"

"That could work. I've always been a sucker for beautiful redheads."

"You can't exactly call me a redhead anymore." She pushed at her white hair self-consciously. "Now, in my youth . . ."

"You're starting to make me forget my commitment not to talk about how hard this has become with your parents and Paul," he warned with a smile. "Let's have a little more of that kissing and stuff right now."

"I can do that."

A LITTLE LATER, after breakfast with Steve, Peggy went down to the basement to check on her experiments. Steve had to leave early since he had surgery that morning. It seemed one of his patients, Conner McCloud, a python, had somehow managed to swallow a stone that would have to be removed. She didn't know how Steve was able to cope with such things, but she knew he had a great love for all animals. He was her own Dr. Doolittle.

It was because of his love for animals that they got together right after she'd found herself with Shakespeare in her life. He was her first pet. She'd taken him from an abusive owner and Steve had helped her nurse him back to health. Because of that, she'd gained so much richness in her life. The two of them had helped her move past John's death.

The basement ran the full length of the house, with French doors that opened into the backyard. Here Peggy had kept plants since she'd moved there with John, fresh out of college. To begin with, it was some herbs and a few early tomatoes. After Paul had moved out, she'd installed a pond and begun working with other botanists from around the world on projects they talked about on the Internet.

Right now, she was observing some high-yield rice plants growing in the pond beside her native lilies and cattails. Her hydroponic gardening had expanded in the last few months to include a new form of bean that was a cross between a pea and a butter bean. It was high-yield and fast-growing to accommodate areas desperately in need of food. The more they could naturally tinker with plants that could feed millions, the closer they came to stamping out world hunger.

Of course there were some plants that were just for fun. She had the beginnings of a lovely, large passion flower vine growing near the windows, in the sun. There was also a grape-colored tomato growing close to it. She planned to surprise some dinner guests with that and a matching lavender lettuce she'd devised.

After being sure all her plants were in good shape, Peggy let Shakespeare inside and set off for the day. It was still early enough that she could ride to the Potting Shed before she had to go to the lab. Being there would make the rest of it easier, she hoped.

Thinking about the Potting Shed made her worry again about what she could do to keep the shop open until the drought passed. She had no doubt the dry weather would go away. It always did. It was tough going for farmers and anyone who relied on good weather and plentiful moisture for their living. She just had to figure out a way to survive until rain started coming regularly again.

She waved to Mr. Stogner, who stood on the corner of College and Fourth streets. He was always out there, walking his spaniel as he ate Krispy Kreme donuts. The little spaniel had such a round belly, she thought Mr. Stogner must share with him.

Peggy loved watching the city come to life in the morning. She'd been raised with the smell of the sea and in a port town atmosphere, but now Charlotte would always be home. It was growing too fast for its own good and losing too much of what was important about living there, but these were only growing pains. She had no doubt the Queen City would thrive and find a way to grow even more beautiful.

Sam was already parked behind the shop, his pickup loaded with fertilizer. She was glad to see he had a job that day. She never had to worry about that aspect of the business, at least about it getting done. There was nothing Sam could do about the weather. The landscaping business was too slow to say they were making a profit, but they were hanging in there. It was nothing a few weeks of rain wouldn't cure. In no time, Sam and Keeley would be swamped the way they normally were in the fall.

"You're up bright and early." Sam came out the back door with a bag of fertilizer on his shoulder. "The store won't be open for two hours. Just come to hang out?"

"I suppose so." She told him about Mai needing her at the lab. "I guess I came to get some equilibrium before I go. That old rocking chair always makes me feel better. I'm glad you convinced me not to get rid of it when we remodeled after the flood."

"I knew you'd still want it to be here." He grinned. "This way you can rock next to your own personal miniwaterfall."

"You and Jasper did a great job on that. I wish we could've kept him on."

"Me, too. But there's not much call for ponds and such right now. Unless we turn into the Sahara down here, I'm sure it'll come back again, bigger than ever."

"Have you heard from him?"

"Yeah. He calls me once a week or so. He's working with his dad right now, and he's not happy about it. I didn't know what to tell him about working with us again. Then it came to me!"

"Oh?" She raised a cinnamon-colored eyebrow. "Did you hear a different weather report than I did?"

"Probably not. But I'm going to need a hand with a new aspect of the landscaping business. I've been reading up on it, and I think it could save us until the drought passes."

"Well, let's hear it."

"I'd like to oblige you, but I'm on my way out to Mrs. Foster's place to fertilize her yard. She's having me plant grass seed and fertilize it. She said she feels rain coming in her bones, and she wants to take the chance. I tried to talk her out of it. Not very hard, but I *did* try."

Keeley pulled her car up beside them, her dark eyes

narrowed as she rolled down the window. "Has he told you his idea yet?"

"No," Peggy admitted. "He's being secretive this morning."

"I promise I'll find you at lunchtime and we'll talk." Sam was halfway in the truck as he spoke. "Come on, Keeley, we're already running late."

6

False Solomon's Seal

Botanical: *Smilacina racemosa*

There are two types of wildflowers with the name Solomon's seal. True Solomon's seal has tiny white blooms that hang down on the stem. False Solomon's seal has feathered white blooms at the end of the stem. Also, false Solomon's seal has reddish purple berries in the fall; true Solomon's seal has green seedpods. Other than that, it is difficult to tell them apart since leaves and stems are so much alike.

PEGGY WALKED INTO THE SHOP through the back door and locked it behind her. It was over an hour before Selena would report for duty. Just enough time to enjoy a cup of tea and sit in her rocker beside the waterfall.

She wasn't able to enjoy her favorite rocking chair as much as she had in the past. She'd thought giving up her position at Queens would give her more time, but instead she was busier.

Some of that was her parents being new to the area. She took them around and showed them the sights as much as she could. After leaving their farm, she knew it would be hard for them to adjust to the city. But even that didn't truly explain her lack of time.

She heated some water on the little electric cooker and took out a tea bag, smelling it as she did. It was orange and spice, her own blend, leftover from the holidays last year. The cooker and teapot were covered in dust, mute evidence of their lack of use. She needed to take stock of her herbal teas as well as her life, and find out how she could spruce them both up.

Finally settled in her rocking chair, Peggy inhaled the aroma of the tea she'd made, sipping it from a Potting Shed cup. The little waterfall cascaded prettily from the rocks in the top pool into the middle and bottom ponds. A few orange koi she and Keeley had saved from certain doom during a wedding landscape project swam in and out through the current created by the waterfall.

She looked around her little shop and was very pleased with the changes brought on by the broken water pipe over the summer. When she'd first opened, she had used what she found there rather than spending money she didn't have on specialized fixtures. Now the shelves were made to hold growing plants as well as seeds and bulbs. The hydroponic garden hanging from the ceiling gave the whole place a wonderful sense of life.

John would have loved it. She sipped her tea and rocked quietly in her chair. This dream that she was living, which sometimes seemed to consume her, would've been heaven for him. Her father loved to garden, but John was even more passionate about it. He could take the sickest plant and make it well. Their love of growing things was exceeded only by their love for each other.

Sometimes she was afraid she had glossed over the rough patches of their marriage and made John a saint. She pushed herself to remember the bad times as well, times they'd argued over his dangerous job or her refusal to quit working at the university. But even in those times, it had been their love that sustained them. She had loved him more in the years before his death than she had when they'd stood before the minister in Charleston to say their wedding vows. She wouldn't have thought that was possible.

There was a loud pounding at the old glass door, which faced the courtyard. Peggy opened her eyes, wiping away tears, and glanced at the wheelbarrow-shaped clock near the door. It wasn't time to open yet. She sneaked a peek around the counter and saw her neighbors from across the cobblestoned way peering into the shop, looking for her.

She wanted to ignore them, but knew Emil and Sofia from the Kozy Kettle Tea and Coffee Emporium never went away that easily. With a sigh for her short-lived peace, she gulped down the rest of her tea and went to answer the door.

Maybe it was just as well she didn't have much time to sit and ruminate if she was going to end up crying and feeling guilty that John was dead. Sometimes she could go days without even thinking about him, thrilled to be with Steve and find her life so full.

Other times, she felt the terrible pain of losing him as though it had happened only yesterday. She didn't know if it would ever be any different.

"Thank God you opened the door!" Emil Balducci pushed his bulky frame through the opening, his well-rounded wife right behind him. He curled his oiled, black mustache and looked around the shop. "You got any problems here?"

"What kind of problems?" Peggy looked around the shop, too.

"Termites!" Sofia put her white Kozy Kettle apron over her blond head and settled her gaze on the ceiling. "They're jumping off everywhere at our place. God forbid it gets like it did that summer in 1962. They ate an entire village to the ground. People with wooden legs had to run for their lives!"

"Not to mention the damage they did to the water supply." Emil proceeded to embellish the incredible tale of the Sicilian village where they'd lived. "We couldn't drink the water for weeks."

"People lay on the ground and died from thirst," Sofia continued. "My Aunt Teresina's tongue got so big, they had to tie it away from her mouth so they could give her something to drink."

Peggy tried hard never to laugh at Emil or Sofia. They believed everything they said, from deadly goldfish that spared their village only because a priest blessed them to relatives who had qualities similar to Paul Bunyan and Babe the Blue Ox. "I haven't seen any termites, but it's always possible."

Sofia pulled a scarf from her pocket. "That's why we brought you this. My cousin used it as an aphrodisiac, but all the termites died when she put it on, so she got out of helping people who couldn't get married and started a business killing termites." She handed the colorful scarf filled with white powder to Peggy. "You spread it around in here, and the termites will stay away."

Peggy took the scarf carefully. "What about you? Don't you need some of this in your shop?"

Emil shrugged his broad shoulders. He looked like a man who had been handsome in his youth, and acted like he had used it to his advantage. But that was a long time ago. "Ah, we called Terminix. We didn't know if you could afford it with business being so bad."

"It's not *that* bad," Peggy protested. "I think we'll get by, even if we have to call an exterminator. But you know, the company we pay our rent to would've sent a termite inspector without you paying for it. It's part of the lease agreement."

Sofia stared at her husband for a long moment before she snatched the powder-filled scarf from Peggy and hit him on top of his black curls. "How many times I have to tell you to read the lease? Now we paid good money we didn't have."

"How was I supposed to know? You said we should do it!"

Sofia smiled at Peggy and patted her hand. "Don't worry about the powder on the floor. I told you it is an aphrodisiac. It might be good for you to bring your Steve down here. You know what I mean?" She waggled her brows up and down.

"I'm going back to finish the baking," Emil declared. "Can I bring you a muffin, Peggy? It will make up for Steve not paying you any attention."

"No, thanks. I have to leave in a few minutes." Peggy wasn't getting into a strange discussion with the couple as to why they thought Steve was neglecting her. She *certainly* didn't plan to talk about their love life.

Sofia shrugged. "Don't worry. You bring him down here. He'll want you."

Emil's laughter bellowed out of his barrel-shaped chest. "He'll want you and every other woman after he gets a whiff of this! Sofia, you stay in the shop when you see him."

Peggy closed the wooden door with the many-paned windows behind them and locked it for good measure. They were impossible. She'd have to think of some way to keep Steve from going over there for the next few days. She shuddered to think what the conversation would be like if they saw him.

By the time Selena came to work, Peggy had taken stock of everything they were low on in the Potting Shed. Some of it they used on a regular basis, like the house plant fertilizer and the new grow lights, but the rest she'd wait for until the stock got a little lower.

"This place looks great," Selena enthused, putting her backpack behind the counter. "And it smells lemony. Not so much like dirt and plants."

"I added a touch of lemon verbena to the floor cleaner. I couldn't believe how dirty the floors were." Peggy gave her a list of things to do if traffic was slow during the day. "Don't worry about any of this if you have customers. But if it's slow like it has been, the shelves could do with a dusting and some reorganization."

Selena glanced at the list. "This could take me a week, even without any customers."

"I'm sure it's not that bad." Peggy put away her rocking chair. "And if you're busy, don't worry about it."

"Does busy include studying for my chem test next week?"

"Not exactly. But you don't have to do all of this in one day, so you can take some time to study, too."

Selena sighed. "What's going to happen to us, Peggy? How is the Potting Shed going to stay open making a hundred dollars a day?"

"I don't know yet. Sam said he has some ideas. Let's hope they're good ones."

"I'll try and come up with some ideas, too. Maybe we can tighten our belts and cut some corners."

Peggy laughed. "That sounds great! Write them down and we'll talk about them." She glanced at the clock on the wall. "I have to go to the police lab. If you need me, call me."

"You know I will. I hope we have a lot of customers, 'cause I really don't like cleaning the shelves."

Peggy left Selena frowning at the cleaning list and drove to the ME's lab a few minutes away. "You're late!" Mai met Peggy at the door to the lab with her white coat in one hand and a file in the other. "You know how important this is. I can't believe you could be late today, of all days."

"I'm sorry. Traffic was bad between here and the Potting Shed." Peggy considered, unkindly perhaps, that Mai needed a tranquilizer. It was only a minute after nine, and they were already walking back to the lab.

"I've heard from the chief three times since seven-thirty. His family wants to bury his aunt by this weekend. He said we better make up our minds about what killed her."

"Did you tell him that's what we're doing?"

Mai shuddered. "Of course not! He's the chief! We have to make a decision about Mrs. Mullis today. I need you to help me do that."

The phone rang and Mai answered it. She held her hand on the receiver and made a face at Peggy. "It's Dr. Ramsey. I guess the chief called him, too. I left all the stuff we took off the body on the worktable. Maybe you could start taking a look at it."

Peggy nodded, glad she didn't have to talk to Harold, and went to take a look at the "stuff." Mai seemed fairly convinced that Lois had had a heart attack. She wasn't sure why she was second-guessing herself.

Of course the information about Lois's cars still being at her house and the ladies from the club not finding a friend who took her to the dry lake was part of the police investigation, not the ME's. Peggy knew she couldn't allow her suspicions on those other matters to color her judgment on the physical evidence.

As far as Geneva believing Jonathon was responsible for what happened to Lois, she felt sure that was simply grief and anger talking. Outside of taking on this project of collecting old bones, the two seemed to have nothing in common.

All of the plant samples Mai had taken from the body were in plastic bags arranged neatly on the long, gleaming metal table. Peggy picked up a marker and a notebook to try to classify what they'd found.

Some of it was simple. There were some blackberry brambles with tiny pieces of fabric caught in them and a stem of purple berries from false Solomon's seal that had been found in her shoes. Most of the botanical evidence was what she would expect to find on anyone who was outside in a rural, forested environment. Nothing special.

Then she came to three small, green seeds. Those took her aback for a moment. She looked at the notation in the folder as to where they were found on the body. For a moment, she stared straight ahead at the spotless, eggshell-colored wall.

The first thing she'd noticed when she'd seen Lois's dead face was that her lips were red. Since it appeared she was wearing eyeliner as well, she'd assumed it was lipstick. Now she wasn't so sure.

"So? What do you think? Anything that could lead to death?" Mai glanced at the collection on the table.

"I'm afraid so."

"I *knew* it!" Mai put her hand down hard on the table. "I don't know why. It wasn't that stuff you told me about her cars. I just knew it!"

"It may not be anything, but these seeds you took out of her mouth are yew seeds. The berries they were probably attached to are deadly poisonous. I saw that her lips were red, but I didn't think about her eating something that colored them."

Mai looked at the green seeds. "I don't get it. They don't look red to me. Do they change color with saliva?"

"No. The seed is almost hidden inside a bright red berry on the plant. They're hard to spot. The berry resembles a blackberry or raspberry. It would take only this small amount to kill her."

"You think she was out there at the lake alone and wanted a little snack? She saw the berries and decided to eat them, not realizing they were dangerous?"

"Did you find any seeds in her stomach?"

"I don't think so. Let's check."

Peggy watched Mai look up the case on the computer. Mai checked everything, but couldn't find a notation of physical evidence that would show them that berries had been ingested.

"I suppose it could be possible she didn't have time to swallow them," Mai suggested. "Could they be that toxic?"

"It's possible, especially for someone who had heart problems."

"So it could still be an accident. Maybe not a natural death, but not a homicide."

"It could be an accident," Peggy agreed carefully. "People, especially children, eat poisonous berries every year. Pokeberries, elderberries, yew berries—they all look harmless enough. Sometimes birds eat them, so people think they can eat them, too. If Lois saw them and ate a few, it could've caused her death."

"We'll have to go back and check to make sure the seeds aren't inside, too." Mai made a note. "But this theory could explain what happened."

"Maybe."

"What do you mean?"

"I've been in touch with Lois's friends from the historical society again. They couldn't find anyone who took Lois to the lake yesterday. They even have a suspect. If they knew about the berries, I'm sure they'd be convinced she was a victim of foul play."

"No way." Mai sat down hard on a stool. "I don't want to know about this. It's not my job. We find the physical evidence on and in the body. That's all. We don't do any outside investigating, except for sending *you* out to look for the yew berries."

"Branches." Peggy shrugged. "All right."

"Really. I mean, that's not our job. The detectives have to check into that other stuff."

"That's fine."

"And why would her friends think this, anyway? She was supposed to be out there with them yesterday."

"She called and told them she couldn't be there because of her lumbago. They weren't expecting her to be there." Peggy glanced at Mai. "To make matters worse, neither of her vehicles was there. I told you how they feel about that."

"Maybe she took a taxi."

"I thought of that. She hated taxis. Her friends said she'd never take a taxi."

"What are you suggesting?"

"I'm not suggesting anything. I'm telling you what they said and what they'll probably insist on telling the chief. I don't know if he'll listen to them. Even if yew berries poisoned her."

Mai stood up again, shaking her head. "No. I won't get involved in this. We have too much to do, and the chief wants results today. We have to give him what we have. We'll have to take another look at the body. There'll be more tests. The detectives have to do their job. That's the way it has to be. Let me know if you find the right branches or berries out at the lake."

LAKE WHITLEY WAS ONLY FORTY minutes from the ME's office. "I don't know how I let you talk me into this," Mai said as she drove. "I have a hundred things to do today, not the least of which involves redoing part of the autopsy on Mrs. Mullis."

"You said we should go and look for yew bushes at the lake." Peggy shrugged. "I thought you meant right away."

Mai glanced at her. "I didn't say *we* should look for yew bushes. I don't even know what yew bushes look like. You're the forensic botanist. You're supposed to go out and take care of these things."

"And I will, but—"

"But you couldn't resist taking a look around at the crime scene," Mai continued. "And for some reason, you wanted me to come along."

Peggy laughed. "Not for some reason. I like you, Mai, and we don't spend enough time together."

"Great! In other words, you want to snoop on Paul and me."

"I wouldn't dream of it. The two of you are coming for dinner on Tuesday, right?"

"Short of an emergency. Or if you keep dragging me off on weird field trips and I never finish my work."

"You'll finish," Peggy assured her. "Paul told me you've decided to paint the house."

"*We* did. Why is that kind of thing always *my* decision?"

"Did I say *you* decided? I meant both of *you*. What color are you doing the dining room?"

"Is this some kind of test? Our house isn't as big as yours, Peggy, so what looks good at your place won't necessarily look good at our place."

"I don't know why you're so upset." Peggy pointed out the turn to Lake Whitley. "I only asked what color you're doing the dining room."

"Rose." Mai looked at her with a belligerent gleam in her dark eyes. "Go ahead. Say it. Paul has said it often enough. Rose isn't a good color for a dining room. A bedroom maybe, but not a dining room."

"I think it's a lovely color for a dining room. Especially since you have those beautiful rose pattern dishes."

"Really? I think it's going to look great. I'm doing the kitchen Sunday Sand and the living room Torrid Taupe."

"That sounds wonderful! I hope Paul's helping you paint."

Mai pulled the ME's van into a spot beside the line of crime scene tape. "Oh, he's helping, or it'll get ugly really fast. We went furniture shopping last week. He didn't want to do that, either. He's such a *man!* Next I think he might want a La-z-Boy and a big-screen TV."

"You mean he doesn't already?"

"Probably. He hasn't said so." Mai's pretty face grew serious. "He said something to me about you and Steve. He's worried about you. He likes Steve. He's just not sure about your relationship."

"I'll tell him when I think he's ready," Peggy said. "It's

been only three years since his father died. I don't want him
to think I'd forget John because I love Steve."

"I think he can handle it better than speculating on
what's happening at your house. He's not a little kid anymore. And he's not stupid. If you don't tell him soon, he'll
catch you guys and confront you. I know you don't want
that."

A knock at Mai's window drew their attention. She opened
it and smiled at the officer on the other side. "We're going
to take another look around."

"Sure thing, ma'am," the officer replied. "Just thought
you should know someone has been out here playing with
our crime scene. We caught this guy a little while ago."

The officer pulled Jonathon closer to the van. The museum director smiled and adjusted his glasses. "Peggy?
Maybe you could tell this man that I wasn't here to disturb
the crime scene."

Peggy thought about what Geneva had said in regard to
his relationship with Lois. "What *were* you doing out here,
Jonathon?"

7

Yew

Botanical: *Taxus baccata*

The yew was the first Christmas plant to be used in Europe, even though its name means sorrow. Sprigs were cut for decoration as we cut holly now, and the tree was the original Christmas tree, brought to England by Queen Charlotte of Germany. Yew has been used as a medicinal plant for centuries and is still in use today. An oil, Taxol, is taken from yew and used for treating breast and ovarian cancer.

PEGGY VOUCHED FOR JONATHON, THOUGH she was reluctant to do so. It seemed odd to her that he'd be out there, apparently alone. Of course she *could* be allowing Geneva's doubts to cloud her judgment. "What were you doing out here?" she asked him again as he accompanied her and Mai to the area where they'd found Lois.

"I didn't realize this was considered a crime scene." Jonathon held back a blackberry bush for the two women. "Why are the police investigating Lois's death? I thought it was obvious she'd died from natural causes."

Mai's dark eyes narrowed. "And what made you think that was obvious, sir?"

"No one would want to hurt Lois. She was the backbone of the group. Besides, those things happen only on TV."

"Not quite," Peggy answered. "Even if there were no suspicious aspects of this death, the ME is required to take a look at anything that's out of the ordinary. Lois may have had a heart attack while she was waiting for the group, but she wasn't exactly at home in her bed."

"I didn't realize. I thought she'd just died, and we'd go on with the excavation." He smiled at Peggy and Mai. "Time nor tide waits for no man. We'll have rain eventually, and everything you see here will be under forty feet of water again."

"I understand your dedication, Dr. Underwood," Mai began, "but we have to clear anyone before they can come into the crime scene. Nothing else can be disturbed until we know for sure what happened here."

"I'm sorry." His large hands went up to his sun-reddened face. "I didn't take much out today. Everything I found is under the tarp over there. I won't touch anything else until you tell me."

Just for the sake of asking the question, Peggy wondered, "Where were you before you picked up the ladies and brought them out here?"

Mai gave her a strange look but didn't comment.

"Am I under investigation? Is there something I should know?" Jonathon glanced nervously back and forth between the two women.

"It's just routine," Mai backed Peggy. "Please answer the question."

"Well, as you know, we got out here quite early. I got up at six, showered, dressed, and grabbed a few protein bars before I left my house to pick up the ladies. I believe I was at Dorothy's house a little before six-thirty, and we were all out here by seven. We picked up Mrs. Waynewright last, didn't we, Peggy?"

She nodded. "My mom and I were together at my house. You were there a little before seven."

"What about before six?" Mai asked.

"I was sleeping." Jonathon shrugged after swatting at a fly. "I slept all night."

"Is there someone who can corroborate your story?" Mai got out her notepad and put on her glasses.

"No. I live alone. I sleep alone. My cats were there with me." He looked at Peggy. "Do I need a lawyer?"

"Not if you haven't done anything wrong," Mai responded. "I'm afraid I'm going to have to ask you to go back to your vehicle and wait."

"Just one more thing," Peggy said. "The ladies said there were some hard feelings between you and Lois. What was that all about?"

"It was something silly. Someone took some artifacts from the museum. I was blamed for leaving the door open, but it isn't true."

"And you think Lois took them?" Peggy found that hard to believe.

"I'd rather not say." He frowned. "It's not good to speak ill of the dead."

Peggy didn't press the point since she wasn't really sure why the ladies found Jonathon suspicious. If he'd accused Lois of stealing something from the museum, she could see where that could cause hard feelings on her side, but not on his. She needed to know more before she could make sense of it.

Jonathon glanced back a few times as he left them, before turning the curve in the path, which led to the dry lake.

"Now would you like to tell me what that was all about?" Mai asked Peggy.

"I don't know. A few of the women in the historical society say he and Lois were having some problems. They think he drove her out here before he picked up the group, and killed her."

Mai's eyes widened dramatically as her pencil scribbled on the pad of paper she held. "Why didn't you say so before?

He could be a suspect if what you're thinking about the yew berries proves to be true."

"I thought of that." Peggy skirted around the edge of where the lake had been. "But I really think it's more likely that Lois got out here and saw the berries, then ate them. It happens all the time. People can't tell the difference between the poisonous berries and the nonpoisonous berries, but they eat them anyway. Thousands of people are poisoned every year that way."

"Why did you question Dr. Underwood if you don't think he had anything to do with it?"

"I guess so I could try to put the ladies' minds at ease. They see murder in this, but I think it's less likely than a tragic mistake."

Mai followed Peggy past the tarp under which the group was preserving what they could find in the thick mud. She looked at the human remains around them and shook her head. "This place could be a nightmare if you're trying to put together any kind of case! Where did all those bones come from?"

Peggy explained about Whitley Village and why the group was out there trying to preserve what they could. "They plan to bury whatever remains they find and keep the artifacts in the museum. You see what Jonathon meant about time being valuable. It won't take a lot to ruin the site for another hundred years."

"Let's take a look at the spot where you found Mrs. Mullis," Mai suggested. "I'd like to get out of here. This place gives me the creeps."

Peggy laughed. "How can it bother you, with everything you've seen?"

"This is different. I see them *before* they get buried. All these coffin parts sticking up, it's like a bad horror movie."

Peggy took Mai to the old post office, explaining they knew the landmarks by the map Jonathon had of the village. "I actually wasn't the first one to see Lois. Geneva Curtis found her, and then we all came over. The mud is a few feet thick in there, and she kept rolling over. Not on her own, mind you. I think she was in the less solid area. There's a small creek running under the mud."

"Have you seen any yew bushes yet?" Mai glanced around her. "I wouldn't know one if it slapped me in the face."

"I've seen a few bushes, but no berries."

"Maybe she ate them all."

"Maybe. They aren't loaded with them, like blackberries or blueberries. Sometimes they don't have any at all. Like any other plant, they have to be mature enough to grow them." Peggy knelt beside the area where Lois's ghastly face had appeared to her.

"So you and this other lady, Geneva, found Lois here." Mai looked at the thick brown mud around what was left of the old post office. "What happened then?"

"We called 911. She looked like she was dressed to be here. I noticed her tennis shoes and jeans. I could tell she was wearing makeup, but the red on her lips was probably berry stains instead of lipstick."

Mai walked carefully along the edge of the shore, looking for anything the police might have missed. Peggy checked the surrounding area for yew bushes. There were several, but none of them had berries. She snipped and saved a few branches. They appeared to have had berries and seeds, which were missing. It might be possible to match the seed to the plant if not the berry.

"I don't see any red berry blotches," Mai told her. "Though I can see where your theory about her eating them could come from."

"The only thing that doesn't make any sense is how she got out here." Peggy sat down on a large rock beside the dry lake and looked across at the small hill that was visible in the middle of where the lake had been. "According to her friends, the taxi idea was out of the question, and none of her other friends or relatives drove her here. Her cars were still at her home."

Mai sat down beside her. "I'd say that doesn't make any sense either, but that's not part of our job, remember? We're just here to speculate on the cause of death. If Mrs. Mullis died from yew poisoning, we can't rule that a natural cause. Then we have to find out if she mistook the plant, as you said, or if someone gave it to her."

"How will we know the difference? It's not like you can examine her and make that decision."

"We'll look again for signs of struggle or bruises that could have come from her being held down and force-fed the berries."

"I'll try to match those seeds to the bushes close by." Peggy glanced at her. "What if we decide she wasn't force-fed the berries? That still leaves the problem of how she got out here."

"We'll file the car information with the detective on the case." Mai shrugged, then stood up slowly, her gaze focused on something in the mud. "Do you see that?"

Peggy looked where Mai pointed. Something gleamed dully in the spotty sunshine. "It looks like metal, but I should warn you, we found lots of bits and pieces of things out here. They have a whole miniwarehouse full of them. Still . . ."

"And maybe it's nothing."

Peggy took off her shoes and rolled up her pants legs. "But it's close to where we found the body. We have to check it out."

"We don't have to do it right now." Mai winced as Peggy stuck her feet in the mud. "We could call a hazmat crew and let them get in there."

"Those little currents of water running through the mud could be a problem," Peggy explained, to keep her mind from wondering what was touching her feet and legs where she couldn't see them. "If we don't grab this now, it could be gone. We'd never find it at the bottom of the mud."

"Is that safe?" Mai asked. "I hope you don't step on something and cut yourself. Dr. Ramsey would kill me if we have to file an OSHA form."

"Thanks for your concern."

"You know what I mean. Just hurry and get out of there. You're making me super nervous, and I'm feeling a little queasy just watching you."

Peggy reached forward and snatched up the gleaming bit of metal. "Got it!" She wiped away some of the mud and looked at her treasure. It was a ring. Hard to tell when it was made. Was it modern enough to be Lois's or one of the other ladies'? Or was it something that belonged to one of the villagers who were long gone?

Not wanting to be in the mud one moment more than she had to be, Peggy held the ring tightly in her hand and waded back to the shore. She let Mai take a look at it as she did what she could to clean up. "What do you think?"

Mai took out an evidence bag. "I think it bears further study." She looked at Peggy. "Now how are we going to get you back to town without having the inside of the van cleaned?"

AFTER A QUICK SHOWER AND a change of clothes, Peggy met Sam, Keeley, and Jasper Wheeler at the Potting Shed. She and Sam had hired Jasper over the summer, before the drought had set in, to work with Sam creating landscape water features. At the time, water features were the hot ticket. As the land dried up, so did landscape ponds and fountains. Mecklenburg County and the counties surrounding it had passed resolutions to do without anything that required extra water.

Peggy had regretted laying off Jasper. He was a nice young man, and they had all worked well together creating the water feature in the shop. But she had to keep the Potting Shed going. She'd also laid off her part-time weekend assistants, Dawn and Brenda.

Now she smiled and waved when she saw the three young people waiting for her on the wrought iron benches in Brevard Court. "Hello, Jasper! It's good to see you again. How's Christie?"

"She's fine," he replied with a ready smile. "She's back in school. Still hanging out with those extreme pollution fighters, but she learned a lot from working with you."

"I'm glad. I'd hoped she wouldn't be angry about everything that happened."

He shrugged. "She's not the kind of person to hold a grudge. Besides, she doesn't blame you for any of it. She blames Sam."

"Me?" Sam jumped a little. "Why me?"

"Because she thinks you were responsible for ratting out the group to the police." Jasper laughed. "Cheer up, Sam. She still wants to go out with you. Who can understand the way a sister's mind works?"

"Hey!" Keeley shoved him. "I'm someone's sister. Don't act like we're all blond."

"Hey!" Sam took issue with that remark. "Let's not get on that 'blonds are dumb' thing, or I'll have to prove they aren't."

"I think we'd better go to lunch," Peggy intervened. "It sounds like all of you have low blood sugar. How about Anthony's? My treat."

They all agreed quickly, and Peggy sent them to the Caribbean restaurant next door while she went to check in with Selena. She was pleased to find her shop assistant taking a Visa card for a few purchases from an urban dweller who had moved into one of the new condos in Center City Charlotte. It wasn't a large purchase, just a few indoor plants, but it made her feel better. They needed much more to stay alive. Rent wasn't cheap in Brevard Court, or any-where else in Center City.

When the customer was gone, Peggy asked Selena how the morning had been. "I've seen better," Selena told her. "What does it take, anyway? Maybe I should dress up like a plant and parade around on Tryon Street to drag in some customers."

"How about we close up the shop for an hour and I buy you lunch next door instead?"

Selena's eyes lit up. "I could go for that. But what if someone comes in and we miss them?"

"They'll come back. Let's go."

Sam saw them come through the restaurant door and waved them toward the table they'd picked out. Peggy wasn't happy to see that Anthony's business was down as well. Normally his café was packed with hungry business-people who spilled out from the banks and other corporate centers. Today, most of the tables in the splashy, colorful restaurant were empty. Maybe it was more than just the drought keeping people out of the Potting Shed.

Before the waiter could reach them, Anthony bounced out of the kitchen. "Never mind," he told the man. "I'll take care of my friends."

"It's good to see you!" Peggy stood up and hugged him. "I haven't been here in a while."

"So that's what's happened to all my customers," he said in his liquid Jamaican accent. "I'm glad there's someone to blame!" He hugged Sam, Keeley, and Selena while they in-troduced Jasper. "I know you! You put that pretty pond in Peggy's shop. I wish I could afford to have you do that here."

"You can't even offer a glass of water unless I ask for it," Selena reminded him. "I don't think the water police would like to see you put in a pond."

Anthony's black eyes widened comically. "You see them?

I haven't seen the water police, but I've heard about them. They dress all in black and come at night to shut off your water. You can't ever get it turned back on if that happens."

"I don't know who you've been talking to," Sam started, "but they're just some guys who work for the city. And they turn your water back on as soon as you pay the whopping big fine they charge you."

"I don't know. I've heard some mighty bad stuff about them. I don't do anything that might bring them here." Anthony shook his head and smiled. "So what can I get you for lunch, minus the water?"

"I'll take the special," Peggy said. "I love the jerk veggie chicken. And I'll have the pineapple mango shake with it. No water. That way we don't have to worry about antagonizing anyone."

The rest of the group had various Caribbean dishes, all with juice or Coke. Anthony thanked them for their order and went back to the kitchen.

"Okay, let's get down to it." Sam grinned at everyone. "I have a way to make some money."

"No melodrama on his part," Selena sniped.

"Never mind." Peggy got between them before the sparring became a verbal battle. They were too much like brother and sister. At one time, she'd thought the two had romantic feelings for one another, but that was before she'd found out that Sam was gay and Selena preferred small, fragile young men instead of Viking giants.

"Jasper came up with a system to grab all the water from the gutters on a house and store it. Then it can be pumped out and used to water lawns and plants."

"Have you tested this?" Peggy was excited about the concept but careful of putting it into practice. It had been a long haul creating a good name for the Potting Shed. She didn't want to jeopardize that out of desperation.

"We have," Jasper enthused. "It works perfectly."

"Yeah," Keeley added. "They waited until the middle of

the night and sprayed water on my mom's roof so it would drain into the gutters. It seems to work."

Keeley's mother, Lenore, was a good friend of Peggy's. "I'm surprised your mother would let them use her water that way."

"She put in a well before the drought started," Keeley explained. "That's why her grass still looks so good while everyone else's is brown and dead. Now the city won't let homeowners put in any new wells. Her garden club hates her."

"But despite all of that rambling," Sam cut in, "the point is that the system works. All we need is some rain to make it viable."

"And some customers," Selena pointed out.

"We already have some of those." Sam beamed. "We contacted all of our regular landscape customers, even those who stopped their service because of the drought. All of them are interested in putting in the system."

Peggy was a little alarmed at how fast this was happening. "You didn't say anything to me about this."

"You made me your full partner and handed me control of the landscape part of the Potting Shed's business." Sam shrugged. "I didn't think I needed your permission. I know this will work, Peggy. Everyone's excited about it."

"Have you installed the systems already?" she asked.

"Not yet. It's going to cost something." Sam sipped his pineapple juice. "I told our customers we'd install it, then bill them."

"What?" Peggy couldn't believe he'd commit them that way, knowing times were hard. "Where are we going to get the money to install the systems?"

"I've worked that out, too. Keeley, Jasper, and I are starting a new part of the landscape service which, I might add, has brought all our old customers back to our roster. We're going to begin dry shrub and tree removal, with replanting at the customer's discretion."

Peggy took a deep breath and digested this news. She trusted Sam, or she wouldn't have given him the landscape business. He'd always been dependable and smart at what he did for them. "Have you considered offering shrubs and trees that are more drought-resistant than what the customers lost?"

Sam grinned and hugged her. "I knew you'd get it! I didn't think about that, but it sounds like a good idea. Can you come up with a list of what would be best for me? I figure once people see what we're doing, we'll increase business instead of losing it like so many other local landscape firms. If our customers' yards look better than anyone else's on the block, regardless of whether or not they have a well, I think we can anticipate some growth."

Selena let out a screech and put down her Coke. "I think Blondie might have an idea there, Peggy! What about giving some workshops on what people can plant that won't require much water? You've got the garden club to start with, and we can advertise from there. That's what people are looking for now, right? Everybody still wants to garden, they just don't know what to do because of the drought."

"I can't believe it!" Sam sat back in his chair. "Selena finally came up with a good idea. I guess all that college is finally paying off."

Peggy was encouraged by the ideas. It was what came of having good people around her. She was about to congratulate them as the food arrived and her cell phone rang. She glanced at the number calling her. It was Geneva. "Peggy, we have to talk. We've considered the consequences, and there's something you have to know about what happened to Lois."

8

Chokeberry

Botanical: *Aronia melanocarpa*

The chokeberry begins its season with white flowers in May, which are followed by large, shiny, dark berries, which are edible and grow for months. The berries have been used to make a tart juice. It can grow to a shrubby six feet tall and has a vase shape. It grows well in bad soil, in sun, or in shade, and does not mind drought. Since it grows rapidly, you do not have to wait long for it to become an impressive, large shrub.

"WE WEREN'T SURE IF WE should tell you about this." Geneva, Mrs. Waynewright, Dorothy, Grace, and Annabelle were huddled together in Geneva's condo in the heart of Center City.

Peggy had agreed to meet them there since it was close to the Potting Shed. She couldn't imagine what was so dire that all the women looked as though the end of the world had come. "Maybe you're right," she said to Geneva. "You should be talking to the police. I work for the ME, which is about as different as a daffodil and forsythia."

"We thought we should talk to you first." Grace poured them each a cup of ginger tea. "After all, the police already know about this. No one has connected it yet to Jonathon's involvement in Lois's death."

Peggy sipped her tea and crunched on a lavender butter cookie. It was really quite good, though normally she didn't like the taste of lavender. "All right. What shouldn't you tell me?"

Geneva glanced at Dorothy. "This happened last fall when we first began working out at the lake," Dorothy said. "We had some of the bones, particularly skulls, stolen by a man who was working for Jonathon at the museum."

"Did you tell Jonathon about it?" Peggy questioned.

"Yes. He said he was going to fire the man." Dorothy closed her eyes briefly, then opened them wide. "We believed him, and he didn't come to the site with Jonathon again. But one morning, Lois and I went out early, by ourselves. There he was, big as day, stuffing those poor people's bones into a cloth bag. I wanted to walk away, but Lois insisted on calling the police."

"What happened?" Peggy wished they'd stop pausing dramatically. This way, it was going to take hours to drag the story out of them. She was anxious to find out what Mai had learned about the gold ring they'd found.

"They arrested him. There was a hearing and Lois testified against him. He went to prison, but he might be out now. If you could've seen the look he gave Lois!" Dorothy shuddered. "I'm telling you, that man could've killed her."

"Where were you?" Peggy asked. "I thought you both were at the lake and called the police."

"Do I look crazy to you?" Dorothy put her hands on her big hips for emphasis. "I went back to the truck so he wouldn't see me. Lois stayed there and pointed him out to the police. He knew she turned him in. Then she insisted on testifying against him."

"So now you think this bone thief killed Lois?" Peggy wasn't sure she could keep up with the number of suspects in a case that truly wasn't a case yet.

"Maybe." Geneva paced the floor and pushed aside the heavy, green velvet curtains to look down into the street.

"What we think happened is that Jonathon is friends with him. He wouldn't even testify against him. He left that up to poor Lois. Together, they may have lured Lois out to the lake and killed her."

Peggy didn't plan on telling them any of the information she'd gathered during what was becoming a long day. They were clearly speculating on what had happened to their friend. "No one knows if Lois's death was an accident or not. The ME is still working on the case. In the meantime, maybe all of you should concentrate on finding out how Lois got out to the lake."

"We have some theories about that," Grace added. "We don't have all the details, but we're working on getting them."

Peggy knew she was going to be sorry she asked, but she had to know. "What are you doing to find the details?"

Mrs. Waynewright, a deep purple beret on her gray hair, held herself very erect and looked across the room at her the way a queen looks at a peasant. Her eyes were steely gray. "It would be prudent *not* to discuss those plans at this time."

The rest of the group agreed with her. "Please, Peggy, can't you talk to the detective on this case and find out what's going on?" Annabelle asked.

"I'll see what I can do," Peggy promised. "I don't know if anyone will do anything without more evidence that Lois was a victim of foul play. But I'll talk to the detective."

THE DETECTIVE IN QUESTION WAS looking at the dark sky as he met Peggy outside the Mecklenburg County Courthouse an hour later. "Looks like we could have some rain." He pulled uneasily at the brown suit he'd worn to testify in court. "I hope so. I haven't been fishing in months with all the lakes closed."

Peggy had left a voice mail on his cell phone and arranged to meet him here. "How about some lemonade?"

Al glanced at her, then at the hot dog vendor close to where they stood. "Since I have a feeling I'm about to get asked for a favor, I'll take a hot dog all the way with that lemonade."

They walked together toward a bench after Peggy bought two lemonades and a hot dog. Their conversation was about Paul and Mai, Al's always imminent departure from the police force, and whether or not there would ever be any decent local fruit again. Between the late spring frost and the drought, there was little to choose from with local produce.

Their relationship was long-standing, and had been through good and bad times in both their lives. Al had once taken a bullet meant for John and had been in the hospital for months, recuperating from the wound. John and Peggy had taken in his wife, Mary, and their two children during that time. There was nothing either wouldn't do for the other.

Peggy explained everything she knew about Lois's death to him. "I know this is probably violating a hundred written rules and about fifty unwritten rules, but the ladies keep telling me this stuff and I can't do anything about it."

Al wiped a mustard smear off his tie with a napkin. "And you think I can? Why didn't you tell Chief Mullis about all this?"

"You should've seen the way he was that night with Paul. I was afraid he was going to suspend him."

"You mean the night you and the ladies broke into Mrs. Mullis's house and Paul was stupid enough to stand around in there with you."

"I guess so." She sipped her lemonade. "There's this question about how Lois got to the lake."

"Just for the sake of argument," Al said, "let's say I know how she got there, and there was nothing out of the ordinary about it."

"Okay." She looked at him suspiciously. "Are you saying that's the case?"

"I'm not saying it's *not* the case." He finished his hot dog and threw the wrapper in the trash can beside them. "I can't tell you anything else. But there's nothing to look into about that. A responsible *family* member took her out there."

With a sudden flash of insight, Peggy sat forward. "Chief Mullis took her out there, didn't he?"

Al rolled his eyes. "I didn't tell you that. But now that you know, you can see why these ladies need to go home and knit something. There's no mystery to solve here. It was a tragic, but natural, death."

Peggy put her empty cup in the trash beside Al's hot dog wrapper as the first drops of rain began to fall on the city. "I don't know if you can consider dying from eating poisonous berries a completely natural death."

The precious moisture began pelting the hot, dry streets and sidewalks. Al and Peggy ran to his SUV and climbed in to get out of the rain. The smell of the downpour on the hot tar reminded Peggy of summer as the heavy rain pushed brown leaves from the drought-bitten chokeberry shrubs around them.

"Do you know that for sure?" Al demanded. "Or is this just speculation?"

"Mai found the seeds in Lois's mouth. She was going back in to look for more. There were berry stains on her lips. I think she either ate yew berries voluntarily or someone forced her to eat them."

Al put his big, dark hands on the steering wheel. "The chief must've dropped her off out there and she got hungry. There's nothing I've seen or heard of that says any different."

"I'm going back to the lab," Peggy said. "I'll let you know if that's true."

"You know the ME's office doesn't investigate beyond cause of death, right?" He yelled as she got out of the vehicle. "We do the why and how. You know that, right?"

Peggy didn't look back or respond to her friend. They

both knew she had crossed an invisible procedure line by
telling him what she knew about the ME's casework so far.
The same could be said for sharing the information she had
from the Shamrock Historical Society with Mai. She was
never exactly a rule-breaker, but she never minded bending
a few rules that didn't make any sense.

Now she knew that Chief Mullis was responsible for
Lois getting out to the lake. That could mean he was the
last person to see her alive. *Hmm.* That disturbed her more
than Lois's disagreement with Jonathon. Al was evidently
unconcerned about that trip to Lake Whitley. How much of
that was blindly respecting a senior officer? Was it possible
Chief Mullis's over-the-top reaction to finding the historical society members in his aunt's house was something
more?

Her cell phone started ringing before she could reach
her truck. It was Steve, but she didn't stop running until she
was out of the rain. It was wonderful to have the rain even
if she still had to spend the rest of the day in her damp
clothes. By the time she answered the phone, he'd left a message saying a surgery hadn't gone well and he might be late
that night. She tried to call him back and got his voice mail.
She closed her phone, refusing to play phone tag.

Peggy sat in the driver's seat for a few minutes, trying to
put all the pieces of the puzzle together. She hoped the ring
would give them some answers, but it might create more
questions. She wanted to think the information she got from
the yew bushes would be definitive, but she'd worked with
botanicals long enough to know they weren't always what
they seemed.

She finally started the truck and pulled out into traffic.
An impatient horn sounded at her. She glanced in her
rearview mirror and wondered what made Charlotte drivers so irritable. The man in the green Volvo glared back at
her and made a rude hand gesture she chose to ignore.

The rain was still chasing pedestrians inside and snarling traffic when she reached the ME's lab. She was glad she hadn't decided to ride her bike today. She didn't mind a little warm summer rain, but the cold autumn variety chilled to the bone.

Peggy looked for Mai after she signed in and found her lab coat. The conference room door was closed, so she took a peek in there. Mai and Harold Ramsey glanced up at her. "Well! Dr. Lee!" Harold said. "Why don't you come in and join us? Perhaps you can help my assistant explain why Chief Mullis found it necessary to call me back early from St. Louis."

Not relishing the idea of joining the two, especially when she saw Mai's glum face, Peggy wanted to back out the door and pretend she hadn't found them. She couldn't do that, of course, so she closed the door behind her and took a seat at the long table.

There were crumbs on the table—pizza crumbs, unless she was mistaken. That would be another thorn in Harold's side if he saw them. It was expressly forbidden to eat in that room. She hurriedly brushed them on the floor.

"Now that we're all nice and cozy . . ." Harold leaned back in his chair. He was a stout, heavyset man who barely fit between the arms of the chair. He had thinning dark hair that he swept forward to cover a bald spot, and wore heavy black-rimmed glasses. "Who'd like to explain what's been going on?"

"I already explained about Lois Mullis," Mai said.

"Shh!" Harold looked at Peggy. "I want to hear what Dr. Lee has to say. No coaching!"

"Harold, I know you're unhappy about being brought home," Peggy began. "But that's no reason to take it out on us. Mai has done the best she could with a bad situation."

"I like team players, but I don't think she's done much of anything with the situation. Otherwise I wouldn't be sitting here. Where are you on the Mullis case?"

Peggy explained about the possibility of yew poisoning

and their field trip to the lake to find the bushes the berries might have come from. "I might be able to match the seeds to one of the bushes. Then we'd know where she got the berries."

"And are you convinced that's what killed the chief's aunt? Because he seems to think you, and I mean both of *you*, have been dawdling. Maybe taking a few too many field trips while his aunt lies in state in our office."

"I can't say for sure," Peggy said. "According to what Mai told me about the cause of death, it could be natural or it could've been brought on by poison berries."

"I assume you told Dr. Lee the same thing you told me about cause of death?" Harold glared at Mai as he got to his feet and began pacing the room with his hands locked behind his back. "Signs of heart attack?"

Mai nodded. "I told her that, but we both felt that finding the berry stains on her lips and the seeds in her mouth at least warranted further investigation. Peggy told me the berries could cause the heart to stop."

Harold's high brow furrowed as he considered what they'd told him. "And your field trip was this morning, is that right?"

Both women nodded. Peggy pushed the pizza crumbs under the table with her foot.

"And have we learned if yew berries were actually the cause of death?"

"I can't tell for sure, sir." Mai swallowed hard. "I sent some blood work to Raleigh, but it might be a while before we know if a toxin was involved. Mrs. Mullis's heart was in bad shape without any poison."

"So it could go either way."

"Yes, sir. Her lungs were in good shape. There was no fluid in them. She was dead before she hit the mud. Without the blood work, I don't know how we'll tell the difference."

"And you found these yew plants near the crime scene, I presume?" Harold questioned his forensic botanist.

"There were plenty of them," Peggy acknowledged. "You see, even though her lips were red from the berries, it's the green seed in the middle of the berry that contains the poison. One seed can kill an adult human. There would be dizziness, possibly vomiting, and heart failure."

"And do we know if the seeds that were found came from those plants at the crime scene?"

"Not yet," Peggy admitted. "I was coming in to look at them, although we don't have the technology here that I need to test them."

"And were you out procuring said equipment and that's what kept you from explaining this to Chief Mullis?"

Mai and Peggy exchanged glances again. "I blame myself for the breakdown in communications, Dr. Ramsey," Mai said. "Normally we don't communicate everything we find to Chief Mullis. We were still working on the case, and I would've given him my report when we were finished."

Dr. Ramsey nodded his head rapidly as he paced, making him look like a tall bird. "That makes perfect sense to me, Sato. I would've done the same thing."

Mai blinked her eyes more rapidly than Harold nodded his head. "Sir?"

"What? I believe in giving credit where it's due. There was no way for you to know that Chief Mullis wanted to be updated hourly on your progress, nor should you have been concerned with making him feel better or getting his aunt out to the funeral home faster. That's not your job. I'll speak to him. You two carry on."

Peggy got up first, too stunned by his words to say anything. The trip to St. Louis must have done him some good. Mai apparently felt the same way, because she didn't speak either. The two women walked quietly to the door and started to leave the room.

"But stop fooling around with this poison berry thing and get me some real evidence one way or the other." Harold had the last word.

Mai and Peggy went to Peggy's workstation. "I know he's hiding something," Mai whispered, glancing over her shoulder as Dr. Ramsey prowled the other side of the lab. "I can't believe he supported what I did."

"You were right." Peggy shrugged. "Why wouldn't he?"

The look on Mai's face answered her question. "We both know why he normally doesn't."

"So did you find any other seeds in Mrs. Mullis?" The question pained Peggy to ask, but she needed to know.

"No. Those seeds I found in her mouth were it. Could they have killed her without her swallowing them?"

"I don't know. I suppose if she'd chewed them, the poison could've been released into her system."

"The lab in Raleigh can probably identify the poison, but it could take months. They're always backed up."

Peggy nodded. "I'll do the best I can matching the seeds to the plants." She held up the plastic bags, which held the seeds. "You can see there's some damage to them. She might've chewed on them."

"Would the effect still be the same?"

"Probably. I'll consult with a few colleagues and have the answer for you. In the meantime, I'll take these seeds to a friend of mine who has the equipment to examine them."

"You can't do that!" Mai's face was suddenly animated. "That would break the chain of custody, and it might make them inadmissible in court."

"I can look at them under the microscope, but I can't make DNA judgments without the proper machinery."

"Let me check on that. There must be someone who has that machinery, so the seeds would still be safe forensically." Mai left to consult with Dr. Ramsey.

Peggy waited, e-mailing a few friends who might've

done more extensive work with yew berries than she had. She especially wanted to speak with Sir Nigel, a British botanist she'd met years ago. Studies had been done in England on using yew berries for various ailments. The problem always seemed to be finding a dosage that wasn't lethal yet did some good.

"I think I have the answer," Mai told Peggy. "Dr. Ramsey said we have a contact at UNCC. He has some equipment you could use. I'll go with you, and we'll do this the right way so the seeds remain in our custody through the process."

Dr. Ramsey put the seeds into a brown envelope, closed it, and sealed it with tape. He put his initials and the date on that seal, then had Peggy and Mai do the same. "Now mind you, use the equipment but don't let anyone else look at the seeds. This lab at the college has been used before. Have Dr. Dillard add his initials when you get there."

"Merton Dillard?" Peggy asked.

"Yes. Do you know him?"

"It's a small botanical world, Harold," Peggy told him. "We've collaborated many times."

"Good. That should make this more efficient. I want an answer by the end of the day."

"I can tell you if these seeds came from these branches," Peggy said. "But it may take a lot longer to know if they killed Mrs. Mullis."

"One step at a time, Dr. Lee." Harold looked at the two women over the top of his glasses. "Why are you still here?"

THE RAIN WAS STILL STEADY on the streets and houses as Mai drove the ME's van down Tryon Street to the UNCC campus on the northern end of town. There were reports of accidents everywhere. No doubt people had forgotten how to drive in the rain, Peggy decided.

They got out on the school campus near the arboretum and greenhouse, Peggy holding the envelope under her purse to keep it dry. Opening the door into the botanical garden was like stepping into another world.

Mai sniffed and put her hand to her nose. "What is that awful stench?"

Peggy sniffed and laughed. "I'd completely forgotten with so much going on. That stench is corpse flower. It must be blooming at last!"

9

Titan arum

Botanical: *Amorphophallus titanum*

This mammoth plant was discovered in Sumatra by the Italian botanist Odoardo Beccari in 1878. The first cultivated garden bloom was at Kew Gardens in 1889 (from seeds sent back by Beccari). The first bloom in the United States was at the New York Botanical Garden in 1937. The plant grows from a large tuber and can reach close to 200 pounds. It is said to be the biggest flower in the world.

"So named for the terrible stench of rotting flesh it gives off." A tall, white-haired man came up and gave Peggy a hug. "A treasure, to be sure!"

Mai moved her hand away from her face long enough to say, "You're kidding me! A flower that smells like rotting flesh? Why would anyone have such a thing?"

"Because they're very rare outside of central Sumatra in Indonesia, where they grow. They've bloomed only a few dozen times in this country since 1937." Peggy smiled at her friend. "Mai, this is Larry Mellichamp, the director of the UNCC botanical garden. Larry, this is Mai Sato, the assistant ME for Mecklenburg County."

"In other words, if this lady thinks Bella smells like

rotting flesh, she knows what she's talking about." Larry laughed, and Peggy laughed with him.

Mai looked at them as though they'd lost their minds. "Do we have to be in here with it to use the flower DNA machine?"

"No, of course not," Larry said. "But I heard you were on your way over here, Peggy, and I knew you wouldn't want to leave without seeing our girl."

"I wouldn't miss it!" Peggy started to follow him into the enclosed garden.

"I'll wait in the car." Mai backed out.

"Nonsense! You'll want to be able to say you saw this," Larry encouraged her. "It may be the only time you have a chance to see the titan arum in all its splendor."

Mai reluctantly followed the two botanists through the garden, the smell getting steadily worse as they got nearer the corpse flower. As they turned a corner, the plant came into view with visitors and photographers appreciating it. "Oh, my God! I can't believe that's a plant!"

"This is Bella. She's six years old. She's young and a little small." They circled the plant, which was easily six feet tall. "Her spadix reached a temperature of a hundred degrees this morning. We expect her to be bigger next time, which may not be for another five or six years."

"This plant probably weighs more than 170 pounds." Peggy was awestruck by the sight. "Those are thousands of flowers hidden inside at the base of the spadix. That's the fleshy central column."

"They look like little red bugs," Mai said. "How big is that flower?"

"The part that looks like an upside-down bell with the burgundy interior, the spathe, usually opens to three or four feet," Peggy said. "This is incredible. I missed a titan arum that bloomed in London a few years back. I had no idea how remarkable it would be!"

"It's almost worth the smell." Mai wrinkled up her nose.

"It doesn't look real. Or if it's real, it looks like it came from another world. But why does it smell so bad?"

"That terrible smell attracts carrion beetles and flesh flies that pollinate it," Peggy explained. "Without it, it wouldn't be able to reproduce."

"There you are!" Dr. Merton Dillard called out when he saw Peggy and Mai. "I had a feeling you couldn't come out here without seeing Bella. She's a beauty, isn't she?"

Mai didn't disagree while Peggy, Larry, and Merton talked about the gigantic flower. There was work to do, however, and Larry promised all of them e-mail photos of Bella the next day.

"You're looking for a needle in a haystack, aren't you?" Merton asked as they left the gardens and walked down the paved paths that led to the central botanical studies area. "Trying to piece together masticated yew seeds with their branches may be impossible."

"We might be able to get something together on it," Peggy said. "It could be important for the case."

"Don't tell me any more!" Merton held up his pudgy hands. "The last time I helped the police, I had to testify in court. I wasn't too happy about that. I don't like large groups of people, especially in stuffy courthouses."

"That won't be a problem," Mai promised. "It would be me or Peggy called to testify."

Peggy was surprised to find Merton working at the lab. She'd started to hug him when she first saw him, then checked herself. She noticed he was still wearing gloves. Merton had come a long way by being out of his house, but he probably wouldn't be interested in that kind of physical contact. The man was obsessed with germs. "I can't believe they got you out to work again."

"Larry lured me here with promises of updated equipment I couldn't afford in exchange for a few hours a week working here. How have you been, Peggy?"

"Just fine, thanks." She glanced at the spray bottle of

Lysol at his elbow. His iron gray hair stood straight up on his head as though glued there.

She reintroduced him to Mai, who attempted to shake his hand. Merton pulled back abruptly. "That's far enough, young woman. I remember you quite well from the last time. What do you want me to look at? I assume someone has killed someone else and botanicals are involved."

Peggy explained what she could about the case. Merton was an outsource. He wasn't supposed to know all the details. It made the study blind, as far as he was concerned. And she was sure he didn't want to know any more. "I just need to know if it looks like these yew seeds could have come from any of these sources." She held out the branches she'd collected from the side of the dry lake.

"Shouldn't be a problem," he said. "I'll give you a call when I've had a look at all of it."

"I don't want to rush you, Merton," Peggy said, "but could you get it done as quickly as possible? We have some time constraints on this case."

"I'll do what I can." He shrugged. "Time takes time."

Again the possible evidence was signed for and resealed so the chain of custody wouldn't be broken. Peggy heard the sound of Merton spraying disinfectant as they left him in the lab. Some things never changed. She couldn't imagine how Larry had managed to get Merton out of his pajamas and his house and back into the lab. The man was a hopeless xenophobe, worried that being around people meant deadly germ exposure.

Mai smiled as she and Peggy bypassed the garden with the titan arum to get back to the van. "That was easier than I expected it to be. Now we can only hope Dr. Ramsey has been able to stall Chief Mullis."

But Dr. Ramsey had not been as successful as Peggy and Mai. He swooped down on them as they came back to the lab, and told them the chief wanted to see them right away. "I apologize. I thought it would be enough that I'm the chief medical examiner. But my absence at the beginning of this case puts you in the hot seat, Sato. He may be willing to hold out another few days if *you* talk to him."

Mai was flustered by the request. "What can I say that you didn't say? I was here, but I don't really know any more than you probably already told him."

Dr. Ramsey nudged her toward the door. "Maybe you can say it differently. Go on. Take your botanical friend with you. Maybe she can find something to say, since this seems to be all her doing."

"I don't mind talking to the chief at all," Peggy said with a smile. "Let's go."

It had stopped raining, but the clouds and dampened atmosphere lingered, creating mist and fog on the streets. The temperature had dropped to a more seasonal coolness that probably wouldn't linger past the next day.

Mai and Peggy talked about the case as they drove to the chief's office. It seemed very simple to Peggy that the chief wouldn't want to bury his aunt before all the possible questions were answered. "Unless he has an ulterior motive."

Mai's face contorted as though she were in pain. "You aren't going to suggest that to Chief Mullis, are you? Just because he drove his aunt to the lake doesn't mean anything. It certainly doesn't mean he was involved in her death. Please, *please* don't say that to him."

Peggy didn't promise anything. It might be good for everyone if the question was asked and answered. That way they could all get beyond how and why Lois was at the lake before everyone else.

They moved slowly through the line of people waiting to be scanned for weapons before entering the police department. Peggy and Mai had left their purses in the van and brought only their IDs inside with them. One man seemed to be having difficulties getting through the metal detector. The officers scanned him several times, and still the buzzer went off. There didn't seem to be anything else he could get rid of that would contain metal, certainly no place he could hide a gun or knife.

Finally they located the problem: a metal clip holding an elastic bandage on his ankle. Once they understood the situation, it was simple to fix and the line moved quickly.

Chief Mullis's assistant, a tired-looking young man with droopy shoulders, met them in the hall as they got off the elevator. "Chief Mullis is in a meeting with Sheriff Bailey. He'd like you to wait in his office. The meeting should be over shortly."

Peggy and Mai took seats across from the huge, cluttered desk. Mai drew in an unsteady breath. "I really don't like this. I don't know if I can be the chief medical examiner if I have to confront people this way. I'm not good at confrontation."

"I hadn't noticed." Peggy smiled at her. "Cheer up. Harold isn't going anywhere for awhile, and you'll get better as you go along. What about that ring we found?"

"It was an old ring. I'm having Bosco look it up on the Internet. Or maybe contact an antiques dealer. I don't know." Mai glanced at the closed door and bit her lip. "David, who does auctioneering on the side, said he thinks the stone is a carnelian. It has some kind of carving on it. It's too dirty to tell exactly what it is, so I'm letting it soak in a cleaning solution."

"Of course it could belong to any of those poor souls who lived and died in the village."

"Or it could belong to the killer."

"Or the victim."

The door to the office opened behind them, and Chief Mullis greeted them as he stepped into the room. "I appreciate you coming by, Ms. Sato." He sat back in his burgundy leather chair and made a pyramid of his fingers as he frowned at Peggy. "I recognize you. You work in the lab?"

"Yes. And I've been helping the Shamrock Historical

Society out at Lake Whitley. I was there when they found your aunt. I'm very sorry for your loss."

He snapped his fingers. "You're John Lee's widow, Paul's mother. You were at the house when those crazy ladies broke in."

It wasn't the way she wanted him to remember her, but she had to acknowledge her involvement. "Yes, I was."

He smiled and sat back again. "John was a good man and a good officer. We worked together several times, coming up through the ranks."

"Thank you." Peggy wanted to change the subject to the reason they were there before Mai fell apart. "I'm also working as a contractor for the ME's office. That's why I'm here."

"That's right! You're the plant person. I can understand why they called you in on this one, although I might question your objectivity, since you're a member of the group and you were on the scene when they found Aunt Lois."

"I can assure you that Dr. Lee is extremely objective," Mai said. "She's worked with us on several cases and her work has always been exemplary."

"That's fine." The chief picked up a manila file folder on his desk. "I said someone could *think* that, not that they did. I don't have a problem with the situation or Dr. Lee, Ms. Sato. My problem seems to revolve around *you*."

"M-me?"

"That's right. I've been looking through your notes, and I don't see any mention of bruising around my aunt's mouth that might be consistent with someone forcing her to eat poison berries."

Mai frowned as she sat forward. "Those are *my* notes. I haven't released them yet."

"I'm the chief of police. The notes don't have to be released for me to see them. Dr. Ramsey was kind enough to bring me everything on this case."

"But we're not finished yet—"

"Unless you have something more than I see in this file, I think you're finished. I see no evidence of foul play. Aunt Lois had a bad heart. She had another heart attack. It's a terrible thing that she had to die out there alone, when she had so many people who loved her." He closed the file and tossed it in Mai's direction. "But sometimes that's the way it is."

"What about the man she helped get arrested?" Peggy jumped in. "How do we know where he is right now?"

"I really don't see any reason to ask where he is," Chief Mullis said. "Unless you're suggesting he was somehow responsible for her having a heart attack, I'd say it's irrelevant to what happened."

"I think there's more to this," Peggy added. "All we're asking for is a few more days. What harm can that do?"

"The harm, Dr. Lee, is delaying Aunt Lois's burial and memorial service. Plus many of those people I mentioned who loved her are concerned about the police holding on to her body. They think there's something wrong, and we can all clearly see there isn't."

"How did it happen that you dropped her off at the lake that morning?" Peggy really didn't mean to ask that question. It just sort of slipped out.

"Excuse me? Are you suggesting I'm somehow involved with what happened to my aunt?" Chief Mullis moved forward in his chair to glare at her. "I think you should leave that kind of conjecture to the professionals. The police department appreciates your help, Dr. Lee. You provide a necessary service. But you're not a police detective."

Peggy felt her temper begin to rise. Why wouldn't the man answer the question if he had nothing to hide? She started to ask him exactly that when Mai put her hand on her arm. "Thank you, Chief Mullis." Mai abruptly got to her feet. "I'll release your aunt's body to the funeral home. I'm sorry for the delay."

Peggy fumed as she followed Mai into the hall. The satisfied look on the chief's face made her even angrier. "What was that all about?"

"I've worked really hard to get here," Mai answered. "I'm not letting something like this knock me back down. I mean, really, Peggy, do you honestly think the chief killed his aunt or was involved in any way?"

They'd stopped walking and confronted each other in the hall, ignoring the people who passed them. "I think your integrity is more important than backing down because the chief doesn't agree with you."

"I asked you not to say that to him." Mai started walking quickly toward the elevator. "I care about what happened to Mrs. Mullis, but he's right. I looked for bruises anywhere on her body that would tell us she'd been physically coerced in some way. There was nothing."

"But we know she chewed on some yew berries," Peggy argued.

"That's true. And it may or may not have caused her to have a fatal heart attack. I don't know if we'll ever be able to say one way or another. But without some reason to suspect that someone forced her to eat the berries, we'd have to conjecture she saw them and wanted to eat them. You said yourself people are poisoned every year by eating something they shouldn't eat. As far as I've heard, Mrs. Mullis wasn't a nature specialist who could identify poisonous berries."

They got in the elevator together. "So that's it?" Peggy asked.

"Unless one of Mrs. Mullis's friends comes up with something else that makes sense." Mai shrugged her thin shoulders. "I can't see anything else to do."

"What about the blood work you sent to Raleigh?"

Mai swallowed hard. "When we get that back, we'll deal with it. I'm not antagonizing the chief about this."

Peggy didn't agree with her, but her arguments were pointless without evidence to back them up. She could only hope Merton came up with something conclusive from the seeds.

They drove back in silence that was neither agreeable nor friendly. Peggy said good night, but there was no response from Mai. She called Steve as she left the lab. She'd already fielded a call from Selena asking if she could close the shop early. There had been only two customers since lunchtime. The rain usually slowed things down, but not so dramatically.

Steve's voice mail picked up. She started to leave a message, then decided against it and went home. When she saw Steve's SUV wasn't in her drive, she parked her truck and plugged it in, then walked to his house. He lived only a few doors down, in another turn-of-the-century house on Queens Road. It wasn't as large or grand as the house that she was fortunate enough to live in, but it was a good, solid redbrick house that would probably stand for another hundred years.

Peggy peeked through the window in the kitchen door. There was no sign of Steve even though it was dinnertime. His Saturn was in the drive, though, so she knew he was here somewhere. She started thinking about his difficult surgery and took out the key to the house that he'd had made for her.

It was still shiny and a little stiff in the lock. She hadn't used it many times. When she stayed with him, she was barraged with phone calls. It always seemed easier for him to stay with her.

She walked through the kitchen and living room. It looked as though no one lived here. Not a thing was out of place, but it was appallingly dusty. A little shaft of sunlight that had dared show itself between the raindrops pointed out a long cobweb that stretched from his TV to the ceiling.

"Steve? Are you here?" she called out as she tried to keep from feeling guilty about being in his house. Her mother would be proud of her. Guilt was an important part of any Southern girl's upbringing. The fact that Peggy could feel guilty about being in a deserted house meant she was in good standing. The irony of why his house was left alone so often wasn't lost on her. She didn't think her mother would appreciate *that* fact.

"Peggy?" Steve came up the basement stairs. "I thought I heard you up here. I guess I had my cell phone turned off. I'm down here with my patient. She's not doing so well."

She went downstairs with him to where he was keeping a small, white dog company. The dog lifted her head at Peggy's approach and whined a little, but she was too sick to make any other effort. "The poor thing. Is this the one you operated on this morning?"

"Yeah. She's had cancer a few times. This time it was in one of her kidneys. But she's a trouper, aren't you, Daisy?" Steve ran his hand down the dog's fur. "I just don't know if she's going to make it this time."

Peggy pulled a chair beside Steve's. "I'll get us something to eat."

"I don't want to leave the house."

"Of course not. But I don't see why we can't eat together anyway. Unless you think Daisy would mind."

"I don't think so." He kissed her. "Thanks."

Peggy smiled, but she knew, as she was going upstairs to order Chinese food, that she'd have to do more than call for take-out. She could give the old house a good dusting while she was at it. Maybe run the vacuum over the carpets. She'd seen a few red roses still blooming at a corner of the house. They were a little leggy, but she could cut a few of them for a vase, if Steve *had* a vase. It was terrible. He knew her house so well, but she knew very little about his home. That was about to change.

10

Black-eyed Susan

Botanical: *Rudbeckia hirta*

This flower has been the state flower of Maryland since 1918. It was named for Olav Rudbeck and his son by the Swedish naturalist Linnaeus in 1753, and coupled with hirta, meaning rough and hairy. It is native to the eastern United States.

PEGGY TIED A KITCHEN TOWEL around her hair after she'd called in the order for Chinese. No telling how long those cobwebs had been there or what was living inside them. She couldn't find a feather duster, so she took out a few more towels and went to work.

The ceiling fans were the worst. It was like gray snow falling on her. She sneezed as the dust came down and wished she had a mask to protect her nose, but kept going. Steve was going to be so surprised when he saw the house!

There was no vacuum. She searched all the closets, but could find only an old carpet sweeper. It would have to do, she decided. The cloud of dust she raised from the carpets made her resolve to buy him a vacuum. Or maybe hire a maid service for him once a week.

The three main rooms were clean, furniture gleaming with polish, when the doorbell rang. She paid the delivery boy, then set the food on the kitchen table. She was going to have to clean herself up before she could eat.

"Is that dinner?" Steve called from the basement stairs. "I'm starving."

"I'll have it set up in a minute."

"Let me give you a hand."

"No! I'll be fine. You stay down there with Daisy."

Steve agreed, though he sounded a little suspicious. He knew her too well. Peggy bustled into the bathroom, the only one she could recall, in his bedroom. Steve had converted what should've been a den or library into a bedroom. He said he didn't want to use the second floor of the house because it would take too long to get downstairs to his patients.

Peggy had never had the opportunity to look through his personal effects before. She'd always been there with him. Now she forgot about washing up as she looked at the photos on his dresser. They were older pictures, probably his parents. It looked as though he had a younger sister as well. Funny, he'd never mentioned her.

There was a mystery novel with a toothpick used as a bookmark on top of a textbook on canine eating habits after surgery. There was also a small pistol. That surprised her. She didn't think of Steve as the gun-toting type.

Cautiously, she opened the closet door and turned on the light. There were several good suits, all black, and a few pairs of shoes. She hadn't realized how few clothes he had. Biting her lip, she opened a green duffel bag she found on the floor. Inside were muddy clothes and boots.

"Peggy? Are you in the kitchen?"

Quickly she closed the duffel bag, turned out the light, and backed out of the closet. She was already in the bathroom by the time he reached the bedroom.

"What are you doing up here? Are you *cleaning*?"

She laughed, feeling awkward. "It was so dusty. I know I'm not much for cooking or cleaning. It was a mercy clean."

"You didn't have to do that."

"I know. I was too dusty to eat. I think you need a maid service."

He put his arms around her and looked at her in the mirror. "One of those provocative ladies in short black dresses with the frilly white aprons?" He kissed the side of her neck.

Peggy looked at him in the mirror. His face was so familiar, so dear. Yet she had known him only a short time. She knew only what he'd told her about himself. She'd taken him on face value. He'd won her heart almost from the first moment she'd run her bicycle into his SUV.

But looking through his things had made her realize how little she really knew about him. The photo of his parents, for instance. Were they still alive? What about his sister? Her curiosity almost got the better of her, but asking about it would be admitting she'd snooped in his bedroom.

"Are you okay?" His dark brows drew together as he questioned her.

"I'm fine. Just dusty. Since you're up here, maybe you could get the food. I'll get something to drink." The man was too in tune with her. It didn't help that she was the worst secret keeper in the world.

"Let's just eat up here," he suggested. "That way I'll make sure you're not polishing the silver on the way downstairs. Daisy is asleep for now."

They ate in the kitchen. Steve took out two china plates and put the chicken and vegetables on his plate; the broccoli and mushrooms on hers. "What did you get into today?"

Peggy dropped the broccoli she'd speared on her plate. "What do you mean?"

"You're always into something." He shrugged. "I know you're looking into Mrs. Mullis's death. Anything happen with that?"

She took a deep breath. "Not really." She told him about

her meeting with Chief Mullis. "I'm sure no one else would ask him to explain himself."

Steve laughed. "I'm sure you're right. Are you satisfied with his answers?"

"I guess I'll have to be." She glanced at him, wishing she'd never looked in his room. Now she felt out of sorts being with him. Was he hiding something important from her? She was going to have to find a way to ask him about his family. Nothing as blunt as her question to Chief Mullis. Why didn't he want to talk about them?

"My days are never as exciting as yours." He put more soy sauce on his chicken. "The horse farm called today. I hope Daisy is doing better tomorrow, so I can go out there. A few of the horses are sick. It's a big account, and I don't want to lose them."

"How many horses do they have?"

"Probably a hundred. Skipper's a friend of mine and a serious horse nut. I think he'd have more if he had more land."

"What kind of horses does he have?" This was as good a place to start as any. She obviously needed to know more about Steve's life. He told her all about the horse farm and what he suspected was wrong with the horses. All the time she was wondering what he was holding back. Why hadn't he introduced her to his friend by now? She wanted to kick herself for questioning what he said, but once she'd started, she couldn't seem to stop. It was driving her crazy.

When they were done eating, they went back downstairs and Steve checked Daisy's vital signs. "No change," he muttered. "Of course, in this case, no change is probably good. Poor old girl." He stroked her fur. "You've really had a rough time."

Peggy watched him. He was so gentle and patient. Not just with the dog but with everyone and everything. She felt secure with that knowledge about him. As far as the little pistol on his nightstand, maybe he was nervous. She looked at the basement door, where pet owners went in and out on a regular basis. It had made her nervous when she'd first opened the Potting Shed. That could be enough to make him want to protect himself.

"You're very quiet." He sat beside her on the old sofa he slept on when his patients needed constant attention. "It's making me nervous."

"Why? Are you saying I talk too much?"

"Not at all. I like how you talk and what you say. But I know that when you're quiet, you're working on some scheme I'm probably not going to like."

She laughed, but it died quickly. "I don't work on schemes."

He traced the side of her face with his finger. "Yes, you do. What is it this time? Are you planning on running away with Mrs. Mullis's body until you can prove what killed her? Or are you thinking about kidnapping her nephew and getting the truth out of him with some botanical truth serum?"

"I can't believe you're saying those things to me!" She forgot about the photo and her doubts for a moment as she defended herself. "I only do things that are necessary. And it's not like those are bad things. I've helped a few people."

"And almost gotten yourself killed in the process more than once."

She wanted to wipe that tender smile from his handsome face. "At least I don't keep secrets." As soon as the words were out of her mouth, she regretted them. The bad thing about words was that you couldn't call them back.

"What are you talking about?"

Peggy got to her feet and paced the limited area in the surgery room. "I'm talking about keeping secrets from each other. I'm sure you have some secrets I don't know about."

It sounded lame to her, but she wasn't really prepared to confront him. Her temper had gotten the best of her, as always. Now she had to try to find a way out of it.

"You keep more secrets than me," he said. "I'm pretty much what you see."

"Everyone has secrets," she persisted. "Like your little sister. Why haven't you ever mentioned her?"

He sat forward on the sofa. "My sister? What makes you think I have a sister?"

She had no choice but to confess at least part of her guilt. "I noticed her in the photos with you and your parents. She's smaller than you, and I assumed she must be your younger sister."

"You were snooping as well as cleaning."

"Not exactly. And let's get back to why you've never mentioned her. I take it you don't see much of each other, since I've known you a year and I haven't met her."

Steve ran his hand across his face. "There's a reason I don't talk about her or my parents."

"As I said, everyone has secrets." Peggy nodded with satisfaction. "You know everything about me and my family. I realized when I saw that photo that I know almost nothing about you."

"There's not much to know. But as far as secrets are concerned, what about Nightflyer, your Internet chess buddy? Have you heard from him lately?"

"No."

"But you wouldn't tell me if you did, right?"

"That's not the same."

"You're right. He's not family, at least as far as I know. I don't think you really know anything about him."

"I don't," she agreed. "But we're talking about *you* right now. Why are you being so defensive about your family? They can't be any worse than my family. At least they don't judge you like you're still a teenager."

Steve took a deep breath. "She's dead, Peggy. That's why I don't talk much about her. My sister was killed in a car accident when I was six. Right after that my mom and dad broke up, and my mom and I moved to Ohio."

"Oh, Steve!" Peggy was devastated. She couldn't believe she'd blundered into a terrible history. "I'm so sorry. I wouldn't have asked if I'd known."

"That's the trouble with snooping. I would've told you at some point. It was a long time ago."

It was unforgivably rude to have asked about his dead sister. But how was she to know? She should have encouraged him to talk about himself, but their conversations always seemed to revolve around what they were doing. What *she* was doing.

They sat together quietly for a long time, the sound of Daisy's breathing the loudest thing in the room. Peggy didn't know how to begin another conversation. Steve seemed lost in his own thoughts. Probably depressed now that she'd reminded him of the loss of his sister.

Her cell phone rang, making her start at the sudden sound. It was her mother. She didn't want to talk to her at that moment, but she supposed that if she didn't, her parents might come looking for her. "Where are you, Margaret? We've been to the shop and now we're here at your house. It's getting late. Is anything wrong?"

Peggy glanced at her watch. It was a little after nine. She supposed that was late for farmers who were used to getting up at dawn. "I'm with Steve. He's sitting with a sick dog."

"Your father and I need to talk to you. Do you think you could come home for a few minutes?"

Peggy glanced at Steve, who was monitoring Daisy. With everything that had gone wrong between them that evening, she supposed she might as well go home. He'd want to stay here tonight, anyway. That might be for the best. They seemed to have reached a painful impasse. "I'll be right there."

"Parent issues?" Steve asked as she closed her phone.

"I guess you could call it that." She shrugged. Where were the words she needed to make this right? "I'm sorry I looked through your room. I was just curious about you.

Sometimes it seems as though I've known you forever, but it's really been only a short time. There's so much I don't know about you."

Steve stood up from his perch on a stool near Daisy. "You're welcome to ask me anything. I didn't realize I was keeping things from you. I would've been glad to give you the fifty-cent tour if you'd wanted it."

She put her arms around him and hoped her kiss would say what her words seemed too awkward for. "I love you. I'll see you tomorrow."

"I love you, too." He smiled at her. "Thanks for cleaning the house, anyway. I guess I'm never home, so I didn't notice how bad it is. There's a beautiful redhead who keeps me occupied most of the time."

"I'd be jealous if I didn't know you don't have enough time for anyone but me and my crazy life. Good night."

"Breakfast tomorrow?" He held her hand. "I have some fresh cinnamon rolls."

"I'll be here."

PEGGY WALKED QUICKLY DOWN THE sidewalk toward her house, careful of joggers in their shorts and tank tops. There was a wonderful row of black-eyed Susans lining the driveway of the house beside Steve's. Their light golden petals and black "eyes" stood out from the dull landscape around them. No problem for them during the drought, unlike the mums on the other side, which were wilted and brown.

She'd really messed up, asking Steve about his sister. But how was she to know? The pistol on the bedside table would've been a better choice to confess her snooping. No matter why he had it there, it couldn't be as bad as the memory of losing his sister.

She'd always been bad about asking inconvenient questions. Her mother still reminded her about a question she'd

posed to their minister when she was twelve. They'd seen
Reverend Mason on the street with a young woman who
wasn't Mrs. Mason. Peggy had bluntly asked him where his
wife was. The good reverend had turned a terrible pasty
color and hurried away. Lilla had explained the virtues of
not asking personal questions of elders.

Reverend Mason had left the congregation abruptly the
following week. Peggy's mother had always told her it was
the result of her rude question. As a child, Peggy had believed her. As an adult, she understood the situation. But
there were still times she wished she could better analyze
the situation before jumping in.

Her father was out in the yard exercising Shakespeare
when she got back to her house. Traffic was still heavy on
Queens Road, but the lighted windows of the houses around
her showed that most of her neighbors were home. Her least
favorite neighbor, Clarice Weldon, was gossiping over the
fence between their yards with her mother. Peggy shuddered as she considered what the two of them might be
talking about. No doubt her mother was pumping Clarice
for information on Steve's comings and goings.

"He seems thinner," Ranson told her, looking at Shakespeare. "Are you sure you're feeding him enough? He's a
big dog, you know."

"He's fine, Dad," Peggy said. "Great Danes are slender
by nature even though they seem large. If he eats too much,
he won't be able to get around as well."

"That might be a good thing, Sweet Pea. This is a handful of dog you have here. Why didn't you get yourself a nice
cat that could catch mice in the house?"

"I don't think there are mice in the house. Shakespeare
might not catch them, but he'd probably play with them and
make them run away."

"There you are!" Lilla waved to her daughter and excused herself from Clarice. As she got close enough, she

whispered, "That woman has no sense of propriety. I've noticed that about a lot of people up here."

Peggy smiled as she opened the kitchen door. That meant Clarice had no information to share with her mother. "I'm going to put on the kettle. Would either of you like a cup of tea?"

"I would," her mother responded. "Peppermint, if you have it. My stomach has been a little unsettled since we found that poor woman in the lake."

"I'll take one, too," Ranson added. "But my stomach has been just fine. Maybe it's because I didn't know the lady."

"And you didn't see her," Lilla reminded him. "It wasn't like Cousin Lou last year. Mrs. Mullis had been dead for awhile and rolling around in that mud. I've never seen a dead person with red lips like that before. I guess it was makeup, but it looked bad on her."

Peggy measured peppermint leaves into the infuser and put on the kettle for hot water. "What are you two doing out this late? Are you taking on city habits?"

Ranson laughed. "Your mother likes living close to grocery stores now. We have to go out every night and buy food, whether we need it or not."

"Well, it's not like at home, where our pantry was stocked with plenty of food I canned over the summer. There's not even any dried apples. We have to be careful now. If something happened that the grocery store wasn't open in the morning, we could go hungry."

Peggy smiled at the idea as the kettle began to whistle. She knew she wouldn't be able to disabuse her mother of the idea, even though it was laughable to think Harris Teeter wouldn't open tomorrow. Her parents had always lived an hour or better from the nearest store. This was a new experience for them.

"Anyway, we were out when it occurred to me that you might know something else about Lois. We had a historical society meeting this afternoon and Geneva had a small memorial for her. Everyone is wondering when the funeral will be."

"The medical examiner hasn't released the body yet," Peggy told her. "It shouldn't be too much longer. I'm sure Chief Mullis will keep you posted."

"Dorothy was telling us that the chief was the one who dropped Mrs. Mullis off out there at the lake. Imagine that! She also said the chief is her only heir. They have one of those agreements like you have with this house. That big house and all those wonderful antiques will go to her nephew."

Peggy put the three cups of tea on the table while her father got the honey and a spoon from the counter. "How did Dorothy find out about the chief dropping his aunt off at the lake?"

"I'm not sure." Lilla sipped her tea without honey before adding a large dollop. "Maybe she knows someone else in the family."

"Maybe." Peggy felt sure the chief wouldn't have shared this information with many people. As testy as he was about it today, she didn't think he'd enjoy answering questions from anyone else about how this happened. Even if Dorothy knew someone in the family, it was hard for Peggy to believe she'd know what happened. But how else could she know?

"Is there anything out of place with Mrs. Mullis's death?" Ranson asked as he fetched some Oreos from the bread box. "There must be some reason the ME is keeping her so long."

"Is that true?" Lilla slapped her husband's hand as he reached for more than one cookie. "I know the ladies think she was killed by that bone digger. They think Jonathon was behind it. Have you found anything like that?"

"Even if she had"—Ranson grabbed two cookies—"she couldn't tell us. Margaret can't give out that information.

But I'd be glad to volunteer my services if you need any help in that vein, Sweet Pea."

Peggy thanked him for the offer. "I think Mrs. Mullis ate yew berries," she confided.

"That's why her lips were so red." He whistled. "Can't let these city people out in the wild without them eating poison berries."

"Do you think Jonathon or the bone thief might've made her eat them?" her mother asked around a crumb of an Oreo she'd popped into her mouth.

"There's no evidence of that," Peggy said. "I think Lois's death is going to be ruled an accidental poisoning. But until the ME releases the report, no one else can know that."

"I won't say a word," her mother promised.

Ranson laughed as he ate the last Oreo. "It's what she *doesn't* say that will get us all in trouble."

11

Honesty (money plant)

Botanical: *Lunaria annua*

Pretty purple or white flowers in spring are followed by thin, paperlike, coin-shaped seedpods, hence the name money plant. The branches with shimmering, dried pods make wonderful arrangements. Plants are self-seeding and will appear again, maybe at a different spot, in the garden for years. It symbolizes both honesty and money. The leaves are edible and very good in salad.

PEGGY WAS UP EARLY THE next morning after spending most of the night in her basement, working on her plant experiments. She'd already called Steve to ask how Daisy was doing. He told her the dog had passed the crisis point and would probably survive this ordeal. He was going to sleep for a few hours before going to the horse farm and checking on his patients there.

Shakespeare had been out, and was munching his food as she sipped her peach tea and looked in the backyard. The old oaks still retained most of their leaves, though it would have been better for them if they'd dropped early. Most of the smaller trees had been leafless for months as they fought to survive. The roots of the hundred-year-old oaks went down a long way, and probably were able to tap into groundwater other trees couldn't find. That was why they lived so long.

The fall air was cool and humid after the rain yesterday. Peggy had smelled acrid smoke in the breeze as she'd walked Shakespeare. The early morning news identified the source of that smell as the remnants of a brush fire the fire department had finally contained before dawn. It was the thing of nightmares, everyone's worst fear. Fire at this point, with water resources low and every stick and shrub tinder dry, could be catastrophic. She didn't want to think about the loss.

But that started her agile mind in another direction with another loss. Lois Mullis. She sighed. Was there anything to the Shamrock Historical Society's feelings about her death being foul play?

Admittedly, there were odd circumstances. Why Chief Mullis would drop his elderly aunt who had a heart condition in a remote area by herself was a question she'd like to have answered. But unless he confessed to killing her out there with yew berries, it seemed to be an open-and-shut case of death by accident. The chief might well be responsible for that accident.

True, there was the bone thief; the ladies wondered if he could've been involved in Lois's death. But her nephew, technically Peggy's boss, seemed to think that was a ridiculous idea. And the original supposition by the ladies that Jonathon was involved seemed lame.

It came back to Chief Mullis again. Peggy took a deep breath and finished her tea. She planned to spend most of the day at the Potting Shed now that her part in the investigation of Lois's death was over. She was going to ride her bike there and enjoy the cool breezes. What was to stop her from riding a slightly different route and possibly passing someone she knew?

She walked by a little honesty plant she'd put in the

ground that spring. It wasn't looking very good. The gray
leaves, shaped like coins, were drooping even after yesterday's rain. She took a moment to put a little more mulch
around the roots. It might not make any difference, but she
didn't want to see the poor thing suffer. Fertilizing it would
be useless until the root system had a chance to mature. She
gave it a kiss for luck, then went to the garage and unlocked
her bike.

She ran her hand over the covered silhouette of the 1940
Rolls Royce, which she and John had talked about restoring.
But it had proven to be an expensive proposition, particularly since Peggy had wanted to convert the engine to run
on hydrogen. She supposed she should sell it so someone
else could enjoy it, but she didn't know if she could stand to
part with the memories.

Putting aside the threads of sorrow, which continually
threatened to ensnare her, she pedaled her bike into Queens
Road and turned on Providence. It was only a few blocks to
Third Street. She couldn't be sure Chief Mullis had changed
his habits, but when John was alive, the chief ran up Third
Street and along Providence Road before turning back for
home every morning before work.

The tires on the bike made a squishing sound as they ran
through standing water on the street. Leaves had gathered,
blocking the drains that should have carried the rain away.
She was glad she'd invested in new tires a few weeks earlier. Hers were getting worn, and she sometimes needed the
traction. They'd cost the earth. She couldn't believe the price
had gone up so much in the past two years. Ironic that the
cost of bicycle tires should be affected by the price of oil
despite the fact that they saved energy.

Peggy caught sight of a runner in a red hooded sweat-
shirt. His legs were bare, stretching down to expensive running shoes. She guessed he was about the right height and
weight to be Chief Mullis, and swerved into a driveway to
make a U-turn to the other side of Providence Road.

A car whizzed past her, throwing cold water on her legs and feet. She'd have to go home before going to the Potting Shed, but she wasn't going to let this stop her. She slowed her bicycle as she reached the jogger.

The man looked up from under the red hood. "Dr. Lee? What are you doing out here?"

"Getting a simple answer, I hope."

"A simple answer to what?" Chief Mullis demanded. "If you want to talk to me, make an appointment."

"I would, but I'm not working on a police case right now. Unfortunately, that doesn't stop me from wondering what in the world you were thinking, dropping your aunt off at Lake Whitley so early in the morning. What time was it? We were there by seven, and she must've already been dead. Were you there instead of running?"

"I don't care if you're curious or not. I'm not talking to you about this."

"If you don't have anything to hide, why won't you answer?" she persisted. "Everyone does stupid things from time to time. No one is blaming you for what happened."

He stopped running, and Peggy jammed on her brakes. Cars swerved and horns blew as traffic brushed by them in the street.

"There's nothing to blame me for, all right? Aunt Lois wanted to be out there early. I told her I could get her out there at five-thirty. She said that was okay. I didn't know her friends weren't coming until so much later. You all left her out there to die, not me."

She was astonished at his hostility. "No one knew she was going to be out there. Everyone thought she was staying home. Didn't you notice how deserted it was?"

"No. I didn't pay any attention. She was always doing crazy stuff. I wasn't happy about being dragged into it. Is that what you want to hear? I loved her, but she was a pain in the butt sometimes. I just wanted to get rid of her that morning."

Neither of them moved. They stared at each other as Peggy wondered what had made him so angry at his aunt. She ignored splashing water and flying debris as she considered what she could say to him.

"I don't know why I'm bothering to tell you at all." He started running again.

She followed him, swerving close to the curb. "Because you know you made a mistake and you're sorry for it. You wouldn't have left her out there if you'd known what would happen."

"No, I wouldn't. But I suppose you understand her insanity, since you're a member of the gang. They do some stupid things. Aunt Lois was lucky nothing happened to her before this."

"Like what?"

"Ask your friends. That's all you're getting from me today. God knows I could use someone like you on Homicide. You don't give up. Now get out of the street before I call one of my boys."

PEGGY PEDALED QUICKLY THROUGH THE city, her mind going over her conversation with the chief. He obviously felt bad for his mistake in judgment, leaving his aunt alone at the lake. He'd expected her to meet up with the rest of the group, but something happened between that time and her death. Was it accidental? Most plant poisonings were, but this seemed to take on some questionable overtones. Lois probably saw the juicy red berries and decided to have a nibble while she waited. The chief was so angry and hostile. Had anyone else noticed his odd behavior?

It could just be a terrible mistake, she considered, as she locked up her bike behind the Potting Shed. But it could also be something more. The longer she was involved with this case, the more she doubted it was an accident, despite Mai's evidence to the contrary.

She unlocked the back door to the shop, locking it again behind her after she'd entered. This wasn't exactly a bad part of town, but the shops had problems from time to time with break-ins. Better safe than sorry. She'd thought that axiom was pointless when she was younger. It made sense now.

Everything in the Potting Shed was in its place. She stocked a few shelves, but it was more for something to do than out of necessity. She didn't need to check the receipts from yesterday to know it had been a slow day. She looked around the shop that had become her home away from home, and hoped Sam's idea about drought gardening was brilliant enough to turn things around.

Her garden club was meeting at the Kozy Kettle that morning. Normally they met on Thursday, but the meeting had been postponed because several members were going to be out of town. It had been just as well for her, with everything she'd done yesterday.

She looked around at the plants available for her talk. She liked to have a fresh specimen to show the group. Her eyes lit on a pretty French lavender plant that had been in her basement for years. She'd decided to bring it here after redoing the shop. It would be an interesting plant for the club to see and learn about.

Selena came through the back door a while later and found Peggy going through a plant catalog. She was listening to the Moody Blues, one of her favorite groups from her college years. Her parents had always frowned on their music because they weren't American. Of course, that made them all the more attractive.

"Who is this?" Selena asked. "And why are they torturing small animals?"

"You have room to talk with the music you listen to," Peggy said. "The Moody Blues was a great band. They may still be. I haven't kept up with them."

"You didn't have to come in this morning." Selena

grabbed her apron from behind the counter that held the cash register. "You could've just come in late for the garden club."

"Thanks." Peggy didn't look up from her catalog. "Next time, I'll call you before I come in, and get the lowdown on whether or not I should be here."

"You know I didn't mean it like that. I just thought you've been busy and there's nothing much going on here right now. You could take it easy for awhile. Like an hour or two, anyway."

"I'm just kidding you. Did you notice that little lizard that's taken up residence on the side of the pond?"

Selena jumped up onto the rocking chair with a screech. "No! Where is it? Maybe Sam can kill it when he comes in. I hate snakes and lizards."

"They're two different things." Peggy kept her laughter to herself. "Besides, Sam better not hurt it. The little fella is cute."

"I've worked here through floods, snow, dead bodies, and spiders, but I'm not working here with a lizard. I don't like them and they don't like me."

"All right. I'll take it home with me. Will that work?"

Selena nodded, her gaze focused on the pond as she searched for the terrible lizard. "Can you do it now?"

"Do what?" Sam strolled into the shop, Jasper and Keeley behind him. All three were wearing incredibly muddy clothes. "Does it involve all of us jumping up onto a chair?"

"Very funny," Selena said. "There's a lizard in the pond. And where did you manage to find enough water to make mud and wallow around in it?"

"Actually, we installed a pricey rainwater reclamation unit," Jasper told her. "And we have orders for three more just like it." He walked up to the chair and gave her his hand. "Let me help you down from there."

Selena made a face at Sam. "At least there are still *some* gentlemen left in the world."

"And I'm sure you could find them if you weren't always relying on the kindness of strangers." As he spoke, Sam's voice went up several octaves and became more Southern.

"Next thing you know, you'll be wearing a dress made from curtains," Peggy observed. "So tell me, just how pricey was this rainwater reclamation unit, and what was *our* cost?"

Sam and Jasper showed Peggy the plans for the units as well as the cost and profit structure. She was impressed with the numbers and the simplicity of their idea. "It's basically catching the rainwater from the rooftop and storing it, then using a pump to utilize it in the garden," she surmised.

"Exactly." Sam beamed. "We also sold a few rain barrels out there. I'm thinking we should stock some in the store. Jasper knows a man who's making them with designs."

"Designs?" Peggy tried to picture that, and failed.

"Yeah. Some of them look like little men with hats," Jasper explained. "They're very decorative."

Keeley agreed. "They were really cute, Peggy. Wait till you see them."

"Okay." Peggy stood up and put her catalog away. "We'll take a few and see how they do. This sounds great, Sam. Maybe just what we're looking for."

"That's why I'm here." He watched her pick up the French lavender plant. "I take it you have garden club this morning. Let me carry that for you."

Peggy wondered if this was a hint that he needed to speak with her alone, and agreed to let him help. "Is something wrong?" she asked as they walked across the courtyard.

"No. Well, not exactly. I just wanted to make sure this is where you want to go with the landscaping, too. We can pretend this side is all mine, but we're partners. I don't want to do this if it seems wrong to you."

She smiled at him as the sunlight caught in the golden strands that framed his face. "I think it's a great idea. Really.

You're brilliant, Sam. You don't need me to tell you." But she loved him for asking.

"Okay. We don't have regular meetings. I think maybe we should. You know, like regular businesses."

"I guess that's left over from you wanting to be a surgeon. All that organization and things laid neatly in place. You should know by now the garden business isn't that way."

He laughed as he put the lavender on a wrought iron table outside the Kozy Kettle. "At least the plant lady isn't that organized, huh? Fine. That's enough new stuff for one day. We'll work on those meetings later."

Sam said good-bye as two members of the garden club saw Peggy. They watched him walk away with gleaming eyes. "Is that your *son?*" Renee Walters checked out his broad shoulders and slim hips.

"No. Although I think of him like my son," Peggy said.

"How can you think of that hotty as anything but an incredible hunk?" Jessica Martin demanded, straightening her pink blouse and tossing her blond hair.

"I guess I never thought about him that way. He works for me. Sam heads up our landscaping division."

Jessica and Renee both took out their Palm Pilots to add his cell number. Peggy smiled as she got ready for her presentation. No reason to tell the two women that they were hardly Sam's type.

After the rest of the garden club had assembled outside the Kozy Kettle, Emil came to take orders for drinks and food. It was the reason they'd first come to an understanding about Peggy holding her garden club meetings there. She didn't have enough room at the Potting Shed, and Emil enjoyed the business on an otherwise slow morning.

"This is French lavender." Peggy showed the group the plant. "It's not the same as we normally think of lavender, because that's English lavender. This plant began as a weed and eventually ended up in the British Pharmacopeia in the late 1700s. They say Queen Elizabeth the First enjoyed

French lavender, but not just the smell; she regularly drank tea made from it to prevent migraines."

The group of twenty or so, two of them gentlemen, wrote down what she said and contemplated the gray green serrated leaves of the plant. The two ladies closest to the plant, a mother and daughter from Carmel Road, leaned closer and smelled it. "It smells more like rosemary than lavender," the mother said. "It seems strange to call it lavender."

"True, although it was probably the first lavender," Peggy told her. "The English lavender we're used to was bred from this."

"How would it be with this drought?" Mary Tillis asked, pencil in hand.

"It would probably be fine," Peggy answered. "It doesn't necessarily need a lot of water. The plant should be trimmed back twice a year, in spring and fall, or it becomes quite bushy. The flower heads can be left on to dry, and you can save the seeds for another plant."

"Does the plant dry well to use in an arrangement?" another lady asked.

"It does," Peggy responded, holding up one of the branches to show the delicate purple flower. "I used to keep this plant in my basement, but now it lives in the Potting Shed and seems to be happy there. I plan on keeping it in a pot of some kind and bringing it in for the winter."

There was a flurry of questions as Emil brought out teas and lattes with bagels and croissants. Peggy answered each one and gave everyone a chance to take a close look at the plant. She cut off small pieces for them to smell, each person deciding if they liked the scent or not.

"Peggy, talk to us about the drought." Suzi Harcourt said. "I mean, my roses are looking really bad. I know Sam did a good job planting them, but I don't have a well and rain hasn't come often enough. They look like they're dying. What should I do?"

"Have you added hydrogel crystals to the soil around the

roots?" Everyone's ears perked up as Peggy asked the question.

She spent the next few minutes explaining about the crystals, similar to those that hold liquid in baby diapers, and how they could be used to keep moisture around plants for longer periods. "The crystals disperse water as time goes by," she explained. "They're probably good for about a month without water before they need to be soaked again."

"Do you carry those at the store?" Suzi asked.

"Some," Peggy answered. "There wasn't ever a big demand for them." *But I can certainly carry more if that will get you into the Potting Shed.*

The garden club members lingered longer than the usual thirty minutes, and almost all of them went back to the Potting Shed with her when it was over. There were just enough hydrogel crystals for each of them to have one pack. Selena quickly took orders for at least ten more.

"Peggy, you need to give workshops on coping with the drought," Mary told her after paying for her purchase. "I know a ton of people who're looking for answers to this thing. No one wants to give up their garden. It would be a big help."

When all of the garden club had finally left, Selena closed the cash register and let out a *whoop*. "That's almost as much as we did all last week! What did you do?"

Peggy smiled. "Talked about the right thing, I guess. Selena, we should think about helping people survive the drought. Mary may be on to something. Let's take out an ad in the *Observer*. Maybe you can get your friend from the TV station to cover a drought workshop for gardeners."

"I'll see what I can do. Maybe this is our turning-around place. It sounds like Sam has the landscaping under control. Maybe we can make some money in the shop, too."

Peggy's mind was flying with a hundred ideas, but she glanced into the pond and back at her assistant. "Where's the little lizard? You didn't kill him, did you?"

Selena shook her head. "Me? Are you kidding? I had Sam take him with him when he left. I'm sure he'll find a good home for him or Keeley will kill him. You know how she is with anything alive."

Peggy was about to agree with her when six solemn-faced women, all of them wearing black, filed into the shop. "We need to talk," Geneva told her.

12

Shamrock (White clover)

Botanical: *Trifolium repens*

The name shamrock comes from the Celtic word for clover, seamrog. It has three leaves and is considered lucky. It is said the Irish saint, Patrick, used the shamrock to illustrate the Holy Trinity to the people of Ireland. There seems to be an ongoing debate about which form of clover he actually used: trifolium dubium, trifolium repens, or trifolium pretense. It is probably a mystery that will never be solved.

"Your mother told us what happened," Dorothy said. "How could you leave us in the dark that way?"

Peggy glared at her mother, who shrugged and looked the other way. "I don't know what she told you, but whatever it was, she should've known better."

"Lilla told us the medical examiner is going to rule Lois's death an accident," Grace charged. "How *could* you? We *trusted* you."

A customer with a baby in a backpack came into the shop and stared long and hard at the group of women. Peggy took this as a sign and moved them out of the shop. She certainly didn't need to scare off anyone who might spend money. "Let's go out and sit down."

They sat around the same table the garden club had, but for Peggy, the talk about French lavender was much more enjoyable. She didn't see where she had much choice but to explain the circumstances of Lois's death to them. She never should have trusted her mother to keep her mouth closed. Funny, but she had never thought of her that way before. She knew Lilla was desperate to make friends in her new home. It was as good an explanation as any for her breach of trust.

"So she was poisoned"—Annabelle deciphered Peggy's brief explanation—"by yew berries?"

"She had them in her mouth." Peggy clarified. "Whether or not the poison actually killed her, or if it caused her to have another heart attack, could be up for debate. But there was no sign she was forced to eat them. The ME had to assume she didn't know what they were, and ate them on her own."

"Of course she knew what they were!" Annabelle protested. "She grew up here. I'm sure she has them in her yard. Most of us do."

The other ladies nodded, but Geneva spoke out. "But who knew they were poisonous? I thought for sure my cousin in Spartanburg used to eat them all the time."

"You can eat the red berry part," Peggy explained. "But the green seed in the middle is deadly poisonous. Lois had more than one seed in her mouth."

"That's crazy!" Grace declared. "That can't be all there is to it. I don't believe it."

"It may be difficult to take in, but it appears to be what happened." Peggy felt sorry for the ladies and wished there was a better answer, although murder didn't seem to be a better answer to her.

"What about her quarrel with Jonathon?" Grace demanded. "Maybe he tricked her into eating the berries."

"The chances are he was with at least one of you when

she died. We know he picked us up to go out to the lake. He started with you, right, Geneva?" Peggy tried to make them think logically about what had happened.

"Yeah. I guess that was about six. Maybe sooner." The sulky tone of her voice said more than her words. Geneva didn't want to think her friend simply made a mistake.

"The ME and the police detectives checked everything. There isn't any reason to believe Lois was killed. She made a mistake thousands of people make every year, but it cost her her life." Peggy smiled at them. "Believe me, it's better that she died this way than thinking someone killed her."

"She was still alone out there." Annabelle's voice wavered.

"Because her stupid jackass of a nephew didn't want to be bothered taking her out there at a decent time," Dorothy said. "It doesn't hurt that he's the one who'll inherit her house."

"Please don't think of it that way," Peggy encouraged. "Chief Mullis knows he made a mistake. I don't think it was something he did on purpose."

"Easy for him to say," Mrs. Waynewright accused, her thin lips in a taut line. "She's gone now and he's still here. Who knows it wasn't something subconscious?"

"I guess, from what Peggy is saying, we'll never know for sure," Geneva said. "We all got messages saying Lois's funeral will be tomorrow. I guess all we can do now is pay our respects."

"I think we should give her that designation from the DAR anyway," Grace said. "She had the oldest ancestor of any of us, as far as we know. He was a major in the Revolutionary War at the age of sixty-six. I think we should see if we can have the sash and plaque buried with her. What good will it do us now?"

Mrs. Waynewright cleared her throat. "There was always a question about whether my ancestor was older than hers."

"Even so"—Geneva ignored her—"I think Grace is right. We should bury them with Lois."

The group slowly got to their feet and took turns thanking Peggy for her help. "I didn't really do anything," she protested. "I'm sorry about Lois. I know she'll be missed."

Lilla hung around until the rest of the group had wandered away through the courtyard. "I'm sorry, Margaret. I didn't mean to give things away. It just sort of came out as we were talking this morning."

"That's okay, Mom. They would've found out anyway. It was my fault for saying something I had no business saying."

Her mother smiled. "This group seemed very simple, but it's really very complex. You wouldn't believe the rivalry between all the history groups around here to decide whose ancestors are oldest or better in some way. Back home, it was simple. If you had the right family name, your ancestors were best."

Peggy laughed. "Don't worry, Mom. You'll fit in here, too. That Cranshaw name will open some doors. How many people have you met whose ancestor was one of the first to settle in this country in the 1600s? I think you might be in line for another sash and plaque."

"You're right, of course." Lilla hugged her. "We're going out tomorrow morning to locate the grave of a Revolutionary War captain, which was recently brought to our attention. Would you like to come?"

"I don't think so. Thanks for offering. Give my love to Dad."

Peggy was shaking her head as she walked back toward the Potting Shed and her mother continued out of the courtyard to her car. Their relationship had never been easy, but it had been more than thirty years since they'd lived in the same town. Somehow she had to find a way to survive her parents being in Charlotte. Steve was right. She was going to have to work around her Southern principles to get their attention and respect for her life.

Her cell phone rang. It was Mai. "I thought you might like to take a look at the ring we found now that it's all cleaned up. We're handing it over to the history museum, since we put the Mullis case to bed."

"I'd like to see it," Peggy answered. "Have you released Lois's body yet?"

"This morning. Chief Mullis was here to make sure it all went smoothly."

"I'll be over in a few minutes." Peggy closed her cell phone and went in the Potting Shed to talk to Selena. "I'm going to be gone awhile, but I'll be back to close up."

"Famous last words." Selena smirked without looking up from her book. "How did it go with the black crows?"

"They're in mourning for their friend. In the South it's always been traditional to go into deep mourning for at least the first month. That used to mean you couldn't leave your house and every window had to be covered in black. Your bedsheets were black, too, and all the mirrors had to be covered."

Selena looked up at her. "You're kidding, right? How did they survive?"

"The same way people survived everything else. You do what you have to do. See you later." Peggy left with a smile after catching Selena's attention with her historical point of view. Of course, mourning hadn't been that way for a really long time. She doubted most young people could survive the routine of death as it had been more than a hundred years ago.

She unlocked her bike and rode down an alley to get into Tryon Street traffic since there was construction on College Street. Unfortunately, there was construction on Tryon Street as well. She wondered if road crews ever considered working on roads that weren't dependent on each other.

Surely there were other parts of the city that needed work to be done.

Her cell phone rang again, but it was all she could do to negotiate between the cars, the workers, and the large holes they seemed intent on creating. She didn't stop until she cut down Trade Street, going toward Church Street. She got some nasty looks from drivers who wished they could do the same. One thing a bicycle was good for in Charlotte was getting out of traffic jams.

She pulled into the ME's parking lot and checked her phone. Steve had left a message saying he was going to be done early with the horses and wanted to take her someplace nice for supper. He planned to pick her up at six if she was going to be home by then.

She tried to call him back, but he must've been in a dead zone with no cell reception. It wasn't unusual outside the city. Some small towns still had very little reception. She left him a return message to let him know she expected to be dressed and ready by six.

Peggy locked her bike and thought about Steve. They had come so far, so fast, in the last year. She'd gone from believing she'd always be alone after John's death to sneaking Steve in and out of her house after he'd spent the night. Now she was asking herself if they'd moved too fast.

She had no doubt Steve was a good man. She'd known that right away. But the devil was in the details, it always was. There was a lot she didn't know about him. Because he spent so much time living in her life with her friends and family, he knew everything about her. It made her feel suddenly . . . uneasy.

Maybe it was stupid, but she was in an awkward position with him. Snooping through his personal possessions was like a wake-up call. She needed to slow the momentum of their relationship in order to reevaluate it. It felt like it was now or never to ask important questions she'd somehow forgotten to ask in the hasty jumble that had become her life.

With her acceptable plan in place, Peggy went inside and greeted the security guard at the front desk. She signed in, and he waved her on to the lab.

She saw Mai talking with Harold and waited for them to go their separate ways before she approached the girl. "I hope everything is back on an even keel with you and Harold now."

"As even as it ever gets with us." Mai pushed the strands of her silky, fine black hair from her face. "At least I know what it's like to be the head honcho now. And I'm not ready for it. I hope Dr. Ramsey stays on a while longer."

"You did fine! I'm sure Harold couldn't have done any better himself."

"Would you like to make a small wager on that, Dr. Lee?" Harold had sneaked up behind her, and stood rocking on his heels as he spoke.

"I'd be happy to," Peggy replied. "It was a difficult situation. You know Mai did the right things, the things *you* would've done. You might as well admit it. She does a good job."

Dr. Ramsey sniffed dismissively. "I'd give her a B-minus on her performance. I was called home early from a conference because she couldn't communicate with Chief Mullis. The job of a medical examiner is to work with the rest of the police department. We are *not* an island, Dr. Lee."

"And you are the biggest blowhard I've ever met." Peggy turned away from him. "I'm ready to look at the ring now, Mai."

"I'm sure *you* would've handled it differently," he taunted her as the two women walked away. "I suppose *you* would've accused Chief Mullis of killing his aunt. Yes, that *would* be brilliant, Dr. Lee."

"I'm ignoring you," Peggy yelled back at him, then whispered to Mai, "That man never changes."

"Now that I know he has to take the heat for everything we do in the lab, I feel a little more respect for him," Mai admitted. "Not a lot. And I still want his job. Just not right now. I'm missing something I hope to gain as I go along."

"And what's that?"

"I'm not sure." Mai shrugged. "I'll let you know when I find it."

Peggy watched as Mai took an evidence bag out of a drawer. The ring that had been so encrusted with mud was clean and shining. "It's beautiful!"

"I got a jeweler friend of mine to clean it up once we knew it wasn't evidence. He did a good job." Mai took the ring out of the bag and handed it to Peggy. "He said this is an old ring. He could tell by the quality of the stone and the gold. I'm not sure what the symbol carved into it is. He didn't know, either, but he said it's valuable."

Peggy examined the ring in the light. It was heavy and large, definitely a man's ring. The stone was square with a carving taking up most of the reddish brown space.

"Ah, yes!" Dr. Ramsey joined them in the evidence room. "A very nice sienna-colored variety of chalcedony. Carnelian. You don't see this kind of thing much anymore."

"You certainly don't," Peggy agreed. "Whoever this was made for had massive hands. The carving is intriguing. I wonder if you could find it on the Internet."

"I didn't look, since it wasn't relevant to the case anymore," Mai admitted.

"You mean since there *was* no case," Dr. Ramsey reminded his young assistant.

"Still, it would be interesting to know. You said the museum is going to take it?" Peggy asked Mai.

"Yes. They were very excited about it. I talked to the director, and he's on his way over. I was glad you could come right away. I didn't think he'd come and get it that quickly. Nobody ever moves that fast."

"There are some serious history buffs in this town," Peggy explained. "This is like a pot of gold for them."

"I'm glad we can give it to them." Mai took the ring back

and put it in the evidence bag. "We were lucky to find it in all that mud. I guess everyone out there collecting the bones has made other things come to the surface."

"There's a wealth of things from the past out there," Peggy agreed. "You wouldn't believe anything could still be there after being underwater for so long. There are cups and saucers, pottery, even some personal items that looked like barrettes to me."

"And this is where I leave you," Dr. Ramsey said. "I don't understand people's fascination with the past. I suppose, being a man of science, I don't appreciate hundred-year-old bric-a-brac."

"I guess it must be because you are a *man* of science." Peggy smiled up at him. "As a *woman* of science, I was fascinated by it."

"The bones I could see," he conceded. "The rest, you can keep."

The security guard called the lab to let them know there were visitors at the front desk. It was Jonathon and Geneva, who was the museum docent for that day. "Peggy! I didn't expect to see you here," Jonathon said. "I came by to pick up the ring they found out at the lake."

"Jonathon, this is Mai Sato, the assistant ME. Mai, this is Jonathon Underwood, the director of the historical museum. And Geneva Curtis. She's a member of the Shamrock Historical Society."

Everyone shook hands and said a few nice words. Mai sympathized with the pair over the loss of their friend. "Could I ask why you call it the Shamrock Historical Society?"

Geneva was glad to explain. "It came from our very first member, Captain Marcus O'Malley, who donated the property for a museum. The group that raised money for it decided to call it the Shamrock Society after the large patch of shamrocks where they planned to put the building."

"That's very colorful." Mai smiled. "Here's the ring.

Peggy waded into all of that gook to get it. I suppose she's the one you should thank for saving it."

Mai handed the bag to Jonathon. Geneva gasped when she caught sight of the ring. "Where did you say you found this?"

"Sort of floating in the mud," Peggy answered. "It was close to where we found Lois's body."

"You were lucky it wasn't sucked right down," Mai added. "What's wrong?"

"That ring." Geneva looked at Jonathon. "It's already registered in the museum's catalog. It's been a part of the collection for more than a century. There's no way it should've been out there at Lake Whitley."

Jonathon peered closely at the ring without removing it from the plastic bag. "It may be a different ring, Geneva. They may look the same, but the other ring must be still in the collection. Maybe someone who lived in the village had something similar."

"No way." Geneva was certain of it from the set look on her face to the rest of her body language. "This is the *same* ring. I just want to know what it was doing out there."

13

Phlox

Botanical: *Phlox paniculata*

There are more than sixty species of phlox. All but the Siberian phlox are natives of North America. Phlox are usually tall with thick, glossy leaves. All flowers have five petals on a tubular base. The word phlox comes from the Greek word for flame, probably because of its bright colors. A British naturalist, Thomas Drummond, is credited with discovering this plant, which means unanimity in the language of flowers.

"THIS WON'T MEAN ANYTHING TO what happened to Mrs. Mullis," Mai told Peggy. "You know that, right? There is no case. It's been ruled an accidental death. Officially ruled by the acting medical examiner, me."

Peggy was going back to the museum with Jonathon and Geneva to check out the ring. She'd tried to say all the right words to dispel any fears Mai was harboring about her case, or lack thereof, falling apart after she'd put her *official* seal on it. She'd never do anything to undermine Mai's authority . . . unless something important changed the parameters of the situation.

She sat in the front seat of the history museum's van with Geneva chattering constantly about the ring. "This is the same ring that caused all that controversy a few years back. You don't remember that, Jonathon. You weren't here yet. I was just starting as a docent at the museum. I can't quite recall what all the fuss was about. I'm sure one of the other ladies would remember it better than me."

Jonathon kept his eyes on the traffic as he drove through the downtown area to the museum. "The carving on the ring is interesting. I thought that from the first time I saw it. I haven't had a lot of time to look it up. I'm surprised someone hasn't figured it out by now."

"What was the controversy about, Geneva?" Peggy asked.

"Something about the ownership of the ring and who donated it. There were a few people who claimed it belonged in their family. Like I said, we'll have to talk to Mrs. Waynewright or Annabelle. They've been in the society longer than anyone; well, since Lois died."

Peggy watched another parking deck being demolished to make room for another set of expensive condominiums as they stopped for a red light. Soon there wouldn't be anything but expensive condos in the downtown area. A few weeks ago, she'd gone to look at a rooftop garden in a building where the condos started at one million dollars. That had stunned her.

"I feel responsible for this," Jonathon said as he took off from the light. "I should've kept better records of things going in and out of the museum."

"Are you sure it's the same ring now?" Peggy wondered. He'd been so sure it wasn't, at the lab.

"I don't know. It might've been a knee-jerk reaction to seeing it there when it should've been locked safely in the collection." He glanced at her. "It's unlikely there would be two rings so much alike. I guess we'll see when we get there."

They reached the new history museum, fittingly located on Shamrock Drive. Peggy was getting out of the van as Jonathon's long strides were taking him to the door, keys in hand. Geneva held her back, using the open van door as a shield between them and Jonathon.

"I'm telling you, Peggy, there's something fishy about Lois's death. You finding this old ring just focuses the sunlight into the dark corners. Maybe you should be asking Jonathon about the big slap down between him and Lois the day before she died."

Peggy looked into Geneva's pretty, chocolate-colored face. She guessed Geneva had retired early. She was much younger than most of the other ladies in the Shamrock Historical Society. "I asked him about that when we were at the lake after finding the ring. He said there were some items missing from the museum. He made it sound as though Lois might've been involved."

"As if! Twice we came here and found the back door left open. Jonathon's a sweet kid, but we didn't have a say in who replaced our old director. Most of us feel he could use a little seasoning, if you know what I mean."

"I think I do." Peggy closed the van door and began walking toward the modern granite building. It was two stories, with past flags from Mecklenburg County flying in front. "Do you think that's how the ring got out to the lake?"

Geneva narrowed her eyes and glanced toward the door. "*We* think Jonathon had the ring out at the lake when he argued with Lois and made her eat those poison berries."

"You mean that's what the other ladies will think when they know about the ring."

"I texted all of them on the way over here. We thought he had something to do with Lois's death in the first place. Don't you see that this lends us credibility?"

Peggy didn't really follow that line of thought. Why would Jonathon bring the carnelian ring out there with him if he was going to argue with Lois and eventually kill her? It sounded like desperate thinking to her. She was amazed the ladies felt so hostile toward Jonathon, who seemed to be a very likable young man. What had he done to alienate them?

A few unlocked doors didn't seem like enough to engender such harsh feelings.

They finally went inside. There was no sign of Jonathon. Geneva pointed them in the direction of the museum's locked collection, where several dozen valuable pieces of jewelry were on display.

Jonathon was already unlocking the case and pulling out the drawers. "The carnelian was stored right here." He pointed to the empty space. "I know I didn't take it out. The question is, who did?"

Geneva glared at him. "We have only your word for that, Mr. Director. I suggest we call the police and report this as a theft, and let *them* find out who took it."

"That would be my thinking on the subject as well," he agreed, taking out his cell phone. "No matter what you think, Geneva, I didn't have anything to do with this."

"Possibly those ruffians you hired to come in those times when you conveniently left the back door unlocked did the job for you, Mr. Underwood." Mrs. Waynewright stood at the door to the display area, flanked by Grace and Dorothy. She held her head high under a subdued black felt hat.

Jonathon smiled sadly and shook his head. "I don't know how I've wronged you ladies. I've tried to be what you've needed as a director. I've gone along with all of your suggestions. What do you have against me?"

No one spoke for a moment, then Grace stepped forward. "I'll tell you what we have against you. You're too young to have the responsibility for this place our ancestors struggled to maintain. When Mr. Hawkins retired, the board should've named someone with a little maturity to this position."

The historical society members nodded in agreement as the sound of sirens reached them from the street. Peggy wondered who'd called; when she looked at Grace, she held out her cell phone. "It takes only one button. I always have 911 on speed dial. I called them on our way over here after Geneva explained the situation."

They waited for the police to come to the front door. Geneva let them in and led the way to the showcase.

Peggy was surprised and pleased to see Paul's face beneath one of the blue caps. She didn't act any different because he was her son as he and his partner began questioning the group about what had happened.

Jonathon denied any knowledge of the theft. He admitted he hadn't checked the artifacts in the last few months, as they had been working out at Lake Whitley. "The most I might be guilty of here is some negligence. But I think people could cut me a little slack after I've spent days in hip-deep mud."

Geneva was happy to tell both officers about the back door being left open. "Ask this lady here." She pointed to Peggy. "She works for the ME's office, and she found this ring out at the lake where Mr. Underwood killed Lois Mullis."

Paul beckoned to his mother to join him in the hall as his partner spoke to Grace and Mrs. Waynewright about the ring and the theft. "I should've known you'd be involved."

"That's not fair. It was just as likely you'd find your grandmother out here today. It was the luck of the draw that it was me." She explained about how she and Mai had seen the ring at the lake and taken it in as possible evidence. "Mrs. Mullis's death was ruled an accident, as I'm sure you know. Mai didn't know the ring belonged here. She was just looking for a place to take it, since there was no reason to keep it as evidence."

He looked at his notes in a way that made her heart ache. It was so familiar and so much like John. Paul looked like her, but many of his inflections reminded her of John. Seeing her son in the same blue uniform that ultimately took his father's life was never easy. She didn't think she'd ever get used to it. John would've been proud of him. She was proud of him as well. But never a day went by that she didn't worry about him.

"Was the ring stolen or not?" Paul glanced into the room now filled with angry voices. "It kind of sounds like a museum domestic dispute to me."

"I don't know what to tell you. Maybe if you could get a crime scene team out here to dust for prints, it might settle this once and for all."

"I can't just randomly decide to bring in the crime scene boys, you know that, Mom. The captain would have my head. I can't see where anything besides a misunderstanding is going on here. Do you think those ladies have the authority to press charges against Mr. Underwood?"

Peggy shook her head. "It would surprise me if they have authority to do anything except complain about it, or Jonathon wouldn't be here anymore. They don't like him very much."

Paul's cinnamon-colored brows went up and down. "*Jonathon?* Sounds like you two know each other pretty well. Does Steve know? Grandma just *thought* Steve was too young for you. Jonathon must be all of thirty."

"I'm going to ignore that last remark, young man. Be glad you're too big for a switching! I think you should stick to the case."

He laughed. "Just kidding, Mom. Why don't the ladies like him?"

"I think it has something to do with his age. They thought someone older, more mature should head up the museum." She ran her gaze over her son from head to toe. "Now that I look at you, I tend to agree with them."

"What's that supposed to mean? I do a good job. You know I do."

She took a tissue from her purse and handed it to him. "You could do a much better job if you didn't have spaghetti sauce on your chin, Officer Lee."

"Mom!" he whined, glancing at the group to see if anyone had noticed. But he took the tissue and wiped his chin. "I'm moving to Colorado just so this kind of thing can't happen."

She smiled wickedly. "What makes you think that's far enough?"

Paul's partner interrupted them. "Could I have a word with you?"

The two of them walked down the hall and Peggy went back into the exhibit room. Geneva and Grace were railing at Jonathon, who seemed to bear it all with a stoic face. If it bothered him that they were threatening his livelihood, it was impossible to tell. Mrs. Waynewright stood off to the side, talking on the phone in a quiet voice that couldn't be overheard. Peggy considered that she might be wrong about the ladies being able to press charges.

What did they really have that could be considered police business? Even if it were true that Jonathon had left the back door to the museum open a few times, no one had reported the ring missing. It seemed they might never have noticed, if she and Mai hadn't found it. That didn't seem to be something the police would take seriously. She supposed they could try to get the police to investigate the whole bone thief theory and the museum would need to check the entire collection, which seemed a good idea to her at this time. Whether Jonathon was responsible or not, a valuable historic artifact had been taken out of the case and transported to the lake.

Paul and his partner came back into the room and announced that they would be calling in the crime scene people after all. "We'd like a concise list of everything that should be here," Paul told Jonathon. "We'd also like you to come with us to the station and give a statement."

Jonathon looked flustered. "Are you accusing *me* of stealing the ring? I can't see where there's any evidence of that, and I may know who was actually responsible."

Paul's partner took his arm. "We aren't accusing you of anything, Mr. Underwood. We'd just like you to come with us. If we could swing by your office for that list, that would be fine."

Grace, Geneva, and Mrs. Waynewright watched him walk out of the room with the officer. They stopped speaking until he was gone, then the debate raged again.

Peggy went after Paul as he started to follow his partner and Jonathon. "What happened? I thought this wasn't something you planned to handle."

He shrugged. "You know how that goes, Mom. We got different instructions from Chief Mullis, so we're taking the man to the station. I don't make those calls."

"I see." The chief's part in this situation was making her uneasy again. "I just have this feeling Jonathon is getting railroaded."

"Save me from those feelings." He started walking away. "Don't mess with my case, huh?"

"WHAT ARE YOU AFRAID JONATHON is getting railroaded for, exactly?" Steve asked after they had ordered dinner at the Peaceful Dragon Tea House on Steele Creek Road. "If there's no murder, what's left?"

"I think the ladies are going to try to get him fired," Peggy said.

"Maybe he should be, if he can't remember to lock the doors to the museum and one of their artifacts is missing."

"Anybody could've left that door open," she protested. "There are docents, board members, and historical society people in and out of the museum all the time. As for the ring, unless they did an inventory every day, how would anyone know what's missing?"

Steve sat back in his chair as the waiter brought salads and bread to their table. When they were alone again, he said, "You really like this guy, huh?"

"Don't start. I already got razzed about it from Paul. I like Jonathon, but more important, this whole thing has been blown out of proportion. Those ladies need to start a crochet society or something. They're always poking around where they don't belong."

"That's rich, coming from you." He didn't bother hiding his smile. "How many times have I asked you not to poke around someplace where you might get hurt? I didn't realize crocheting was the answer. We'll stop by the craft store on the way home."

Peggy's gaze was sharp as she looked at him. "I don't crochet, sweetie. And I'm not seventy years old yet. Besides, I work with the police now."

"*Now.*"

She ignored him as she sprinkled some vinaigrette on her salad. "Never mind. Let's talk about your day. How were the horses?"

"Not too bad. I think they'll be fine with some antibiotics. It's kind of like horse flu. Rest, plenty of water, and medicine. I'll go back and check on them next week, unless Skipper calls before then."

"Skipper?"

"He owns the horse farm. He's a retired NASCAR mechanic. He was smart and bought up a bunch of land in Cabarrus County before he quit the circuit. He has a nice place out there. Ever think about living in the country?"

"Not really. I guess I'm a city girl now. Once I left the farm, I never looked back. You see yourself living on a horse farm someday?"

"Maybe. It seems more natural for a vet and a gardener to live outside the city. I could have lots of animals and you could have lots of plants. It would be simple."

"I don't know how simple it would be." She sipped her water. "You like being out there in the mud. I like city streets. They're easier to ride my bike on."

"It's not so much that I like the mud as that I don't mind it, and land is still a good investment."

Peggy absently righted some purple phlox set on the ta-

ble in a cut-crystal vase. She wondered if she could tactfully ask him to talk only about his past. She'd thought of a
slew of things she probably should've asked him that she
hadn't. No wonder she didn't know more about him.

"What's up?" he asked, seeing the look on her face. "I
can see the wheels turning in your brain. It's kind of scary."

"I don't know." She addressed her salad as though her
life depended on it. "Do you hunt?"

"No. I guess I'm too much of a city boy for that. Why do
you ask?"

"How about fishing?"

"Should we fill out one of those questionnaires they have
in women's magazines?"

"There's something to be said for knowing your partner," she told him. "I'm sorry, but I guess finding out about
your family has made me wonder how many other things I
don't know about you."

"I'll be glad to tell you anything." He paused as the
waiter returned to top off his iced tea and her water. "We've
known each other for over a year now. I guess I didn't think
about it. What do you want to know?"

She shrugged while questions burned through her brain.
She had to be careful how she asked what she needed to
know. "Do you ever just go out hiking or walking in the
woods?"

"Sometimes. Mostly if I'm looking for you. Otherwise,
I'm kind of busy. I try to run a few times a week. That's
about the extent of my active social life."

Peggy wanted to continue asking him questions: Were
you in the military? What was your first girlfriend like?
Why didn't you get married when you were younger? But
their dinner arrived and neither of them had finished their
salad. She put the questions to the back of her mind and
tried just to enjoy a meal with the man she loved. She was
curious, but she could leave it alone for tonight.

"So how are negotiations going with your parents finding out that we are quasi living together?" Steve glanced at her over his rice vermicelli with vegetables.

"Fine. This is really good seitan." She tried to change the subject. "Would you like to try some?"

He took a sip of his tea. "You haven't talked to them at all, have you?"

"No. It's been hectic."

"It's *always* hectic."

"I think things will settle down once it isn't so new," she prophesied. "They need time to adjust, just like we do."

"It's not just your parents, Peggy. It's Paul, too. I saw him when I was leaving your house the other morning. He always asks me if Shakespeare is sick."

"Mai knows," she triumphed. "We talk about it sometimes."

"Really? She guessed, right?"

"Sort of."

"What, exactly, do the two of you talk about when you talk about us?"

Peggy took her time chewing her food before she answered. "This and that. Mostly we talk about Paul not knowing that we're together."

Steve leaned forward slightly. "Lovers?"

"Yes."

"You can say it. It's all right."

"It's not a big deal," she disagreed. "I say it all the time."

"Say it just for me, then. Humor me."

Peggy glanced around the crowded restaurant. "Lovers."

"A little louder."

"Lovers! We're lovers! Is that about it?" Her temper started to rise. He was treating her like a child. Heavens, she *felt* like a child. She put down her fork. "You're right. I'll talk to them all right away. I'm an adult. I can sleep around if I want to."

He frowned. "That's not exactly what I had in mind." He covered her hand with his on the white linen tablecloth. "You can sleep around only with *me*. I love you, Peggy. I wish you'd marry me and we wouldn't have to worry about any of this."

Stunned, she was thrilled when her cell phone rang. She was never so happy to hear Merton Dillard's voice as she was at that moment.

14

Red Cedar

Botanical: *Juniperus virginiana*

The volatile oil from this plant has been used medicinally with great care, since it is a deadly poison. The fresh leaves were used to cure blisters. The oil has been used in making perfume in Europe, where it is a principal agent in white rose extract.

"I HAVE TO TAKE THIS," she whispered. "Police business."

Steve nodded as she walked to a secluded corner of the restaurant. Merton was talking, but Peggy wasn't listening. She was thinking about marrying Steve.

It wasn't as if they hadn't talked about it before, but it was always in a random-futuristic sort of fashion. This was different. There was a change in his tone. The resolution to their immediate problem with her family made the subject more threatening.

Threatening?

She wasn't sure how she felt about getting married again. There were the practical aspects of their lives, such as their homes, Steve's business, and her family. But all of that flew through her mind, ending up with just one idea—he wanted to marry her.

Steve was a wonderful man who had changed her life and made her feel that there was more than work. But was she ready to marry again?

"Peggy? Are you there? I can't remember how many times it's polite to ask before assuming a cell phone has lost service," Merton rambled. "I don't want to tell a stranger about my findings. I guess we'll need some kind of code to let me know it's you, now that our connection has been compromised."

Dragged away from her visions of what a fifty-something widow wore to her second wedding, Peggy realized she'd ignored her friend. "I'm sorry, Merton. You were saying?"

"Is that you, Peggy?"

"Of course it's me." Her tone was a little sharp, she realized. She had a lot on her mind. "It's me. What did you find about the yew seeds?"

"Good enough! I don't think I mentioned yew to begin with, just seeds. You must be Peggy."

"And?"

"I couldn't find a match for any of the seeds with the samples you brought me. Are there any more branches?"

"Hundreds more." She glanced back at Steve, then looked away quickly, before he saw her. "I don't know if I can get samples from *all* the bushes out there."

"No one said forensic botany was *easy*, Dr. Lee," her friend chided her. "Did you tag the bushes you got samples from the first time?"

"Yes." She sighed. "All right. I'll go out and get more samples. Although it doesn't really seem to matter, since Mrs. Mullis's death has been ruled an accident."

"You know the ME will want to cross all the Ts and dot all the Is. If you don't know that already, let me assure you of it. Everything has to be neatly tucked away in a file cabinet somewhere. When do you think you can get those samples?"

"I'm not sure."

"I'm going out of town Saturday night, and I won't be back until Monday."

"Okay, I get it. I'll go out tonight and find some more."

"I was hoping you'd say that. I'm not salaried, you know. I get paid by the days I work. No work tomorrow? No pay."

"That's fine, Merton. I'll cut more branches before I go home. It's not a big deal. Thanks for calling." Peggy closed her phone and panicked, wondering if she could sneak out of the restaurant without Steve noticing. It seemed unlikely. Even if he didn't see her leave, he would probably come and find her. One way or another, they were going to have the conversation. She took a deep breath, squared her shoulders, and marched back to the table and her cold seitan.

But Steve was getting to his feet before she reached him. "I'm sorry," he apologized. "One of my patients has swallowed something she wasn't supposed to. I'll have to check on her."

Peggy smiled, her heart pounding. "That's perfectly fine. You have to tend to your patients. I completely understand."

"That's very generous of you. It doesn't have anything to do with the 'M' word being tossed around over dinner, does it?"

"Of course not. I'm sorry you have to go so we can't discuss it right *now*."

"We came together in my Saturn, remember?" He wrapped his warm hand around her cooler arm. "It'll just take a minute. You can come in, if you like."

"Maybe you could drop me off at the house." She went for the least amount of time for them to talk about marriage. "I need to go out to Lake Whitley again and collect more yew samples."

"It's going to be dark soon. With everything going on out there, maybe I should go with you." He smiled at her as they stepped into the cool night air. "I'll feel safer that way. You can see me in action and I can watch you collect yew.

And we'll have plenty of time for you to feel uncomfortable about the idea of getting married again."

Peggy was trapped. She knew there was no way out. She was going to have to take Steve out to the lake with her. And talk about marriage. She wished she knew what to say. "That's really great!"

They got in the Saturn and started down Steele Creek Road. Peggy kept the conversation away from marriage by talking about anything and everything she could think of. She ran out of words by the time they'd reached Steve's patient's home.

He turned off the engine after pulling in the driveway and looked at her. "If you don't want to get married yet, that's okay. We don't have to pretend it's not there. I don't want to rush you into anything. Well, I *do*. But I won't."

Peggy blinked, and tried to think of something light-hearted to say. All she could come up with was "Thanks. It's not that I don't want to . . ."

"I understand . . . I think." He reached behind the seat for his medical bag. "It's a long ride out to the lake. Maybe you can explain while we're driving."

Great! Peggy pushed a bobby pin back into her hair too hard and bit her lip when it hurt. He was right. It was half an hour from here to the lake. She'd better think fast.

It wasn't that she *wouldn't* marry Steve, if she were going to marry anyone. It wasn't that she had meant to lead him in this direction, although she had known this time would come. Steve was a good man with slightly old-fashioned values that would dictate that they should get married. Not that she was exactly comfortable with the idea of sleeping with him without the benefit of clergy. Otherwise, she wouldn't have such a hard time telling her family and the rest of the world. She still didn't want her snoopy neighbor, Clarice, knowing about it. She supposed that spoke volumes. Who was she to call Steve old-fashioned?

A petite, dark-haired woman opened the door as they

approached the small frame house. "I'm so glad to see you, Dr. Steve. Alma is so sick. I don't know what she's eaten this time. I hope you can help her."

The woman put her hand on Steve's arm and looked invitingly into his face. Peggy smirked. She was flirting with him! Maybe her pet wasn't sick at all. Steve was an attractive man, and Peggy didn't blame the woman for thinking about him that way. She didn't *like* it, but there wasn't much she could do to prevent it from happening, short of tying him up in her basement.

The woman looked past him and smiled. "Oh, you brought your mother with you. How nice!"

That was a little unsettling. Peggy raised her chin and held out her hand to the other woman. "I'm Dr. Margaret Lee. I'm Steve's fiancée. Nice to meet you."

Steve glanced at her with a raised brow, but didn't say anything. The woman congratulated them, then led Steve to her pet. She looked a little disappointed, but Peggy decided she could get over it. It was bad enough she was flirting with Steve, but then she had the nerve to suggest Peggy was his mother. That was too much!

Peggy glanced into a mirror as they walked behind the woman. The fiery red hair that had plagued her so much as she was growing up wasn't there anymore. No one would be likely to call her "Carrot Top" now. Her face didn't look that bad, but maybe she needed to think about dyeing her hair. Steve wouldn't want everyone thinking he was going out with someone old enough to be his mother. Maybe that was what she was afraid of from the beginning. Steve was eight years younger than her, and good-looking besides. Someday she might look like his grandmother!

"Alma!" The woman searched for her pet in the great room. "Come out! Dr. Steve is here to see you."

They were standing in the center of the room waiting for Alma when a large iguana finally waddled toward them.

"There you are, you bad girl!" The woman picked up the

large lizard, which was difficult for her to hold. "She's been like this all day, Dr. Steve. I think she ate another pencil or something."

Steve put down his bag and took the iguana from her. He sat down in a chair to examine the creature while Peggy sat down across from him to watch.

"I think you're right, Mrs. Bishop. Alma probably ate something bad again. Has she been spitting?"

"No, not today. She's pooped a lot, though. Do you think she'll need surgery?"

"Probably not." Steve carefully felt the lizard's round belly. "She'll probably pass whatever it is. Even though she's not spitting, if she's going to the bathroom, she's still okay. Give me a call in the morning and let me know how she's doing. Any idea what she ate?"

"My son's hamster is missing. Do you think Alma could've eaten it?"

"No. She's a vegetarian. She should be fine, but we'll see how she is tomorrow."

"Thank you so much for coming." Mrs. Bishop took Alma from him. "She's bad, but she's my baby. I don't know what I'd do without her. You're the best vet in the city, Dr. Steve."

"Thanks." He smiled and wiped his hands with a towelette from his bag. "Alma is one of my best patients."

"I suppose you have a lot of patients." She stroked the iguana as she spoke, but her eyes were on Steve. "I remember when I first met you. You were new in town and didn't know anyone. We almost made it out for dinner one night."

Peggy was surprised to see a blush rise on Steve's face before he responded. "We did. I appreciate you still bringing Alma to me. I hope you find the hamster. Good night, Mrs. Bishop."

Steve and Peggy didn't speak again until they were in the VUE. "I hope you aren't taking all of that in and getting ready to throw it back at me," he said.

"I wouldn't have guessed your patient was an iguana."
She skirted a bed of purple pansies that seemed to be doing
better than average. The Bishop lawn was a healthy, suspect
shade of green, too. They were obviously watering.

She couldn't mention the wisecrack about her being his
mother. It might be stupid, but she felt vulnerable about the
age difference between them. Steve would only reassure
her that it didn't matter, and then she'd feel worse. "I didn't
realize you could treat so many different species. Dogs.
Horses. Lizards."

He started the engine. "Don't blow me off, Peggy. You
know what I'm talking about."

"I'm guessing you met her before you met me. That
doesn't bother me. You're an attractive, single man. Why
wouldn't she want to go out with you?"

"Fine." He turned back away from town, toward the lake.
"We won't talk about Mrs. Bishop. Let's talk about getting
married."

"I thought you said you wouldn't push."

"You were fast enough to claim me in front of Mrs.
Bishop. Why throw me away now?"

"I don't know what made me say that. I guess I didn't
want her to go on about me being your mother, which is
biologically impossible."

"I'm sure it was biology that made you tell her we're engaged. In the animal kingdom, unlike plants, we tend to
want to claim our mates so that other animals stay away
from them. You were just marking your territory, so to
speak."

"Not a pleasant thought."

He laughed. "No matter how much you love plants,
Sweetie, you can't be one. You're an animal like the rest of
us, with certain needs and desires that have to be satisfied.
I hope that's where I come in. At least I *thought* that was
where I came in, until your parents moved up here and
made me your girlfriend."

"I'm not sure what you mean by 'girlfriend.' My parents, and Paul, are just concerned about me. They don't want me to make a mistake."

"No. Paul doesn't want you to forget his father. Your mom and dad want you to be their little girl again. You can have a girlfriend who hangs around and talks trash with you, but you can't have a man friend who spends the night."

"Steve—"

"Peggy, you have to tell them, or we can't go on. If it would make it easier, you can say we're going to be married. We could be engaged for awhile."

"How long is 'awhile'?"

He shrugged as he turned onto a less traveled road where there were no streetlights. "I guess as long as you want it that way. I'm okay with that as long as everyone realizes we're a couple and we share a bed. I don't have to move in full-time, but I don't want to keep lying to Paul. I'm not good at playing games with people."

Peggy considered his words. Maybe he was right. She might not be ready to marry again . . . just yet . . . but if she ever was, she'd want it to be Steve. "I love the way you are. I wouldn't want you to be any different. Maybe we should do the engagement thing for awhile."

"That works for me." Steve took her hand and kissed it. "You know that I have absolutely no feelings for you as my mother whatsoever, right?"

"I certainly hope not." She squeezed his hand. "I don't think of you as a son."

"Then we're good to go! When do you want to announce our engagement?"

"How about Tuesday night at dinner? Everyone will be there. It seems like the perfect time."

"Tuesday it is." He brought the SUV to a stop. "I think we're here. Where's the lake?"

Peggy got out and turned on the miniflashlight she

always carried in her purse. Its tiny beam didn't do much to alleviate the darkness. A bigger flashlight beam bounced around the area from the back of the SUV.

"Good thing I brought these along." Steve took another big flashlight from a dirty duffel bag. "That tiny little thing isn't made for this kind of terrain."

Peggy recognized the bag. "I saw this in your closet the other day, and wondered why it was full of muddy clothes."

"You were in my closet?"

"I was . . . cleaning, remember?"

"What did you *think* I did with it? Why didn't you ask me about it?"

"After asking you about your family, it was hardly the time to bring anything else up."

Steve turned off his flashlight and set it down in the duffel. He took Peggy in his arms and kissed her. "I get dirty sometimes going out into the field and treating animals. It's a simple explanation, nothing too deep or dramatic."

"I suppose." Really, she would've been happy just to stand there with him in the dark and not talk about the duffel bag or any of the other doubts that had plagued her for the past two days.

He rummaged around in the bag and brought out a few more things. "These are dart guns. I use them to tranquilize animals I can't approach while they're conscious. The GPS is for walking around in the woods at the horse farm. Does that make you feel any better?"

Peggy wanted to put the whole thing aside. She felt ridiculous enough that she'd had so many doubts about him over one picture and a pistol on his bedside table. She could even be philosophical about it: How well did anyone know the person they fell in love with?

They heard a sound from the general area of the dry lake, but the trees and shrubs muffled the noise. Steve pulled Peggy behind him and took the pistol out of the duffel bag. "Shh! You stay here and let me check this out."

She knew he couldn't see her face, but she stuck her tongue out at him anyway. "I'm not staying anywhere. If you're going down there, so am I."

He didn't respond, and she followed him away from the SUV. There was a bright light, hidden by heavy red cedar trees. As they came around the thick stand of trees, Peggy could tell the light was focused on the area where the historical society had been gathering bones and artifacts. She took careful steps as they wove their way closer and closer to the light, thinking of bone thieves working in the dark.

Of course, the police were long done with the crime scene and nowhere to be found. The security guard the museum had hired to watch the site had quit after they'd found Lois. The police had learned he hadn't been at his post the night before Lois died.

The situation was making her nervous. Maybe she should've stayed behind and called 911. The trees and bushes swayed in the light breeze that chased the clouds from the sky, allowing some starlight to penetrate the night. Peggy could hear someone whistling, but still couldn't see anything beyond the underbrush that surrounded the lake.

As she and Steve rounded a point between the brush where the police and the historical society had accessed the lake bed, she saw a figure standing in the deep mud. It appeared to be a man in high boots and a T-shirt. He was sifting through the bones he'd found, tossing what he wanted to the edge of the lake. A sizable pile of bones and artifacts had formed, the bright light gleaming on them.

"Let me call the police," she whispered to Steve. Neither one of them was trained to confront someone who might use deadly force to defend himself.

"He'll be gone by the time anyone can get out here."

Steve nodded toward the man, who was already climbing out of the mud to look at his haul. "You said this was illegal and bad for your historical society. You call the police. I'll hold him until they get here."

15

Staghorn sumac

Botanical: *Rhus typhina*

Native Americans made a drink from the staghorn sumac's crushed, red fruit. It is now known to be very high in vitamin C, and may have helped tribes stay healthy before the coming of the Europeans and diseases they had never encountered. The tannin-rich bark and foliage were used as a tanning agent.

PEGGY WOULD'VE ARGUED THE POINT, but Steve was already creeping toward the man, and she didn't want to give him away. Filled with terrible visions of the bone thief shooting Steve, she took out her cell phone and whispered into it when the 911 operator answered.

The darkness seemed terribly quiet. She couldn't even hear cars going by on the main road.

"What is your address?" the operator asked.

Peggy wanted to shush her. The woman's voice sounded very loud in the night. "I don't have an address. I mean, I have my home address, but I'm not at home. I'm at Lake Whitley, and a man is out here stealing bones and artifacts. Can you send someone?"

"We can't send someone without an address," the

operator told her. "Lake Whitley is a big place. I'm sure you wouldn't want officers wandering around out there until they find you."

"All right," Peggy said. "I'm at the scene of Lois Mullis's death."

"Why are you there? That area is off-limits. You should leave immediately."

"I'll leave if you'll send help," she whispered back. "My . . . boyfriend . . . is confronting the thief. He needs help."

"You should both leave right away," the operator persisted. "That's no place for you and your boyfriend to hang out."

It was all Peggy could do not to scream at the woman. She took a deep breath and calmly said, "My name is Dr. Margaret Lee. I work with the medical examiner's office. I'm out here collecting samples, and this man appeared. Can you send someone?"

"Why didn't you say so?" the operator responded. "I have someone on the way."

Peggy closed her phone and turned back to try to locate Steve. The bone thief was sitting on the ground. He carelessly tossed a few leg and arm bones aside and rubbed an old skull on his shirt to clean it. He held several artifacts up to the bright light. One looked like a ceramic chamber pot.

Peggy couldn't see Steve in the darkness but knew he was out there somewhere. Her heart was racing as she clenched her hands into fists, feeling powerless to prevent something terrible from happening. She wanted to do something—she certainly couldn't stand there and let Steve get hurt.

All of her was focused on the scene in front of her. It was like being caught in a living nightmare as she relived those awful moments when Al had come to her door to tell her that John was dead. For weeks, she'd imagined what it had been like when John was killed. She'd walked by the house where he'd been shot, wondering about it and visualizing the scene from start to finish. Surely this couldn't happen twice in her life.

Finding a heavy piece of wood she could use as a club, Peggy advanced on the bone thief with every intention of hitting him if necessary. She'd never really hurt another human being in her life, but this was different. She had to be strong.

Her ears strained for any sound of Steve advancing on the man. She couldn't hear anything except a few crickets. How could he walk through the leaves and brush without making any noise?

She moved to the right of the light and hefted her piece of wood to her shoulder, hoping she looked menacing. She also hoped Steve wasn't coming from the left. He might accidentally shoot her if he was aiming for the thief and was startled when she jumped out. There was no way of knowing. She'd have to take her chances.

Suddenly Steve came out from behind what looked to be a large staghorn sumac bush, its bright red leaves almost gleaming in the weird lighting. He leveled his gun, using two hands. "Don't move! You're under arrest!"

The man fell facedown and put his hands behind his head. Steve seemed uncertain what to do next. Peggy jumped out with her piece of wood. "And don't look up!" She turned to Steve. "I have my nitric gloves. We can tie his hands together."

Steve looked amazed to see her. "I don't think we should do that. What are you doing out here? You were supposed to stay by the Saturn. You could've been hurt."

"So could you," she countered. "I can't believe you'd come down here like this. What were you thinking?"

" 'Scuse me," the man on the ground said, "what're you doin' here? You're not cops. I'll just get up now and be on my way."

"I don't think so!" Steve moved a little closer to the thief. Peggy raised her club.

"Okay. Okay." The man lay back on the ground. "If you're gonna rob me, take what you want and get out. I've got work to do."

"Work?" Peggy demanded. "Undoing years of preserved history! People have died here. You could at least show some respect."

"Respect?" His laughter cackled in the silence. "These people don't know if you respect them anymore or not, lady. My wallet respects them enough for both of us."

"I don't think you can reason with him," Steve told her. "Did you call the police?"

"Yes. They should be here soon."

The light skimmed another article that didn't look old or dirty. It was a woman's pocketbook. "Watch him." Peggy put on another pair of plastic gloves. She leaned down and grabbed the purse, holding it up to the light so she could look at it.

It was a burgundy Louis Vuitton bag. Very fashionable and expensive. Definitely leather, and still shiny and new. She opened it carefully and began sorting through the contents without removing them. There was a spray flask of White Diamonds perfume. Obviously an older woman's bag. Her heart beat a little faster. Could this belong to Lois?

"What is it?" Steve swatted at a mosquito.

"I think it might be something important." She didn't want to speculate until she knew for sure.

As soon as her gloved hands located the wallet, she opened it and gasped. "This *is* Lois's pocketbook. It's not full of mud, so it had to have been on the shore. Her car keys are in here. She must've lost it when she fell into the lake."

"Which may or may not have anything to do with her death," Steve said.

"Yes. Although it seems odd that it wasn't found right away. If she'd dropped it before she fell in the mud—"

"—it would've been found during the initial search of the area," Steve concluded. "It couldn't have happened that way."

"Which means we need to know where this man found the pocketbook." Peggy inched closer to the man on the ground. "I really am with the police department. Where did you find this pocketbook?"

"Like I'm going to tell you."

"Why not? You're already caught here. You don't have anything to lose, and you might help our investigation."

He turned his muddy face toward her, the shadows making it look like a mask. "What's in it for me? Are we cutting a deal here or what? If I have valuable information, I expect to be rewarded for it."

"What do you want?" She thought about how much money she had in her purse. "I think I have twenty dollars. Steve, how much do you have?"

"I don't think that's what he means, Peggy." Steve shifted closer to the man.

"No, that's not what I mean, *Peggy*," the thief mimicked. "I mean, I've already been in prison for this once. I don't want to go back again."

"Then why were you doing it again?" she demanded.

"Because it's easy money." He shrugged. "If you're with the police, you can cut me a deal for the information. Then I'll take whatever you and Stevie have in your wallets, too."

Before Peggy could agree to any deal, the sound of sirens pierced the night. Blue lights flashed from the parking lot, making the play of light and dark on the dry lake and trees even more bizarre.

"You better go up and explain," Steve said. "I don't want them to get the wrong idea."

Peggy stared at the contents of the purse again. She hated to leave it without knowing everything that was inside. But Steve was right. The police probably wouldn't look favorably on coming down there and finding them with a man on the ground between them while they held a gun and a club.

She walked up the hill with only one backward glance to be sure Steve was all right. Police officers were gathered in a large group pointing at the lighted area. They challenged her as soon as they spotted her. Peggy put up her hands as a defensive response. "I'm with the ME's office. I have ID."

"Take it out slowly so we can see it." The officer in charge looked at it with his flashlight. "I think we're here to rescue you, Dr. Lee. Is everything all right?"

Peggy relaxed. She knew him. He'd worked with John several times. "Sergeant Fletcher! Good to see you. How's your wife doing?"

"She's fine. The boys are still keeping her busy. What are you doing out here?"

Peggy explained that she was involved in the Mullis case and was there to collect yew samples. "We saw the man stealing the bones when we came up," she explained. "They've had a lot of trouble out here with people stealing bones and artifacts from the old Whitley Village now that the lake is dry."

"That's right." He glanced around in the darkness. "That used to be out here, didn't it? They say weird stuff goes on out here at night. I had officers refuse to work out here during the investigation. Funny how it can show itself after all these years."

"My . . . *colleague* . . ."—she wasn't going to say boyfriend again—"is down there with the thief. We caught him red-handed. Not just with the historic artifacts and bones, either. I think he might have something from the Mullis investigation."

"Is it something Forensics might be interested in?" Fletcher asked.

"I'll be glad to take a look at it and save you some trouble," she offered. "I have some gloves and evidence bags with me."

"That would be a big help." He grinned. "If it's something you think is important, that's fine. Just be sure to sign off on the evidence. I don't want the captain to think we lost something."

Sergeant Fletcher and his officers went down to the lake to retrieve their prisoner. Peggy was right behind them, eager to get a better look at the purse.

PEGGY HAD STEVE SPREAD A piece of material on the ground beside a small holly bush. It would do for an evidence cloth. She could transfer everything into one of her plastic bags when she was done searching through the purse.

Steve knelt next to her on the hard, dry ground. He held the flashlight so she could see as the police were dismantling the thief's lighting system.

Carefully she removed and wrote down everything she found. There were bits of clutter in the purse: a few sticks of gum, a single pearl earring, and some breath mints. There was even a dried violet preserved in a small piece of plastic. They were things Peggy thought would be found in any woman's purse. There was some loose change in the satin-lined bottom, but otherwise there was no money. She wondered if the thief had already stripped that.

She found a gold-colored ring box, opened it, and was disappointed to find it empty. The spot inside where the ring had been was the right size for the carnelian ring. Maybe this was a sign that the ring *was* part of Lois's death. It seemed obvious to her on seeing the box that Jonathon might have been right and Lois had the ring with her.

She had to talk with Harold and see if they could wangle an interview with the man who'd been arrested there.

Sergeant Fletcher had already taken the thief, Snook Holt, away. She needed to know where he'd found the purse and how it had been overlooked in the search of the area. It might mean nothing, but . . .

"What are you thinking?" Steve asked.

"I'm thinking this might be important." She looked up at him and realized what he'd done. "I can't believe you *did* that. You talk about *me* risking my life! I've never done anything like that! You could've been killed."

"I wasn't. It's okay. I know how to handle a gun."

"And how is that?" she demanded. "Why does a mild-mannered veterinarian even own a gun? I understand the dart gun, but why did you bring the pistol?"

"I have to travel a lot of dark, deserted roads. I thought the pistol would be a way to stay safe. I never know who or what I'm going to encounter."

"You looked like a TV cop out there just now," she complained. "You scared me."

"I'm sorry. I didn't think. I reacted." He shook his head. "I just thought about keeping you safe."

"I guess it doesn't matter. Just don't ever do it again. You didn't get shot this time. Let's go home. I think that's enough excitement for one night."

"What about your samples? Don't you need them for tomorrow?"

She swore under her breath, a Southern lady's prerogative. He was right. She hated it, but he was right. "Yes. I have to get them before I leave."

"Let me help you," he offered.

"I have to fill all these bags." She put the purse and its contents, including the list of everything she'd found, into an evidence bag and sealed it before handing it to an officer who'd see it was placed in the right hands. "I don't know if this will affect the outcome of what happened to the chief's aunt. We'll see."

Steve followed her as she started into the woods, pushing aside brambles from long-dead wild roses. "You don't have to do this," she assured him. "You've already done enough for one night."

"But it will be easier if I hold the flashlight for you, won't it?"

She admitted it would be, and thanked him for offering. She was ready to get done with the process and go home, where she could have a chance to think about everything that had happened.

She carefully marked each bag of yew cuttings with a tag that matched the one on the bush from which she took the cutting. She had ten bags filled a little faster than she'd expected. There was a pale, thin moon above them that had a colored ring around it. "Usually that ring means rain," she said. "I hope it's right." The breezes sighed around them like lost spirits looking for peace. She shivered. No wonder people got spooked out here at night.

The process went along smoothly. After only about an hour they were packed up and headed home. This time, a police guard was left at the site.

It was nearly midnight when they reached her house. Queens Road was quiet. Most of the old houses around hers were sleeping. Peggy didn't get out right away, though she knew she should. She glanced at Steve. He was staring back at her. She looked away quickly, gathered her purse and sample bags, then reached for the door handle.

"I know you don't want to talk about this." His voice was deep and sincere. "If you're that uncomfortable with the idea of getting engaged, we don't have to. I just thought it might make things easier. Your parents aren't going back home this time. We need a long-term solution."

"I don't know what to say right now," she confessed. "I need time on my own to think about this."

"I know. I'd hoped it would be an easier decision for you. I guess I'll say good night."

Steve stayed where he was as she said good night and

walked up to the house. He pulled out of the drive after she was inside. She closed and locked the kitchen door and reset the alarm. Shakespeare got up from his spot in the pantry and shook himself awake before he trotted over to her, to let her know how happy he was that she was home.

"I'm glad to see you, too." She scratched the place behind his ear, then put the kettle on the stove for tea. "I think it's going to be a long night."

PEGGY SPENT MOST OF THE night alternating between looking at her plant experiments and rocking in her chair. It was hard to think about Steve without thinking about John.

John had been a wonderful man whom she'd loved with all her heart. She had never thought about spending time with someone else, not even after he was dead. She'd thought she would just go on alone. That seemed fair, considering the incredible life they'd had together.

Then Steve came along, and he seemed so perfect. In all honesty, he *was* perfect for her life the way it was right now. She loved him, and hated to imagine her life without him.

By the time daylight was beginning to seep around the edges of her backyard, she was completely confused and miserable. She was obviously shallow and self-absorbed. She didn't deserve Steve. She hadn't even known his sister was killed when he was a child! What was this world coming to?

Peggy heard the kitchen door upstairs open, and Paul's cheerful voice calling her name. She went up the basement stairs with Shakespeare at her heels. It would be good to talk with another human after a long night of conversations with the dog and her plants.

Paul was already on his way toward the stairs to the second floor. Peggy called his name, and he laughed. "I thought I might be able to surprise you again. That last time was funny. The look on your face was priceless."

"Good morning to you, too." Maybe she wasn't in the mood for human companionship after all. "What are you talking about?"

"Come on, Mom. I have cinnamon rolls in the kitchen. I'll make you some tea. I think we need to talk."

Peggy went along with him. His arm was around her shoulder, and short of throwing it off, she had no choice. The long night was catching up with her. She wasn't sure if she was fit company for anyone.

"I know about Steve," Paul said as he put water in the kettle after they'd reached the kitchen.

She sat down hard in one of the chairs. "I'm not sure what you mean."

"I know you and Steve are doing it."

The only thing worse than this conversation had to be the one she'd had with her son when he'd seen two dogs mating in the Weldons' yard. She put her hands over her eyes and tried to sound polite. "I think I may be too old to 'do it,' as you so colorfully describe it."

"It's okay. I wish you'd trusted me enough to tell me before you told Mai. I feel kind of weird knowing my mother and my fiancée were talking about sex. But I'll get over it."

"Mai guessed. I didn't tell her."

"Which makes me feel even worse." He took off his uniform jacket and hung it on the back of a chair. "What kind of cop am I if I don't see the clues?"

Peggy couldn't help noticing that Paul always sat in the same chair he'd occupied while growing up. It made her smile. "A good one. You just don't always see what's close to you. Like me with Steve."

Paul answered the shrill voice of the tea kettle and poured hot water into their cups. "Is something wrong?"

Peggy had started to tell him when her parents came through the kitchen door. Both of them were still in their robes and slippers. Her mother's hair was in curlers, and her father's hair stood straight up on his head.

"There you are!" Lilla stormed into the house. "I've been trying to call you since last night! Did you watch the news? They caught the bone thief out at the lake. He probably killed Lois."

Yawning, Peggy explained that she had been at the scene. "I know all about it. I can't believe you were trying to call me all night to tell me that."

"And where were you? I suppose your boyfriend is upstairs somewhere, waiting to try to sneak down and pretend he didn't spend the night." Lilla looked triumphant.

"That may be going too far," Ranson warned.

Peggy got to her feet. Enough was enough. "He didn't spend the night, Mom. Steve and I are having problems. But we have been sleeping together."

"I'll take some coffee, unless you have something stronger," Ranson said to Paul as he sat down.

Peggy looked at her family. "So you all knew all the time?"

Lilla took a chair and shrugged. "Not *all* the time. But we're not dense, Margaret. We've lived on a farm our whole lives. Everyone knows when it's mating season in the barn."

"So what happened with you and Dr. Steve?" Ranson took a cinnamon roll from the box. "Did he dump you for some floozy?"

"Paul will shoot him if that's what happened." Lilla calmly took Peggy's cup of tea as Paul brought it to the table. "I wish you'd drink regular tea, Margaret. This herbal stuff isn't very good."

Peggy sat back down and put her head in her hands. "It might be worse than that, Mom." She told them what had happened. She guessed it didn't matter anymore. They might as well know all of it. When she'd finished, she looked up at them.

Ranson glanced at Lilla. "I don't know. That doesn't seem so bad to me. The boy wants to do what's right."

Lilla glared at him, then turned to her daughter. "You

were absolutely right to send him packing last night. A woman has to teach a man how far he can go and what's expected of him."

"What are you talking about?" Peggy couldn't believe her ears. "I thought you didn't want me to get remarried."

"These are modern times, Margaret." Her mother patted her curlers and frowned. "The days of prolonged mourning are over. You've been widowed what, two or three years? Give it another good while to plan the wedding, and you'll be fine. I can't imagine anyone who could fault you. Except maybe Cousin Milbern. But who cares about him?"

"I wasn't *planning* on marrying Steve," Peggy said. What had she let herself in for? "We talked about getting engaged."

"Margaret Anne! You aren't exactly a spring rose, you know. Steve is a fine-looking man. A professional, too. I like veterinarians."

Ranson nodded. "I had many doctors who looked after our animals at one time or another. It's a good profession."

It was too much for Peggy to take in all at once. She excused herself, telling them she had to take a shower and get ready for work. Her parents nodded and ate the cinnamon rolls. Paul followed her from the kitchen.

"I'm sorry it worked out like this," he told her. "It makes me feel less guilty being happy with Mai knowing you're not knocking around in this big house by yourself."

"Thanks." She hugged him. "I'm sorry we couldn't talk about this before it came out."

"I'm fine." He kissed her cheek. "I just want you to know that I understand, and I don't have any strange feelings about you being with Steve instead of Dad. I know you loved Dad. And I think he'd like knowing you were with someone like Steve."

Peggy kissed him. "Thanks, Paul. It means a lot to me."

"So what are you going to do?"

"I'm going to see if I can bully someone into letting me

interrogate Snook Holt." She smiled at him and wiped away the tears that came to her eyes. "Then I'll probably give Steve a call and see if he still wants me."

Paul ruffled her hair with his hand. "You are such a romantic, Mom. How could he resist?"

16

Salvia

Botanical: *Salvia officinalis tricolor*

Sage and salvia are forever intertwined, as sages are salvias. Salvia is the Latin name for the genus. Through the years, gardeners and healers have come to differentiate them as sages for healing and salvias for decoration. Salvias are tall, spiked flowers that are multicolored and long-lived.

As Peggy was headed out the door to badger someone into letting her talk to Snook Holt, her cell phone rang. "I can't open the shop this morning," Selena told her when she answered. "I've got some kind of bug, and I don't think I can get out of bed today."

There wasn't much to say, except "Get better. Take all the time you need. Call me if I can do anything." Peggy closed her cell phone after listening to a few minutes of Selena's symptoms. She depended too heavily on that girl. At times like this she realized how fortunate she was that Selena wasn't sick more often. She'd been lucky to find her.

It looked like rain again. Knowing she'd have to find time to go to the lab between customers at the Potting Shed, she decided to drive the truck. The engine started easily after she'd unplugged the vehicle. She was on Queens Road shortly after, headed toward Center City.

True to the forecast, a few sprinkles hit the windshield as she was coming up College Street. She parked behind the Potting Shed and hurried inside. A few minutes later, a delivery of potting soil showed up, and then Sam came in with Keeley and Jasper. The day was off and running quickly.

"I tried some lemon juice on these age spots," the truck driver told her as she signed for the potting soil. "You were right, Peggy. It fades them."

She handed him the bill of lading and smiled. "It works every time, Jack. People have used it for hundreds of years. But you have to be careful and protect that bleached skin from excess sun."

Jack flashed her a bright white smile courtesy of his newly capped teeth. With his new toupee and dark tan, he was a changed man since his wife of fifteen years had left him. "I'm trying to get back into the dating scene, you know. Those pretty young things out there don't want you if you're not perfect."

"Maybe you should look for someone not quite so pretty and young," she advised. "There are other places you can meet women besides bars. Church. Grocery stores."

"You're just lucky you and Steve found each other so easy." Jack started back toward the cab of his truck. "If I could meet somebody that easy, I'd run my truck into some-one's bike, too."

She waved to him, not telling him that it would have to be the other way around if there was going to be anything left of the lucky woman. She thought about Steve as she went into the Potting Shed. Jasper was checking the pH of the pond while Sam was on the phone. She considered call-ing Steve, but the situation seemed inappropriate for a phone call. They needed to have a long, heart-to-heart talk about their relationship and how much she missed him. Hopefully, he missed her as much.

"We went over to install one of the systems at Denise Rogers's place," Keeley said. "She wasn't there, and the housekeeper didn't know anything about it. She threatened to sic her dalmatian on us. Nice, huh?"

"You should've called ahead," Peggy reminded her. "With the price of gas, those kinds of mistakes can cut into profits quickly."

"We had an understanding." Sam slammed the receiver down. "She knew we were coming today. What's so important it couldn't wait?"

"I don't know. But you might be better off not having that kind of understanding." Peggy sat down in her rocking chair. "Tea?"

"I'll take some." Jasper got up from the pond and dried his hands on his jeans.

"No time," Sam told him, walking toward the back door. "If we can't work on Denise Rogers's system, we'll move on to the next and catch her on the way back through the list."

"What's the rush?" Peggy asked. It wasn't like Sam to be so impatient. "That attitude isn't going to do much for customer relations."

Sam pointed to the courtyard, which was being pelted by large raindrops. "This could be over with a few good rains. We have to get the systems set up while the drought is still here."

"I don't think it's going away that quickly," Peggy said. "You're going to give yourself a coronary, Sam."

"Maybe. But I want to have at least five hundred of these systems installed before I do."

She smiled. "I get it. Good luck."

Jasper asked where they were going, and Sam took out his Palm Pilot. "The Evanses live over by the university. We can be there before ten."

"The university!" Peggy jumped up from the rocker. "Can you take something to the botanical garden for me while you're out there? I completely forgot about getting these samples to Merton."

Sam looked shocked. "You? Forgot something? I don't believe it. I'd believe you paid Mrs. Rogers not to be home so you could have me deliver whatever it is before I'd believe you forgot something. You must've been sidetracked. What's up? Are you and Steve getting married or having problems?"

He was so close to the truth, it stunned her. For a moment she could only stare at him with what had to be a blank expression on her face.

Sam glanced at her and then put his Palm Pilot in his pocket and crossed the shop floor to wrap his big arms around her. "I guess it must be problems. I don't think anyone looks like that if they're getting married." He smiled down at her. "Unless you don't want to get married."

"You were right the first time," she confessed. "We'll have dinner and talk about it sometime. Right now, my yew samples are running late. Thanks for the sympathy."

"Just let me know when you're ready to talk about it." He squeezed her tight. "And if Steve is giving you a hard time, I can pay him a little visit."

Peggy laughed at the evil look on his handsome face. Unfortunately, the effect was ruined by her recalling how many times Paul had looked the same way when he was about five years old. That was one thing about getting older; everyone seemed to become more childlike. "Just get out of here, and don't forget my yew samples in the truck."

Sam smiled and was gone, trailed by Keeley and Jasper. In their absence, the shop was very quiet. Peggy wished someone, even a salesman, would come in. She'd straightened and primped the shop until there was nothing left to do.

She finally pulled out her laptop and started working on

some flyers for her drought workshop. She was intently
making notes about all the plants that would create a sturdy,
drought-resistant garden when the courtyard door opened.
It was the ladies from the Shamrock Historical Society. She
couldn't believe she was glad to see them, but boredom
could do strange things.

"Margaret." Her mother approached her with Grace,
Annabelle, Dorothy, Geneva, and Mrs. Waynewright standing behind her. "We want to talk to you about what happened at the lake last night."

"We sure do!" Geneva pushed her way to the front. "The
police told us that nothing was unusual about the case at the
museum where the carnelian ring was stored."

"Can you imagine that?" Grace nudged Geneva aside.
"All this time we were looking at Jonathon being the killer,
and it really was that awful Snook Holt."

"First of all"—Peggy stopped her—"you don't even
know for sure he's the man Lois testified against."

"Are you saying you think it's *still* Jonathon?" Dorothy
asked.

"I saw the bone thief on TV this morning," Mrs. Waynewright told them. "It was the very same man. He was out
there stealing those poor people's bones right under the nose
of the police. He probably hurt Lois because she saw him
out there again."

"I'm sure he knew her right away, and was looking for
revenge." Annabelle added her own theatrics to the discussion by pretending to plunge a knife into her chest.

"We feel so bad for suspecting Jonathon," Grace said.
"We have to find a way to make it up to him. Even if he is a
little careless sometimes."

"Of course, the door in the museum *can't* be left open
again," Mrs. Waynewright told them. "We can't abide that
sort of behavior."

"But how did the thief get the ring?" Lilla asked everyone in general.

"We may never know," Geneva whispered. "In the meantime, there's poor Lois getting her hair done for the last time."

The ladies all sniffled appropriately. Peggy didn't share her finding Lois's purse with Snook Holt last night. The ladies certainly didn't need to know what was really going on, unless she wanted it plastered all over the news by tomorrow morning.

"It's a terrible thing," Peggy sympathized, trying to get them to go back outside. She'd been wrong. Boredom was better than this. "I'm glad you came to tell me."

"We didn't come to tell you about it," Geneva said. "We came to take you over to the cemetery. You have to get some training if you're going to help us identify graves."

Peggy explained about Selena. "I'd love to come, but I need someone to be here at the store. I can't just go running off with you, even though I'd like to."

Lilla's face brightened. "Your father is just sitting around at home today. I'm sure he'd love to come and watch the store for you. I'll call him."

There were no words that came to mind to thank her, so Peggy said nothing. The day just wasn't working out the way she'd planned it. Maybe there was a good reason for it, but she doubted it.

HALF AN HOUR LATER, Peggy waved good-bye to her father and got into the museum van. Her mother smiled at her, and Geneva thanked her several times for going with them.

"We're swinging by the museum to pick up Jonathon. It's the least we can do after misjudging him." Geneva grinned at Peggy in the rearview mirror, then turned the van sharply into the museum parking lot. "This kind of thing is a treat for all us history nuts."

Peggy didn't doubt it. Jonathon got out of his car and climbed into the van, sitting beside her. When the door was closed, Geneva squealed the tires as she left the parking lot.

"It's good to be part of the group again." Jonathon smiled and nodded at all the women. "I hear Lois's funeral will be tomorrow. I ordered a wreath from the museum. I hope that's all right."

All the women agreed that a wreath was perfect. Peggy asked him what flowers were on it, but he had no idea. She sat back in her seat, ruminating on how people could ignore the meanings of flowers they used at important times in their lives.

"I'm glad you're with us today," Jonathon said to Peggy. "I guess this must be your first grave-hunting excursion."

The target today was a lone Revolutionary soldier's grave abandoned years before. Or at least that was what they were looking for. Grace explained that they had only an old account of where the soldier should be buried. They weren't sure if the grave was still there.

"It's in a cow pasture," Annabelle explained. "I brought some spray stuff I got on the Internet that's supposed to make people smell like cows, so the cows don't bother them."

"Did we ever get permission from Mr. McWhirter?" Geneva asked as she took off from a stoplight. "I don't remember if we did or not."

Dorothy looked over the top of her reading glasses. "I don't recall right now. It seems like we heard something from him. Mrs. Waynewright, do you remember seeing that letter?"

Mrs. Waynewright was the secretary of the society. "No, dear. I remember you sending it, because we wrote it together, but I don't remember getting a reply from the gentleman."

"It doesn't really matter," Geneva said. "We're within our legal rights to visit the grave since Mrs. Waynewright is a direct descendant. McWhirter can't keep us away."

Dorothy grimaced. "Remember that time we had to sneak into that abandoned cemetery out by Salisbury? Those terrible dogs! I'm not sure what we would've done if Mr. Hawkins hadn't been with us. He took that bite like a man."

"After that, the dogs seemed fine with us being there." Annabelle shrugged.

"But poor Mr. Hawkins had to have rabies shots. He was such a gentleman about it." Mrs. Waynewright sighed in appreciation.

Peggy put her head in her hand. What had she let herself in for?

Jonathon tapped her shoulder. "Don't worry. It's usually not that bad. I've gone out on hundreds of these expeditions through college and with these lovely ladies. I haven't been bitten or pitchforked yet."

"I totally forgot about that time the old farmer pitchforked Mr. Hawkins!" Annabelle threw her hands up in the air. "That was another strange experience."

"It sounds like you've had quite a few," Peggy observed. She glanced at her mother, who seemed completely all right with the situation. Maybe she had done similar things in Charleston.

"I'll stay close by in case someone decides to attack us while we're looking for Zachary Miller's grave." Jonathon smiled at Peggy. "It should be an interesting experience."

Peggy ignored the tales of past expeditions as the ladies talked. She focused on Jonathon, lowering her voice as she asked, "Did you find out anything about the ring?"

"Nothing more than we knew before. It's quite old. Possibly from the time of the Civil War."

"You mean the War Against Northern Aggression," Mrs. Waynewright reminded him. "You *are* from the South, Jonathon. We do *not* refer to that war as the Civil War."

He grinned at her. "You're so right, Mrs. Waynewright. I wasn't thinking."

Jonathon looked back at Peggy. "As I was saying, we think the crest on the ring belonged to a specific battalion or company. We're not sure which one, since much of that information has been lost. It was expensive, so the ring was probably given to the company commander. That would make it a one-of-a-kind artifact."

"Any ideas on how the ring got out to the lake?" Peggy asked, even though she was pretty sure Lois had taken it out there.

"No. We—I should say the police—don't think it was stolen. Someone had to have taken it out there, but we don't know who did it or why." Jonathon's dark brown eyes revealed what he was really thinking but unable to say; he believed Lois took the ring.

"But you're sure it's the same ring?" Peggy pressed for more information.

"Yes. We had good pictures of it. It's definitely the same ring."

"Don't you have video surveillance in the museum?"

"Not yet. But we're working on it since this happened. It won't happen again. Do you have some idea of who took it?"

"No," she lied. It was for his own good, she reminded herself. He was right not to mention anything about Lois stealing the ring. He'd just gotten back into the ladies' good graces.

Geneva put the brake down hard. "We're here." They all rocked back and forth in their seatbelts before they began piling out of the van. Each person had a backpack, and Mrs. Waynewright carried a small American flag that would be put on the grave to mark it once they had established it was truly Zachary Miller's resting place.

Peggy looked at the hill they'd have to climb to reach the cow pasture where the grave was reported to be. Dorothy brought out her GPS locator and explained how they'd know when they found the grave.

"Of course that's all new stuff," Annabelle said. "There are plenty of other ways to find a grave." She took out a tree branch that was stripped of its leaves. "I prefer dowsing for it. My willow wand never lets me down."

"How does that work?" Peggy asked as she followed them up the hill.

"They say, or at least your father says, the graves fill up with water that's retained by the clay," Lilla explained. "Therefore, the wand is responding to the water being held underground. It's like when Mr. Peters came to dowse for our new well when you were a girl and our old well went dry. Don't you remember that?"

Peggy couldn't say that she did. Being a scientist, she'd dismiss this kind of folklore out of hand. But being from the Low Country in South Carolina, she'd been raised with hoodoo and other superstitions that came true more times than her scientific mind could explain.

"Anyway, it works." Annabelle's voice was strained as the ladies threw themselves up the large hill. The recent rain had made the top layer of red clay muddy, leaving them all with red stains on their boots and jeans.

Jonathon caught up with Peggy and slowed his long-legged stride to match her shorter one. "I know it seems like a lot of nonsense, but sometimes folklore is accurate."

"You don't have to tell me," she said. "I was raised in the South. I know every superstition there is. Some of them I even believe. I wouldn't dare disagree with any of them, for fear that would be the one that would come true."

"Do you have some idea about the ring?" he asked. "I know you said you didn't, but I kind of felt like maybe you did, but didn't want to say anything."

Peggy applauded his perception, but didn't change her mind about telling him what she knew. "I felt the same way about you. You think Lois took it, don't you?"

He glanced around before lowering his voice even more. "Yes, I do."

She was thinking about the interview she'd hoped to have with Snook Holt. The interview that was dwindling away with the rest of the day while she looked for an old grave.

"I wouldn't accuse her of that again even if she was alive. Not only was she on the board of directors for the museum, all of the remaining directors were her lifelong friends, like Mrs. Waynewright. Plus her nephew is the chief of police. I don't want to know where an accusation like that would take me now."

"Maybe one of the other ladies took it out there."

He shrugged. "It's possible. But why would they do that?"

"Why do you think Lois would do it?" she questioned. "Does that make more sense?"

Jonathon glanced around again, but the other ladies were yards in front of them. "There was a connection between Lois's family and that ring. At least that's what she said. I don't have all the details. I don't dare ask now. Maybe she took it from the museum because she planned to keep it. Or maybe she planned to sell it to Snook Holt."

"Are you two coming or what?" Geneva demanded from the top of the hill. "We don't have all day to do this!"

As Peggy and Jonathon hurried up the hill to reach the rest of the group, she considered his accusations. No wonder he didn't want to voice them to the group or the museum board of directors. It was unlikely to bring him anything except a pink slip.

Still, what he'd said about Lois having some connection to the ring was curious. She tended to agree with him that Lois had taken the ring from the museum. But why take it out to the lake? That part didn't make any sense. The idea that one of these ladies would sell an important family heirloom that would set her up a few more rungs on the historical ladder seemed ludicrous. There had to be a better explanation.

"We already found the cemetery, thanks to my GPS," Dorothy told them.

"Yes, but my wand will help locate the graves that may have sunk since they were placed there," Annabelle said.

Peggy looked across a pretty meadow that had thousands of red salvias, which were barely holding their heads up after the rain. Normally they would've been gone in September, but the drought had helped them linger into fall. And sure enough, there were at least a hundred cows munching grass in the pasture. Somehow the fence had come down near the hill, but the cows seemed to ignore that.

"Okay, let's get started," Geneva said. "I'll take photos of the site. Peggy, you get the shaving cream for the upright headstones. I'll put you in charge of the rubbings as well, but call me when you can read the tombstone. The rest of you know what to do."

"Good thing I was out for my constitutional," a man's gravelly voice interrupted them. "I don't take with no trespassers on my property. Law says I have a right to shoot first, and it looks like I might have to do just that."

17

Heartleaf Philodendron

Botanical: *Philodendron scandens*

In 1793, Captain William Bligh—the Captain Bligh of Mutiny on the Bounty—brought this vine from the West Indies to the Royal Botanic Gardens in England. All parts are poisonous due to aroid toxins, including calcium oxalate. The roots were used as an antioxidant, preventing disease and infection for native tribes. The toxins cause low-level skin irritation as well as burning and swelling of the lips, throat, and tongue.

THE FARMER BIT DOWN ON the chewing tobacco that was lodged in his right cheek. He shifted his old shotgun as though it was too heavy for him.

Without thinking about what she was doing, Peggy stepped between him and the rest of the group. "We're only here to look for Captain Zachary Miller's grave. Is he an ancestor of yours?"

It must have suddenly occurred to Jonathon that Peggy had put herself between him and the shotgun. He did the noblest thing possible, and stepped between Peggy and the farmer.

The farmer, who'd been considering Peggy's question,

got riled up again when Jonathon moved. He motioned with the shotgun for him to go back to where he had been. "I don't know what you all are talkin' about. Just get off my land."

Geneva stepped forward. "We can't do that, sir. We're from the Shamrock Historical Society, and one of our members is related to Captain Miller."

Grace stood beside her. "So she has as much right to be here as you do."

Mrs. Waynewright waved her hand. "Be off with you, old man. We intend to find the captain's grave and honor it. He was a hero of the American Revolution and my ancestor, and deserves a better fate than sleeping in this cow pasture."

The farmer spit on the ground. "Who you callin' old? You look like you could'a been in the war yourself."

Before the discussion got any hotter, Peggy encouraged all of them to step back. "My name is Peggy Lee. What's your name?"

He chuckled. "Like the singer? Are you kin to her?"

"No. Your name?"

"Marcus Miller McWhirter."

Mrs. Waynewright eyed him with a cold stare. "My great granddaddy was named Marcus Miller. I suppose we *could* be related."

"You one of them Huntersville Millers, or part of the Miller clan from around Goose Creek?" The farmer looked interested instead of angry. Peggy thought it was a start.

While Mrs. Waynewright exchanged family information with Farmer McWhirter, the rest of the group moved closer to the headstones gathered under a huge, old oak tree. "This tree was probably here when they laid these people to rest," Peggy told them. She put her hand against the rough bark and considered all the things the tree had lived through. Still, it was standing, protecting the dead who slept beneath it.

"Here's the shaving cream and the squeegee." Geneva handed Peggy her gear. "Let's get to it in case our friend over there decides not to be so friendly. You never know if the Millers get along or not."

Peggy took the equipment, watching Jonathon as he took photos and observed the graves. There were three headstones with a large sunken space between them. She stepped around that area and knelt on the ground to put the shaving cream on the first headstone.

"I'll bet that's Captain Miller's grave," Jonathon said. "Probably his wife beside him. That's why there's no headstone. People didn't think wives needed to be recognized back then. It was enough for them to be laid beside their husbands."

"That's amazing." Peggy shot shaving cream into her hand, then smoothed it on the worn stone. Her mother had told her about this technique for reading old tombstones years ago. The white shaving cream filled in the letters and dates so historians could read them. She brought the squeegee down over the stone to take off the excess, and sat back with a notebook and pencil to record her find.

"These are probably two of their children," Jonathon said on the other side of the sunken grave area. "Probably older children."

"I think I found Captain Miller," Peggy called to the other ladies, who all rushed to her side. The tombstone inscription filled in with shaving cream read "Captain Zachary Miller, Revolutionary War Hero and County Judge for ten years. Born 1750. Died 1820. God loved him."

"That's him," Annabelle said. "Everyone come and take a look."

Peggy thought it was remarkable how quickly people could go from being enemies to blood relatives. Farmer McWhirter rested on his shotgun with the business end in the hard earth. "Well, I'll be! I never thought much of this little cemetery bein' out here. My daddy even thought about takin' it all out, but the preacher told him he'd burn in hell if he did."

Mrs. Waynewright brought out her bouquet of red, white, and blue silk roses. She placed them on the captain's grave and stood the flag beside the tombstone because she couldn't push it into the hard earth. Dorothy played a recording of "God Bless America" with her MP3 player. When the little ceremony was over, silence filled the wooded area.

Farmer McWhirter wiped his eyes on a dirty handkerchief. "That was beautiful. You all come up to the house for some lemonade. My wife just made some gingersnaps. I know she'll want to meet you."

Peggy's cell phone rang, and she walked away from the group to answer it. It was Dr. Ramsey, in fine form. "Where are you, Dr. Lee? And why was my chain of evidence broken today?"

"Hello, Harold. I have no idea what you're talking about." She watched as the others started toward the old white farmhouse in the distance.

"I'm talking about those yew branches you gathered from the lake. You had some delivery driver take them to the university, where he gave them to Dr. Dillard. What were you thinking?"

Peggy realized she hadn't been thinking clearly that morning. She'd given crime scene evidence to Sam so she wouldn't have to go to UNC Charlotte. The worth of the evidence was destroyed by her not taking them there herself.

"I'm sorry. I don't know what I was thinking." She chastised herself mentally a million times before his response.

"Fortunately for you, the branches didn't match the seeds he's been looking at. Get over here to the lab as soon as you can."

She started to protest that it was stupid for him to yell at her when the evidence didn't match anyway, but he'd already hung up. She supposed he'd simply tell her the lesson was for the future. The forensic evidence could've made an important difference in the case, and it would've been botched because of her. As a scientist, she could certainly appreciate that fact.

Jonathon had remained behind with her. He was examining the other tombstones, taking pictures of them and using paper and charcoal to take rubbings from them. "Trouble?"

"Not really." She put her phone away. "This has been interesting. My only question is how any of you manage to stay alive doing this. I don't know why you were so surprised by Lois's death. How many times do angry property owners come after you with guns?"

He laughed. "It's never happened to me before. I can't speak for the ladies. They seem determined to put themselves in harm's way."

Peggy walked beside him to the farmhouse, listening to him talk about history as though it had happened yesterday. A great deal of passion and pride was displayed by this group when it came to claiming their heritage. She certainly didn't want to disparage the theory that Snook Holt had come across Lois at the lake and caused her death, but there were aspects to that idea that made no sense.

The question of how a man Lois would never have trusted could get her to eat anything, much less poison berries, was at the forefront. Without signs of coercion, she had to assume Lois ate the berries willingly.

There was also the carnelian ring. It obviously had bearing on the case. It had been out there, and she believed it arrived in Lois's purse. Surely Lois wouldn't have taken the ring out if she knew Snook Holt was there.

Peggy thought about the puzzle while she and the others ate gingersnaps and drank lemonade with the McWhirters before heading back to the van. The ladies were happy with the standing invitation to visit the site whenever they wanted. That and dedicating Captain Miller's grave was a good day's work for them. They all fell asleep on the way back to Charlotte while Jonathon drove.

PEGGY CHECKED IN ON HER father when she got back to the Potting Shed. He was asleep in her rocking chair, his chin resting on his chest. She smiled at him fondly, then shook his shoulder.

Ranson jumped up in surprise. "You sneaked up on me, Sweet Pea. Are you back from your historical expedition already?"

"*We* are." Her mother joined them. "It was wonderful. You should've been there." She went on to describe the event and meeting the McWhirters. "You would've been proud of your daughter. She almost backed up a man with a shotgun trained right on her heart."

"And why would that have made me proud?" He glanced at Peggy and frowned. "You had all those prime old ladies out there, and you were willing to sacrifice yourself. I thought I taught you better."

She laughed. "Any business while I was gone?"

"One woman came in to buy fertilizer for her African violet. I managed to sell her some tulip bulbs with it."

"I hope she plans to put them in pots." Peggy got behind the cash register. "Otherwise, I hope she has one of Sam's new watering systems. The soil's too dry and hard to plant them."

"I'd like to see one of those contraptions," her father said. "Think that could be arranged?"

"I don't see why not. I'll talk to Sam about it."

"Talk to her about that later, Ranson." Lilla yawned. "I'm tired and dirty, and you know that's not a good thing for me."

He shook his head. "You'd never guess you've spent most of your life on the farm."

"Not in my youth, dear. I'm still a city girl at heart."

Lilla waved to Peggy. "I'll talk to you later. Any luck with Steve yet?"

"I haven't had time." Peggy shrugged and sat down in the recently vacated rocking chair. "But I'll talk to him tonight."

"Good. We still have plenty of time to plan an engagement party for Tuesday night. I hope that's not rushing you."

Peggy said good-bye to her parents without answering her mother's question. She wasn't sure if it was wise to plan an engagement party when one half of the couple didn't know they were getting engaged. She took out her cell phone and tried to call Steve, but could only reach his voice mail. What if he didn't want to get engaged now? Just because her parents and Paul thought it was a good idea didn't mean Steve would.

The door to the shop opened, and a woman pushing a small cart full of houseplants stepped in. Peggy helped her get the cart past the doorway, wondering why she had so many plants and hoping she wasn't going to return them. Like any other store, she sometimes had people who weren't happy with what they bought and wanted to bring them back.

"Can I help you?" Peggy asked after closing the shop door.

"I hope so. Are you the owner?"

The woman looked as though she'd been crying. Peggy immediately sat her down in the rocking chair and put on some tea. It was blueberry with a touch of borage. "I'm Peggy. I own the Potting Shed."

"A friend of mine, Jolie Lamonte, told me if anyone could help me, it would be you." With that, she sobbed uncontrollably for a few minutes.

Peggy made the tea and put a mug of it in the other woman's hand. "Of course I know Jolie. She's a very dear friend. What's your name?"

"Rachael Woods. I live over in the Dilworth area. I've taken care of my mother for the past three years. She died two days ago. Now I have all these plants." She spread her hands at the cart. "I want to take care of them, but I don't know how. I think all of them are dying. What am I doing wrong?"

Peggy sipped her tea and took a good look at the plants. "Well, let's see. I think this little cyclamen needs to be re-potted. I'm sure it'll be fine with some new soil and a bigger pot. And this Christmas cactus has overgrown its pot, too. See how the soil looks? It's used up all the nutrients. As far as this philodendron is concerned, I think we may have to reroot part of it. It may survive that way. It's hard to kill one of those."

"I'm no good with plants," Rachael cried. She accepted Peggy's offer of tissues. "I just can't stand the idea of anything else dying right now, you know? If I can save them, I want them to live."

"I don't think that's a problem." Peggy opened a bag of good potting soil and set Rachael to work taking the plants out of their containers while she rounded up a few new pots. It took only a few minutes to put the plants into their new homes. "You can take these fertilizer pellets with you. Use one a month on each plant. Be sure to keep them out of drafts."

They tackled the philodendron next. Peggy very carefully removed the only good leaf left on the plant. She didn't want to imagine what kind of abuse the poor thing had endured. Usually philodendrons were the safest bet for a new gardener. "We'll just put some new soil in this little pot and stick the end of the leaf in the soil. Water it a little. Don't let it get too dry, but don't drown it, either. It should be fine."

Rachael sniffed, her hands and dress covered in soil. "I don't know how to thank you. Jolie was right. You've been such a big help."

When the younger woman burst out crying again, Peggy hugged her tightly and tried to comfort her. The shop door opened again, this time to admit Sofia from the Kozy Kettle. For once, Peggy was glad to see her. It took the Sicilian woman only an instant to take the girl in hand and lead her toward another cup of tea and something sweet at her shop.

Sofia glanced at Peggy as though she had made Rachael cry. Peggy shook her head to deny it, but it was no use. A few minutes later, Emil ran across the courtyard and let himself into the Potting Shed. "What's wrong over here? Did that girl try to take your man? You know that happens sometimes. It might be for the best, since you aren't good for each other, anyway. He likes the animals and you like the plants."

Peggy started adding up what she'd put together for Rachael. "That's not the problem," she explained. "She was crying because her mother died and I saved her plants."

Emil rolled his expressive dark eyes. "You can believe that if it makes you happy. You come over and eat when you get done here, and we'll talk about it."

"I have ten other places I have to be, Emil. But thanks for the invitation. Can you help me get this cart over there?"

Emil picked up the cart and carried it across the brick courtyard. Peggy noticed that someone had left an ICEE in one of the big flower pots she maintained for Brevard Court. She took it out and dropped it in the trash can. The bright rust and red mums looked none the worse for the experience.

Rachael was still crying when Peggy got to the Kozy Kettle. She took out her credit card when she saw the cart full of plants. Peggy ran the card, happy it was good and she wouldn't have to tell the girl she couldn't buy what she needed.

"I won't ever forget what you've done," Rachael said as she signed the receipt.

"You take care of yourself and those plants," Peggy

advised, giving her a copy of the transaction. "I'm sure your mother wouldn't want you to go on this way and make yourself sick."

Sofia crossed herself. "No. Not like my Cousin Gena. She made herself crazy when her mother died. We had to lock her in the attic for months. Then her father died. What a mess!"

Peggy didn't wait to hear more of the story. She went back across the courtyard and closed the Potting Shed. She started home, intending to look for Steve. He was probably in his basement with a patient, and that's why he wasn't picking up the phone. She was sure he wasn't ignoring her when he saw her name and number on his caller ID. Surely he'd at least talk to her.

Her phone rang as she closed it. "Peggy, you have to get over here," Mai told her. "This is officially still my case, and I need to know where we are as far as those berries are concerned."

"We're nowhere right now," Peggy told her, not planning to go near the lab until she'd talked to Steve. "Merton says none of the branches I've given him match the seeds you took from Lois."

"Then we need more branches. She didn't get those berries out of the air. We need to know where they came from, now that we know Holt was involved."

"Have they charged him with her death?"

"No. They're waiting on evidence, waiting for *you!*"

"I can't cut branches off of every yew bush out there," Peggy said. "There are hundreds. Besides, that doesn't explain your findings. You said there were no bruises and you didn't think anyone had forced Lois to eat the berries. Surely you don't think now that she willingly took poison berries from a man she would've been afraid of?"

"I don't know what to think right now," Mai admitted. "But I have Dr. Ramsey and Chief Mullis breathing down my neck. I need you here to back me up."

"If it's any help," Peggy said, "I think this whole thing is about the carnelian ring. Did you see the contents of Lois's pocketbook that we found at the lake?"

"I've been going through it all day. Are you talking about the ring box?"

"Yes. I think if we can figure out why Lois took that ring out to the lake, we may be closer to figuring out why she died. The yew berries could be from anywhere out there."

"But that may not be true either," Mai argued. "Please, Peggy. Come to the lab. What else are you doing that's so important? It's past six, so I know the shop is closed."

Peggy couldn't bring herself to admit she was going to look for Steve and ask him if he still wanted them to be together. She liked Mai, but this wasn't something she wanted to discuss with her. It was bad enough to start the day discussing it with her family. "All right. I'll come over for awhile. I'm not sure what good I can do, but I'll be there in a few minutes."

"Great! I'll schedule a conference with everyone."

"Is everyone me, you, and Harold?" Peggy asked, but the phone was dead. Apparently Mai had raced to schedule that conference. Why did she have the feeling she had volunteered to walk through a minefield?

She tried calling Steve again. There was still no response. A feeling of dread was creeping into her. Steve never went this long without answering. Even though she hadn't left him a message, he had to know she'd been calling him all day. If he'd wanted to talk to her, he would've called.

Maybe it was just as well. The whole thing could be a mistake. It had taken her parents and son to convince her it wasn't a mistake. That said something in itself. She wasn't sure what, but maybe it was better to leave things as they were. When she recalled how angry and frightened she'd been the night before, she tried to summon some of that frustration. But all she got was a strange feeling of emptiness.

She parked the truck in the lab parking lot, not surprised to see how many techs were still working. There was a growing number of crimes in the city and always a shortage of good help. It was one of the reasons she'd agreed to do this work. It brought her a lot of satisfaction to solve cases, but it also made her feel as though she was doing something good for the community.

"Dr. Lee." Harold loomed up out of the stainless steel and green paint in the lab. "How nice of you to join us."

Peggy's cell phone rang. It was Steve, of course. "I'll just be a minute, Harold."

"Dr. Lee," Chief Mullis addressed her, "I see we're all here. Shall we get started?"

18

Spanish bayonet

Botanical: *Yucca aloifolia*

Spiky Spanish bayonet will tolerate a wide range of soil conditions but usually needs full sun. Little maintenance is required to keep the plant growing. The pronuba moth pollinates most yuccas. The plants and the moths share an interesting biological dependency on each other; the moth needs the plant as much as the plant needs the moth.

PEGGY SIGHED AS SHE TURNED off her cell phone. Steve was going to have to wait.

She sat down at the long, battered conference table with Harold, Mai, and Chief Mullis. Before they started talking, Captain Jonas Rimer and Detective Al McDonald joined them. A few pleasantries were observed; Peggy knew Jonas's wife, Georgette, and asked after her since she hadn't seen the couple in a few months.

Chief Mullis killed that notion quickly. "Are we here for the social hour or are we here to find out what happened to my aunt?"

Everyone was quiet after that, with only the sound of shuffling papers filling the room.

Harold finally cleared his throat. "Even though I was *not*

the acting medical examiner at the beginning of this case, I'd be happy to take over now."

Mai gasped. "There's no reason to do that, Dr. Ramsey. I think I can handle following through on this."

"I simply meant I have more experience on a homicide than you, Sato. I'd hate for anything to be missed while we try to piece together what happened to Mrs. Mullis."

"What do we think happened to her?" Peggy pushed her way into the conversation.

"It's pretty obvious." Al opened his folder. "Mrs. Mullis helped prosecute Snook Holt. He got out of prison a few months ago and apparently went right back to his old habits. Chief Mullis dropped his aunt off at Lake Whitley to meet her group. He didn't realize Holt was out there at the time."

"When Holt saw the woman who sent him to jail"— Jonas picked up the story—"he wanted revenge. He forced Mrs. Mullis to eat poison berries, then pushed her into the mud."

Chief Mullis nodded in agreement. "That's the way I see it. Thank you."

Peggy cleared her throat and glanced significantly at Mai.

Mai nodded and swallowed hard before saying, "We can't support that theory, Chief Mullis. There was no sign of your aunt being forced to do anything. No bruising around the mouth, as you might expect in this case. No bruising on the arms, shoulders, or neck. I believe she ate the berries willingly."

"You're saying she killed herself?" Chief Mullis demanded.

"No, of course not." Mai shuffled her papers without looking at them. "I'm saying Mr. Holt didn't force her to eat the berries. Maybe he talked her into eating them."

Chief Mullis exchanged looks with Jonas and Al. "I suppose something like that could happen. Aunt Lois was older. We all know older people are more likely to be victims of scams."

"That's the most outrageously stupid thing I've ever heard anyone say!" Peggy brought her hand down hard on the table. "This woman was smart as a whip. She couldn't be fooled that easy. She wouldn't have taken berries from that man. All the ladies in the group talk about him like he's Jack the Ripper. There's no way he convinced her to eat anything!"

"Do you have a theory, Dr. Lee?" Chief Mullis asked.

"Not exactly. I know what *didn't* happen. She didn't eat those berries because Snook Holt held them out and offered them to her."

"Not having a theory doesn't help in this case," Jonas told her. "At least we have something to go on the other way."

"It's the wrong something," she maintained. "And what about the ring?"

The three police officers looked at her blankly. Harold put his head in his hand, and Mai shuffled her papers for the tenth time.

"What ring is this?" Chief Mullis wondered. "Because I haven't heard anything about a ring being involved in this case."

Peggy wanted Mai to explain, but the younger woman shrugged and shook her head. "There was an antique man's carnelian ring in the mud when Mai and I visited the site to get some cuttings from the yew bushes around the dry lake." She went on to explain where it had come from and why she thought it was important.

"You say Mrs. Mullis had a ring box in her purse?" Al wrote down the information. "Why weren't we told about this?"

"Because until yesterday, you didn't think there was a case," Peggy said. "Until Steve and I happened on Mr. Holt, everyone was calling her death an accident. Now it's a homicide, and I think the ring may be important."

"If this ring is so valuable, why didn't Snook go after it when it fell into the mud?" Chief Mullis asked.

"It's not entirely the dollar amount that makes the ring valuable," Peggy explained. "If you were a historian, you'd understand. But I agree with you. If Mr. Holt had seen this ring, he would've jumped in after it the way I did."

Jonas was sketching on his notes. "Which brings us back to Snook killing Mrs. Mullis. Only now we have a stronger motive. He robbed her of this ring as well as wanting to take revenge."

"I don't think that's what Dr. Lee is saying." Al glanced at her. "No matter what else happened, there's nothing to corroborate the idea that Snook gave those berries to Mrs. Mullis and she ate them willingly. It doesn't matter about the ring or the revenge if we can't prove he got her to eat the berries. Is that about right, Dr. Lee?"

"That's exactly it, Detective McDonald." Peggy smiled at him. "Thank you for clarifying that. I think the ring is important, but not as important as why Lois ate the yew berries."

"There's a thing called proximity," Chief Mullis told her. "Snook was out there at the lake. He knew my aunt, and conceivably wanted revenge. She had a valuable ring. This may be circumstantial, but a lot of circumstantial evidence adds up to hard facts."

Jonas nodded. "I think to ignore those facts would be a mistake. I'll talk to the DA. I believe he'll want to go ahead with the case even though Forensics isn't exactly in our corner on this one."

Chief Mullis got to his feet. "We're burying Aunt Lois tomorrow. I assume you'll have whatever you need for this case by then, Dr. Ramsey."

Dr. Ramsey stood up and shook his hand. "You can count on me."

With a nod to the rest of them, the chief left. Jonas followed him while Al hung behind a moment. "Sorry, Peggy.

I did what I could. For what it's worth, what you're saying makes sense to me."

She thanked him, but when Al was gone, Dr. Ramsey rounded on her and Mai. "We need something else to put this together," he said. "Sato, look over the body again. Maybe you were mistaken. Maybe you missed something."

Mai picked up her folder. "You heard the chief. We don't have the body. She's probably already been embalmed. There's nothing else to look at."

"Go back over the photos and the evidence you collected, then. And you"—he pointed at Peggy—"always the troublemaker. You go out to the lake and cut down every yew out there until you find the one that matches the seeds Sato found. You have the weekend. Don't waste any of it."

PEGGY DIDN'T WASTE ANY TIME taking off her white lab coat and heading for the parking lot. She grabbed a handful of evidence bags and gloves, stuffed them in her purse, and took out her cell phone.

She'd apologize to Steve for calling him, then not answering his return call. Something life-threatening had kept her from answering. She didn't know what that was yet, but she'd think of something. Somehow it seemed indefensible to call a man you'd wronged, then go to a meeting when you had a chance to make up.

She didn't exactly regret the decision, it just sounded bad. The call was going through when she saw Al standing beside her truck. Immediately, she stopped the call. Better to do that than risk asking Steve to wait a minute while she spoke to Al.

"I was wondering if Ramsey was going to keep you in there all night," he joked. "I have an offer to make. You can say no if you like."

"It was an evidence matter," she explained. "Not that it

made any difference, but I had to put up my house and shop as collateral, swearing I'll never break the chain of custody again."

He laughed. "It sounds weird hearing John's wife say that. I never thought I'd be working with you on a case. What do you think he would've made of that?"

"I don't know. I ask myself that all the time. I guess he'd be happy I have something to do that pays the bills." She opened the truck and stuffed her heavy purse inside. "What is it you want to ask me?"

"We're questioning Holt in a few minutes. I was wondering if you'd like to sit in."

Peggy showed her surprise at being included in such a matter. "You mean help you question him?"

"Not quite. Captain Rimer kind of agrees with your theory about how Mrs. Mullis *wasn't* poisoned. Not to the extent that he's willing to confront the chief about it like you did. But he thought you might like to listen to Holt's answers and see if any of them jibe with what you're thinking. You'll be observing. He won't even know you're there."

Peggy knew this was a concession to her everlasting curiosity. She could make some valuable allies and possibly hear something that could make a difference to this case.

On the other hand, she needed to make up with Steve. The only way that was going to happen was if she saw him. The longer they were broken up, the harder it would be to put them back together. She refused to be pressured by her family's opinion, but she loved Steve and didn't want their relationship to be over.

Of course, she hadn't made that call yet. Steve was probably at home tending one of his patients. What harm could a few minutes listening to them question Snook Holt be?

AN HOUR LATER, she realized she'd made a mistake. Al had questioned Holt for awhile, then Jonas had stepped in.

Chief Mullis had a go at the man. No matter what they said, Holt said the same thing.

"Let's start at the top." Jonas relieved the chief, sitting opposite Holt at the little table in the pale green interrogation room. "You were out at the lake collecting bones again, which is a violation of your parole. You're going back to jail. You know that, right?"

The prisoner wiped his nose on his sleeve. "But that don't mean I'm guilty of hurtin' anyone. I never hurt that woman. All I did was find her pocketbook."

"But what did you think when you first saw her out there?"

"I didn't think nothin'. I didn't see her. I went out there at night. That way no one's around. I wouldn't be out there in the morning, like that other officer said. I sleep in every morning. I'm no good till lunchtime."

"But you hated Mrs. Mullis because she got you thrown in jail," Jonas persisted.

"I don't hate no one. It's bad for you. And she wasn't the only one who told on me. What do you think? I can't go around killin' everybody."

"You had her pocketbook. Are you saying you didn't take anything out of it?"

"I might'a taken some cash. I didn't touch no credit cards. And there was only ten or fifteen dollars in there. Just barely enough to eat at McDonald's."

"You expect us to believe you found the pocketbook, stole the money, but didn't take the ring?"

"What ring? I don't know what you're talkin' about."

Peggy looked up as Al joined her behind the one-way glass while Jonas continued questioning the prisoner. "I bet you never thought it would be this way," he said.

"That's for sure." She glanced at her notes. "The next time you go in there, could you ask him where he found Lois's pocketbook?"

"Sure. What difference does that make?"

"None, maybe. If he has an exact location, it could narrow my search for the right yew bush. Also, I'm curious to know why no one found it out there after we found Lois."

"Will do."

"He asked for representation," Peggy reminded him.

"I know. Somebody's on the way. In the meantime, we can still talk to him." Al nodded and left the observation room.

Peggy watched him go back into the interrogation room and say a few words to Jonas. Al walked around the table, then approached Snook. "Where did you say you found that pocketbook?"

"I didn't say. Nobody asked me."

"Well, I'm asking," Al continued. "Did you take it from the woman before or after she was dead?"

Snook sniffed. "No. I don't touch dead people. Only their bones. 'Sides, I saw on the TV she was dead before I went out there."

"Then where did you find it?"

"Where's my lawyer? I know my rights. I get a Coke and a lawyer. You can't take that away."

"You got your Coke and your lawyer is on the way," Jonas assured him. "Now answer the question: Where did you find the pocketbook?"

"I found it stuffed in an old cedar stump with a big bole. It was a few hundred yards from the lake. I thought it was somethin' they hid over there—you know, them people from the museum. I went out there and they had things thrown everywhere. I thought it was one of them. But it was that old lady's pocketbook. Like somebody put it there for safekeepin'."

"What about the ring you found inside of it?" Jonas asked.

The door to the interrogation room opened again, and Peggy was surprised to see Hunter Ollson, Sam's sister, walk into the room. Hunter looked a lot like her brother: tall, blond, and beautiful. The royal blue wool suit she wore complimented her flashing blue eyes. "My client has answered all the questions he's going to answer for right now," she said. "Don't say anything else, Mr. Holt."

"Mr. Holt?" Snook scratched his head and laughed. "Nobody calls me that."

Peggy knew Hunter was a struggling young lawyer trying to make her mark on the world. She applauded her efforts and respected the system that brought her there. But she wished Snook would've given a little more information. Of course, if he truly didn't know anything else, there wouldn't be much to say.

Was he telling the truth about finding Lois's purse in a stump? If so, Peggy felt certain Lois didn't hide it there. Someone didn't want it to be found right away, but didn't feel it was valuable enough to take it with them. Or was afraid of being caught with it. She believed Snook would've gone in after the ring if he'd dropped it in the mud. That made him a victim of circumstance and returning to his bad habit of robbing graves.

The issue of the purse being hidden definitely pointed to another person being with Lois when she died. Whether or not that person was responsible for her death was another question. It was possible this other person didn't realize the yew berries were poisonous, and panicked when Lois died. It was also possible the person with her was a friend.

Peggy got up from the hard wooden chair she'd occupied and stretched her limbs. If she hurried, she could still talk to Steve that night. She groaned inwardly as Al and Jonas joined her in the observation room to ask her what she'd thought of the interrogation.

"Did you get anything?" Al asked her.

"You definitely narrowed my search for yew branches to somewhere around the lake where there are dead tree stumps a pocketbook could be stuffed in."

Jonas smiled. "Sounds like my job. I'm always looking for the needle in the haystack."

"It *does* make me feel someone else was there with Lois," Peggy told them. "Someone had to hide that pocketbook."

"I think you're taking what Snook said at face value," Jonas said. "He'd say anything at this point to keep us from thinking he killed Mrs. Mullis."

"I don't think he did." Peggy looked for her purse, then remembered she'd left it in the truck. Her ID card around her neck had been enough to get her in the building.

"Why doesn't that surprise me?" Al chuckled. "You always root for the underdog. But sometimes the underdog is guilty."

Jonas took her elbow to walk with her to the front door of the police station, leaving Al behind at his desk. "Something's bothering me about this case," he confessed. "Have you heard or seen anything that could link Chief Mullis to it?"

Peggy considered her words carefully before answering. "He dropped her out at the lake hours before the rest of the historical society would be there. He admitted to me that it was a mistake on his part. I'm assuming it wasn't a malicious mistake."

"Before Snook was brought in, there was some talk about the chief being involved. Possibly not homicide, but manslaughter. It's common knowledge that he inherits the estate from his aunt plus a sizable chunk of change."

"Do you think he could hurt his aunt?"

"I've known the man for a long time. I wouldn't like to think that. But there were also rumors of fights between the chief and his aunt. I don't know what to think at this point. Everyone else likes Snook for what happened to her. And it may be as simple as her eating the berries and someone pushing her into the mud and hiding her purse. Or someone could've tricked her into eating the berries."

Peggy frowned. "I'm not sure how you'd trick someone into eating poison berries."

"Hell, Peggy, I wouldn't know a poison berry from a

regular berry. Who's to say Mrs. Mullis was any different? If someone offered me a handful of fresh berries, I'd probably eat them. What if that was what happened to her?"

"But by no stretch of the imagination could that have been Snook Holt."

"No."

They'd reached the front door, and Peggy didn't know what to say. Jonas was thinking along the same lines she was, but there was no real suspect; except perhaps Chief Mullis. He'd seen Lois last. He had motive and opportunity. But this wasn't a suspect who could be brought in without exacting proof. "I see your point. I'll keep my ears open. If anything else develops, I'll let you know."

"Great. I hope I'm wrong." He smiled at her. "Good to see you. You take care out there."

Peggy went out to her truck, thinking about what Jonas had said. Hundreds of possibilities whirled through her mind. She was inside the truck with the engine started before she realized she'd totally forgotten to call Steve.

Before she left the parking lot, she decided to call Steve again. Instead, she found a message from him. He was going to be home by nine. There was plenty of time. She'd go home, change clothes, then go to his house. There was still time to get past this problem before the end of the day. But just barely.

FRESHLY SHOWERED, WEARING A SLINKY black dress she'd bought six months before but hadn't had the nerve to wear, Peggy walked to Steve's house at eight-thirty. She carried a heavy Harris Teeter tote bag in each hand. She'd let Shakespeare out, checked on her plants, and pushed her self-confidence into high gear before she left the house. It didn't matter anymore if anyone knew she'd spent the night at his house, and that was what she planned to do . . . unless he threw her out.

The short walk in the brisk autumn air gave her time to think about what she wanted to say and how she wanted to say it. She loved him and hoped he loved her.

All the energy and enthusiasm she'd built up during her walk past the old houses *whoosh*ed out of her when she saw Steve's Saturn was gone. Deflated like a tired, old balloon, she stood in his driveway for a few minutes, staring at a thriving patch of Spanish bayonet, trying to figure out what to do next.

She didn't want to waste all the buildup to confronting him and apologizing. The key to his front door was on her key ring. Peggy decided to let herself in and wait for him.

The old house seemed deserted when he wasn't there. She looked around the dark kitchen and great room, but not too closely. If she wanted to learn something about Steve, she was going to ask him from now on. No more snooping. If their relationship was going to work, she would have to trust him and believe in him.

She turned on the light in the kitchen and unloaded her bags. Inside them was everything she needed to create a romantic dinner for two. It took a lot to pull it all together, including candles, incense, and a couple of bottles of red wine. She put her best lace tablecloth across his plain wood table and started on the food. If there was one thing she was sure about with Steve, it was food. Whatever happened after the dinner would be up to them, but she knew this would be a good way to break the ice that might have formed between them.

Not long after she mixed the cream into her special Alfredo sauce, she heard the key in the front door, and he walked into the house. It registered in her brain that it was odd for him not to use the kitchen door, but her heart was beating so fast, she was afraid she might have a heart attack when she finally saw him. She turned out the kitchen lights and let the beautiful meal and cozy candle glow speak for themselves.

He walked into the kitchen and stood in the doorway, looking puzzled. Peggy froze, the welcoming smile on her face fading like yesterday's flower. "Who are you?" she asked the strange man who was staring at her. "And where is Steve?"

19

Euonymus (burning bush)

Botanical: *Euonymus alatus*

The nineteenth-century botanist Robert Fortune brought the species to England and America from its native China. The name comes from the Greek for lucky, despite the fact that it is poisonous. Perhaps it refers to the brilliant foliage in fall, which makes hikers and gardeners feel lucky to see it. The plant is showy with its bright red leaves creating its nickname, burning bush, since it looks to be set afire.

THE MAN, WHO LOOKED TO be older than Peggy, stared at her for a long moment, then smiled. His hair was white, and he had a dark tan that emphasized his features. "Steve didn't say anything about entertainment."

Peggy wished she could crawl into the oven and disappear. Or, more to the point, that she had exercised some degree of sanity before coming here. She was incredibly good at getting into tight places. Much better than she needed to be.

But there was no way out. She held her head high and stared the man down. "Don't be rude. Where's Steve?" Years of teaching at Queens University added strength and command to her voice. She may have *felt* ridiculous, but she didn't have to appear that way.

"He had to make a stop, but he'll be here soon. I'm Skipper Hall, from the Lazy Z horse farm in Harrisburg. I'm sorry I intruded."

"I suppose it couldn't be helped." She turned on the kitchen light and blew out the candles. "I guess we'll just wait for him."

He smiled. "You must be Peggy. Steve talks about you all the time. I'm sure he'll be here as soon as he can."

She shrugged, glancing awkwardly around the kitchen. "Good. I've already uncorked the wine."

Skipper moved to pull out a chair for her. "I hope you're not planning to leave."

Peggy was thinking exactly that, but smiled and took a seat. If he could be gentleman enough to respond so kindly to what could've been an embarrassing situation, she could at least stay until Steve got there. It seemed destined to be that kind of day.

Skipper was good company as they waited. He told her about his dream to own a horse farm when he was a child. "I didn't think I'd have to come all this way to make it happen. Steve called me after he'd moved here and told me about a great deal on some land. I flew down and closed on it, and haven't looked back."

"That's wonderful," she exclaimed. "Have you known Steve a long time?"

"We were in the Air Force together. We never lost track of each other after that. Mostly it was meeting for drinks at airports when one of us was going through town. It's great living so close we can see each other more often. He's a good vet, too. The horses love him."

Peggy had a thousand questions she wanted to ask him. She didn't want to sound overly nosy or like she didn't know anything about the man she'd been seeing for a year.

She casually took a sip of wine after pouring a glass for each of them. "Were you in school together?"

"High school." Skipper nodded. "My family moved, and we were separated. But it's like we're destined to keep finding each other again."

"His childhood sounds as though it was painful."

"Not that you'd ever get him to admit it, but it was a hard time for him. He and his mother were very close. I think that's the only thing that got him through."

"I haven't pushed him for information about that time in his life. I can see it still hurts him to talk about it."

"It was a long time ago. I'm sure he's worked through it. Steve's like that. You could ask him whatever you want."

They heard Steve's Saturn pull into the drive. The headlights shone briefly in the kitchen window. Peggy took a large sip of wine. "Thanks for your help, Skipper."

"No problem, ma'am."

"I wish you'd stay and eat with us."

"I have a feeling Steve might not like that. But it was nice meeting you."

The kitchen door opened, and Steve looked at the two of them with a rapidly developing frown. "Did I miss the memo about dinner?" His eyes took in the uncorked wine bottle and Peggy's slinky dress. "Or would one of you like to tell me what's going on?"

Skipper put one arm around Peggy's shoulders. "I thought I'd get better acquainted with the little woman. We arranged to meet here while you were out getting horse liniment. She's a gem, my friend."

Steve's frown deepened. "If I wasn't so sure that I was the one who suggested you wait here for me, we'd be stepping outside. Peggy doesn't cook real food often enough for me to share it with anyone."

"I made it for you, of course." She stepped to the side so that Skipper's arm dropped away from her. Losing the contact made her feel vulnerable, and she wrapped her arms around her midsection. "I asked Skipper to join us, but he didn't think you'd want him to stay."

"And he's right." Steve handed his friend a receipt and held the door for him. "Your liniment is in the back of the Saturn. I'll talk to you tomorrow."

Skipper smiled at Peggy before he took his cue and started out of the kitchen. "I know you're happy that I kept your lady friend company until you got here."

"Whatever. Get out while you still can. Don't ever try to eat my Alfredo again." Steve barely waited until Skipper was out of the door before he closed it and locked it.

"Dinner smells great! I really don't mind if the wine has been breathing too long, either."

"I can heat it up," she volunteered. "The cream separates a little sometimes, but—"

"There's something I need a lot more than pasta or wine," he said, advancing toward her. "I tried calling you back ten times today. Once I think I almost talked to you, but you hung up."

"I'm sorry. I tried to call you, but I kept getting your voice mail, and then I had to go into a meeting. I *wanted* to talk to you."

"I wanted to talk to you, too." He put his arms around her. "Are we okay? Is this preengagement jitters, or are you really that angry at me for asking?"

"I was angrier at myself than at you. It just took me a while to realize it." She looked up into his face. "I'm so sorry I didn't ask you the questions that would've given you the opportunity to tell me about yourself."

"I'm not sure exactly what that means." He shrugged. "Basically, I didn't mean to keep anything from you. I tried to find some way to bring it into a conversation, but there never seemed to be a right time to say it. Maybe it was just lack of trying because everything was so right between us. I'm sorry I didn't just blurt it out earlier."

"So we're both sorry." She wiped tears from her eyes.

"But I still love you very much, and if that engagement offer still stands, I'd like to give it a try."

He kissed her, his brown eyes intent on her face. "You know being engaged means getting married someday."

"I'm aware of that."

"You'll have to tell your family."

"They already know. And not just about us getting engaged. Apparently I wasn't fooling anyone by sneaking around. I'm surprised it wasn't on the news one night."

"And they were all good with that? Even your mother?"

"Even my mother, bless her heart. She told me I could be out of mourning now."

"And here you are, still wearing black." His hand followed her side and made a rustling sound against the dress. "This one I like. Why haven't I seen it before? Is it new?"

"Not exactly. I was just holding on to it for the right moment." She kissed him and smiled. "Would you like me to heat up that pasta now?"

"Never mind the pasta." He kissed her hand, then held it as he led her out of the kitchen. "I could use a little warming up instead."

"I WANT TO KNOW EVERYTHING that happened to you from the moment you were born until I ran into your Saturn at the coffee shop."

He laughed. "That's a lot to talk about."

"I already know more than I knew before," she admitted. "I know you were in the Air Force. Skipper told me."

"What else did Skipper tell you?"

"Not enough. Start talking."

"There's really not much to say. My father left when my sister died. My mom raised me. I was lackluster in high school. Never even tried out for science club with the other geeks. I joined the Air Force, came back, and decided to go to college."

"And you went to school and became a veterinarian."

"And we all lived happily ever after."

"No wonder I don't know much about your past! I thought it was my fault. Now I see it's because you don't like talking about it. What about everything that happened in between? What about girlfriends and your first car? You can't keep those things secret anymore."

He groaned. "Why do I have a feeling that's all about to change?"

She kissed him and snuggled close to his chest. "Because you fell in love with the wrong woman. You know I have to understand everything."

"And you're insatiably curious, can't stand anything being secret, and are just plain nosy." He kissed her nose to soften his words. "I'll start at the beginning. I was born a little small but feisty. My mother said my hair was curly until I was three; then it turned straight. My favorite toys were animals, hence the profession."

"Maybe not that far back," she complained. "Let's talk more about your ex-girlfriends from high school up, and don't leave anything out."

"Maybe we should wait until after we get some sleep. I hate to put on horse liniment unless I'm completely awake. No telling where it could end up."

"I suppose that's fair." She yawned. "I have an early date at the lake again, looking for more yew branches."

"You must have enough of those to make a whole yew tree by now."

"You'd think so. But it has to be the right yew tree."

"Or the right person."

"What?" She sat up in his bed and looked at him. "Of course! That's the answer. It's not the yew berries. It's the person who gave them to her. Lois had to know and trust the person who gave them to her. That's why Snook isn't guilty!"

"Great name. I love the people you meet, Peggy. But

what happened to Lois eating the berries by mistake, no one feeding them to her?"

"Her pocketbook being stashed in the tree negates that idea, because we know she had the carnelian ring in it. I think whoever fed her the berries did so to get the ring, then pushed her into the mud. Lois wouldn't have been able to walk that far after eating that number of berries."

"But the killer didn't go in after it?"

Peggy agreed that it seemed a long shot. "Maybe it dropped into the mud and whoever was with Lois didn't see it at the time. Jonathon said there's a spring under the mud that keeps it moist. It also keeps it moving. That's why it took us a few minutes to find Lois. The question still remains: Did Lois go out early to meet this person and give them the ring, or did this person surprise Lois and decide the time was right?"

There was no response from Steve. She realized he was asleep. Smiling, she laid her head on his chest and listened to his breath and heartbeat. Being engaged would be good. It was a new start to a new life. Marriage was far enough off that she didn't have to panic . . . yet.

If she'd been home, she would've gone downstairs and worked on her projects in the basement. She didn't want to leave Steve, so she lay quietly until she finally fell asleep.

AN INNER ALARM WOKE PEGGY at six a.m. She kissed Steve, they showered and shared cold pasta for breakfast before they went their separate ways for the day.

Peggy went back to her house, refusing to think about all the complications that would arise from being with Steve all the time. The whole his house-her house argument stayed out of her consciousness as she let Shakespeare out and put on a kettle of water for tea.

The phone rang at the same time the kettle whistled. She

answered one while she reached for the other and poured the water into her cup. "Good morning, Paul. Are you on your way home?"

"I could ask you the same thing." He chuckled. "I noticed you weren't home last night when I drove by the house."

"All right. I give up. My truck was plugged in. The bike was in the shed. How could you tell I wasn't home?"

"I stopped in. Shakespeare thought it was you. Did you patch things up with Steve?"

"Not that it's any of your business, but yes. We're on for the engagement dinner on Tuesday. Maybe we should make it a double wedding. How about you and Mai joining in?"

"That was a cold, cruel thing to say. You know she isn't ready for that yet. I *know* she isn't."

"Because you ask her every day?"

"Not anymore. Anyway, good news 'bout you and Steve. Will you live in our house or his?"

"I'm not thinking about that right now. Go home. I'll talk to you later."

She closed her cell phone and sat down to look at her garden outside the kitchen window and sip her tea. She was fortunate to have the big oaks that shaded the backyard from most of the sun. Even so, the drought was hard on everything growing. The holly bushes were wilting along with the burning bushes and marigolds. The dogwoods with their red berries, were the only trees that still looked healthy. She didn't know how much longer anything would survive unless they started getting regular rain again.

Hating the water restrictions that prevented her from helping her plants, Peggy switched on her laptop to check her e-mail. She was part of several focus groups of botanists from around the world who discussed their projects in the hope of solving world hunger through better horticulture.

There was an e-mail from Sir Nigel about the yew berries.

Apparently all parts of the plant were poisonous except for the berry. He also told her that chewing on the seeds could release enough poison to kill Lois.

She replied and thanked him, asking him about his own projects at the institute that were connected with their yew studies.

Like every other day, there were hundreds of e-mails to sift through. Even with her spam blocker on the highest level, she still received scams from people who claimed to represent everyone from the IRS to the wife of a foreign dignitary who needed help sending money out of her country. All of them were just ways for the unwary to lose money at best, and their identity at worst.

She deleted those e-mails gladly, wishing she could send each of them back and tell the senders how stupid it was to send them out. Unfortunately, that would probably give her computer a virus, and she'd just gone through that recently.

Peggy glanced through the remaining e-mails, noting one familiar name after another. She knew Dr. Mendosa in Costa Rica was working on a grain plant that would have a shorter growing season and fare better in hotter climates. Dr. Kingsley was e-mailing about her edible cotton project that seemed promising.

There was one e-mail that didn't fit in with the rest. She would've deleted it for spam, but in the subject line was one word that caught her attention: *Nightflyer*. The e-mail address was different from any of the ones her old chess partner had used before. He'd told her he would try to contact her occasionally after going underground to escape from people he worked for at the CIA.

It sounded bizarre to think about it now. But she knew him too well to doubt his true involvement in things larger than most people understood. Several times he'd helped her solve cases with information no one else was privy to or willing to share.

She bit her lip as she clicked on the e-mail. *Dear Night-*

*rose, I am doing well if not living happily ever after. I stay
constantly one step ahead of the men who are hunting me.
I'm sorry I can't contact you more often. I would not en-
danger you for anything. I hope you are staying out of
trouble and are content with your life. I will write again
when I can. All my love, Nightflyer.*

It seemed there would be no complex chess match between them online, where they could chat about whatever
was going on in the world and she could ask him for advice
about what she was doing. She missed those days, but they
had come to an end soon after she'd met Steve. Those long,
lonely nights with only the Internet for company seemed to
be behind her. She didn't miss them.

Peggy knew she couldn't answer Nightflyer's e-mail.
He'd explained the situation to her. As soon as he'd sent the
e-mail, probably from some wireless café, he'd be gone.
There was a certain romance to it that had almost captured
her imagination. But she wasn't the kind of woman who
could leave everything behind for a man. She was happy
with her life and the second chance she'd been given for
love.

Her last swallow of tea accompanied her final reminisc-
ing. She shut down her laptop and went upstairs to change
her clothes. Shakespeare followed her up the marble staircase, and back down again when she was done. He looked
at her sadly and whined a little.

"I suppose you want to go out to the lake," she said to
him. "I'll warn you, I have to go over to the Potting Shed
for a delivery before I go out there. No falling in the pond
again. You're too big to go swimming in there."

The Great Dane thumped his tail hard on the old wood
floor. Peggy took that as a promise to behave, and put on his
harness and leash. She'd be happy to have his company out
at the lake. Too much was going on out there for her to feel
comfortable alone.

With Shakespeare beside her in the truck, she drove to

the Potting Shed to wait for Sam's rain barrel delivery. Lois's funeral was at four. She'd have to be back from the lake by then and to have left the yew branches at the lab. Merton wouldn't be at the university until Monday, so there was no point in going all the way out there.

Peggy let Shakespeare into the shop as the delivery truck arrived. The man was nice enough to put all of the barrels into the storage area in back before he left. She thanked him and gave him a nice rosemary plant for his wife.

She was getting ready to bring Shakespeare back out to the truck when the Shamrock Historical Society van pulled into the parking lot beside her. She groaned and closed her eyes. This wasn't a good way to start the day.

20

Agave

Botanical: *Agave*

Agaves were a major source of material for clothes, food, paper, and juice for early Mesoamericans. It wasn't until later that Europeans found they could make tequila from the plant. Commonly referred to as the century plant, agave does not live for a hundred years, but it is long-lived, possibly thirty years, and may take a long time to flower. It has many names for various types, from parryi van truncate (artichoke) to agave americana marginata, which grows to soaring heights.

WHAT PEGGY HAD COME TO think of as the militant arm of the museum, the Shamrock Historical Society, spilled out of the van. Jonathon was with them. She could only guess that the ladies had adopted him since he'd been forgiven for his sins. Apparently all question of him killing Lois had been resolved to their satisfaction.

"Peggy"—Grace was the first to reach her—"we need your help."

"We have to get into Lois's house," Geneva continued. "There are things in there that don't technically belong to Lois or her descendants. Chief Mullis is holding an auction

there next week, and an appraiser is going through on
Monday to catalog the items."

"Some of the things actually belong to the museum,"
Jonathan said. "At least that's what the ladies tell me. I've
informed the board, but without the chairman they can't act,
and he's in Switzerland until the end of the month."

"I understand what you're saying." Peggy tried to stop
the tide of emotion flowing over her. "But I'm the wrong
person to talk to about this."

"If you're talking about that stubborn horse's back end,
Mullis, you're barking up the wrong dogwood tree," Dorothy told her. "We already tried talking to him. He said if he
found out any of us went in there to look through Lois's
things, he'd send us to jail."

"First of all, he can't just send anybody he wants to jail,"
Peggy assured them. "But going into his house—"

"—*Lois's* house," Mrs. Waynewright reminded her.

"The house belongs to Chief Mullis now," Peggy said. "If
you go in without his permission, he can have you charged
with breaking and entering. If you take anything, it will be
stealing."

Geneva smiled broadly. "That's why we came to see
you!"

"You're a member of the Shamrock Historical Society."
Grace giggled. "But you weren't there when he talked to us.
You could go in and look for the items. Mullis didn't say
anything about arresting you."

Peggy would've laughed at the preposterous statement if
she didn't believe Grace and the others were serious. "It
doesn't matter if he threatened me or not. I can't go in there
without the chief's permission."

Mrs. Waynewright sighed. "As you get older, it's harder
to lose things of personal value. They become like members of your family."

"The museum is missing several items that Lois took
home to clean or categorize," Annabelle explained. "It's not

right for Chief Mullis to sell those. They belong to the museum."

"You'll just have to hope she has something in her will to protect those things." Peggy refused to be drawn into the discussion. "Jonathon, you have to know better than this."

He shrugged. "I wish there was another way. But what the ladies say is true. Everyone takes a few items home from time to time, to make the job of cleaning them less of a burden on the museum. I don't know how valuable the artifacts are that she had, but they could be lost at the estate auction."

"Mullis doesn't want anything in there to remind him of Lois," Annabelle said. "He told us the sooner he gets the place cleaned out, the sooner he can tear it down and build a new house."

"All that history lost." Mrs. Waynewright shook her head. "Such a pity."

"We thought maybe you could convince that handsome young son of yours to go with you and pretend you had a legal right to be there," Geneva suggested. "After all, the two of you work for the police. Mullis might be fooled into thinking you're there for something to do with the case."

"That's not going to happen." Peggy smiled at them to lessen the harshness of her words. "I wouldn't involve Paul in any of this."

"You mean you'd be willing to do it on your own?" Dorothy enthused.

"Thank you, Peggy!" Grace hugged her. "I *knew* we could count on you."

"I didn't say I'd break into the house to look for anything." Peggy tried to get herself out of the position they'd put her in.

"Of course not!" Geneva stepped forward and gave her a set of keys and instructions to disable the alarm system. "We wouldn't expect you to do that."

After a series of hugs from all the women, they piled

back in the van with Jonathon and squealed the tires leaving the parking lot. Peggy stood watching them with the keys and alarm code, wondering why they'd picked on her.

She pocketed the keys and went into the shop to get Shakespeare. He was asleep next to the pond while a little lizard cavorted through the leaves and across the stones. Selena may have thought Sam got rid of it—or there was more than one.

There was a knock on the front door. Peggy looked up, not sure if she wanted to answer it. She recognized a professor from Queens University. Smiling, she left Shakespeare sleeping and opened the door. "Professor Burris! I haven't seen you in a long time."

"That's because you gave up teaching and went into business," he told her.

He'd always reminded her of a sharp-tongued Santa with his long white beard and flowing white hair. He was a little rotund as well, to complete the image. But instead of a bright red suit, he always wore gray tweed and smelled of pipe tobacco. He wasn't a jovial kind of person, voted again and again as students' least favorite history professor at the university.

"That's true," she agreed. "What brings you here today?"

He looked around as though he was uncomfortable. "I have a problem, and I thought you might be the person to solve it for me."

Peggy couldn't imagine what that could be or how he would've thought of her. "I'll do what I can to help."

"My problem deals with a lady friend." He pointed at her and snarled, "No laughter! And no words of wisdom about older men with girlfriends."

"I wouldn't think of it." She smiled despite herself. "I don't normally give advice to men with lady problems, but—"

"Don't be impertinent! I'm here to consult your horticulture skills, Dr. Lee, not your matchmaking abilities! I don't need your help finding a woman, if that's what you mean."

"All right." She was beginning to regret that she'd opened the door. Professor Burris's personality left a lot to be desired. She couldn't imagine who'd want to date him. "Tell me what I can do."

"I want to grow some plants. I have a sunny window in my apartment. I also have a small balcony that may be appropriate for a pot or two. My lady friend is very partial to plants. She hasn't visited my apartment yet, but I've been to hers and she has plants everywhere. I believe she'll experience disappointment in me if I don't have plants."

Peggy turned her head to keep from laughing. He wanted her to set him up with plants to impress his girlfriend. It was always amazing, the things that could happen in a day. "I'll be glad to help you out, Professor. Did you want to pot these plants yourself or take home some already in pots?"

"Don't use all that jargon with me. I need to understand what I've brought home. I'm sure my lady friend will expect me to know what I'm growing."

"Then follow me, and we'll get started."

Peggy led him to the workbench she'd had installed, and picked out an aloe plant to start with. "This is aloe. It's relatively easy to grow. It likes sunlight, and you said you have a sunny window. Here's a pot that should be the right size. This soil, with a little sand mixed in, should be fine for it. You need to water it once a week or so. It can handle being dry."

She watched the fastidious professor dig into the soil and pick up the aloe to put it in the pot. It was hard for him to hide his distaste at actually getting dirty. She supposed he'd never gotten that far into a subject before.

When he was finished, she rounded up a large philodendron that was root-bound and needed to be transplanted. "This is a little bigger, but the plant is easy to care for. A philodendron will be happy with lower light and water once a week. Just add some soil to this pot and move the plant into it, then fill in around it until the soil's firm."

"Will my lady friend recognize these as beginner's plants?"

"Not at all. Many seasoned gardeners have these plants as well. I can recommend a book you can read that will tell you more about them, and you can learn as you go."

"What about my balcony? I assume I'll need something fairly hardy to survive out there."

Peggy suggested an agave. "This agave should do well on your balcony. It will be easy to take care of, and doesn't require much work. It will get bigger before it flowers, then dies back. That means changing its pot again probably in six months or so. Your lady friend should enjoy it. This one is a Weber's agave. It's one of the biggest and fastest-growing. See the fleshy, blue green leaves? It's a gorgeous plant as it grows."

She helped the professor load his Subaru with his purchases. She'd been surprised that he hadn't haggled over any of the prices. He'd been a quick learner who was obviously motivated to take good care of the plants. "I hope this works with your lady."

"I appreciate your time, Dr. Lee. You were always quite talented when it came to living things. I saw in the paper that you've recently turned your sights to dead things as well."

"You mean the forensic botany." She nodded.

"I mean Lake Whitley. I was out there twenty years ago, during the last drought. It wasn't as severe as the one we're experiencing, so our findings were limited. But it was an impressive site."

"Yes, it is. I only wish the circumstances had been different. Finding a dead woman wasn't part of the plan."

"In history, one takes what one finds at face value until one does the proper research." Professor Burris lifted his chin and looked down his long, straight nose at her. "What was it that woman was killed for?"

"I believe it was a ring." She thought she might as well

be honest with him. "I found it out there, but it's part of the museum's collection. No one seems to know where it came from or its value."

He cleared his throat. "I'd be happy to take a look at it for you. Give me a call at my office when you're ready."

Peggy thanked him and watched him drive away with his load of plants. Maybe it would be good to have a fresh opinion.

ON HER WAY TO LAKE Whitley, Peggy made a detour and ended up at the small, one-story home her parents had purchased in Myer's Park. It was close to where Paul and Mai lived. Peggy had been worried that her parents might smother the young couple with their attention, but that hadn't turned out to be the case. Mai and Paul worked unusual hours, and Ranson and Lilla had joined several country clubs along with half a dozen special-interest groups like the historical society.

Peggy found her parents enjoying coffee on the back terrace of the house. They were with another couple, whom Lilla introduced as neighbors. She exchanged pleasantries with the older couple, then pulled her mother into the green and gold kitchen. "I'm giving you these keys and alarm instructions. I'm not going to break into Lois's house looking for artifacts the society thinks belong to them."

Lilla frowned as she looked at the keys on the counter. "They'll be devastated. Those artifacts belong to the group."

"Was it normal for Lois to take things from the museum?" She was thinking about what Jonathon had said and of the carnelian ring.

"There's been so much taken from the lake in the last few weeks," her mother fretted. "Everyone has tried to do their part. We haven't taken any of the bones, but each of us has some pieces of history we dug up. These haven't been cataloged for the museum yet. Ask Jonathon, if you don't believe me. We all just felt like it would be easier to take everything in already cleaned."

"But you don't know anything about cleaning artifacts," Peggy insisted. "Weren't you afraid you might mess one up?"

Lilla shrugged, her lilac silk blouse falling gracefully across her thin shoulders. "Not really. What's to mess up? Everything is caked with mud. I've just washed them off with water, no detergent. That's what Jonathon said."

"Whatever you ladies think is best." Peggy didn't want to argue about it. "But I'm not going into Lois's house, and neither is Paul. And I don't want you to ask him and jeopardize his job. Okay?"

"I wouldn't do any such thing!" Lilla drew her petite figure up and glared at her daughter.

"What's keeping you two?" Ranson peered around the door. "I have only so many interesting farm stories. Are you arguing about something?"

"No."

"No," Peggy said, backing down from the conversation with her mother. "I'll see you at Lois's funeral. I have to go back out to the lake and cut more yew branches."

"Be careful out there," Ranson warned. "Maybe you should take Steve with you. I hear he knows how to handle a gun." He grinned at his daughter, then shook his head when she didn't return his humor. "You can't worry over it the rest of your life, Sweet Pea. Some things happen and no one knows why. I hope you aren't still mad at the man."

"We've made up," she explained. "I have to go if I'm going to be back in time for the funeral. I'll talk to you later."

"She sure didn't get my sense of humor," Peggy heard her father say as she was leaving.

"Good thing," her mother remarked. "At least she has *some* sensibility."

Back in her truck, Peggy answered her cell phone. "Hello!"

"Sorry," Steve said. "Wasn't I supposed to call if I got done early?"

"Yes. I'm just leaving my parents' house," she explained, backing out of the drive. She admired a beautiful young mayapple her father had planted despite the drought, swearing he would keep it alive with the water he caught while waiting for the cold water to turn hot. It seemed to be working.

"That explains it." Steve laughed. "What are you and your mother arguing about now?"

She told him about the keys and Lois's house. "Are you home yet?"

"No, not quite. I'm just getting to Eastway. Why?"

"I hate to ask, but since you aren't busy, how would you like to take another ride out to the lake?"

"I don't know. The last one didn't end up so good."

"I'll pick you up on the way. You can park your Saturn over at the furniture store until we get back."

"And how is this supposed to make a difference?"

"I'm driving," she told him. "Last time, you were driving. It makes all the difference in the world."

He finally agreed, and Peggy picked him up a few minutes later.

"I can't believe you have to go back out there again," he said, pushing Shakespeare to make room in the truck. "How many yew branches does Dr. Ramsey need?"

Peggy explained as well as she could. "The case can't actually be wrapped up until we know where the berries came from. If I find the yew bush out at the lake, it would make sense of what the police are saying about Snook Holt."

"Which you don't believe is true."

"No. But I don't have a better answer. Snook was out there. He had Lois's pocketbook. He had a motive because of the trial where she testified against him. He certainly had opportunity, since she was out there at least two hours before the rest of us."

"Sounds reasonable to me. What's your problem with it?"

"It's all based on Lois eating poison berries Snook gave her. Or that she ate the berries and was near death when he found her. Both seem wrong to me."

"And if you don't find the missing yew branches?" Steve asked.

"Then they'll probably prosecute him without them, and how Lois died will be a mystery."

She changed the subject, and they talked about the upcoming engagement party until they reached the lake. Two police officers were standing guard at the crime scene today, and they let her pass when they saw her ID.

It was getting easier to spot the yew bushes she hadn't already tagged and taken samples from than the ones she had. "I've covered all the ones closest to the lake. I guess I'll move further afield."

"Where did you say Snook found the purse?" Steve asked.

"In a cedar stump a few hundred yards from the lake." Peggy looked out at the dark, heavy mud where the lake had been. "You can see Baby Island from here. That's a treasure trove everyone would like to investigate, if anyone could figure out how to get there."

Steve followed her line of vision to what appeared to be a large bump in the surface of the mud. "Why do they call it Baby Island?"

"Because all the babies were buried there." She began cutting yew branches and placing them in plastic bags. "Apparently when Whitley Village was here, people believed newborn babies were bad luck to put in the cemetery. They buried all the stillborn children away from the church cemetery so their little souls couldn't come back and haunt them."

"That's terrible. How does anyone know about that?"

"It's in the museum's archives. They have diaries and family Bibles from out here. They know a lot about the area. These artifacts and the hundred graves are valuable because they've been lost for so long."

"I'm glad I don't do this for a living. At least if one of my patients dies, it gets a proper burial."

Peggy walked carefully away from the lake toward the parking area. She found the old, gnarled cedar stump with the black bole. It was easy to imagine Snook finding Lois's pocketbook here.

There were several yew bushes close by. She cut the top branches from all of them and sealed them in the plastic evidence bags. "If Lois was alone out here and saw Snook at that time of the morning, knowing her friends wouldn't be there for at least an hour, she had to be terrified. You know she'd think he'd hurt her."

"I agree." Steve glanced around the area. "What are you thinking?"

"If I was out here alone and felt threatened, I'd hide. There was no car to give her away. If she could hide long enough, her friends would be here and she'd be safe."

"I suppose so. Especially since she was an older lady. She probably wouldn't have thought of trying to confront him."

"So where would she hide?" Peggy walked carefully around the side of the lake. "None of the trees are big enough for her to hide behind. She could've hidden behind a bush, I suppose."

"What are you hoping to find?" he asked.

"I don't know. Something that makes sense." She had run out of plastic bags, and stripped off her gloves. "I'd like to believe Snook did this, I guess. It would be nice and neat."

"But you're still thinking about Chief Mullis, right? He'd be a messy suspect."

"He definitely would be. But if you think about it, he had as much motive and opportunity as Snook. He inherits everything from Lois, including her estate, which is passed to him like John's family will pass my house. He brought her out here incredibly early so he could make an appointment. He's sorry about what happened, and claims he would do it over if he could."

"And that would help your theory about someone friendly giving Lois the berries."

"Yes." Peggy's cinnamon-colored eyebrows knit together above her bright green eyes. "On the other hand, it makes no sense whatsoever with the carnelian ring. I feel so certain it was involved in Lois's death."

"But maybe you're wrong about it. Maybe it was nothing more than another artifact she took with her, and she dropped it. You said even your mom has a few artifacts."

"I know. I can't seem to have it the way I want it. Anyway"—she glanced around the all-too-quiet area with the spring churning the mud in the old lake—"it would take only a couple good rains before the site is lost again for another hundred years. Maybe it's for the best. There's a bad feeling out here. Maybe it's just all the dead out of their graves. Maybe it's so many people's lives ended here."

Steve put his arm around her shoulder. "No wonder you wanted me to come out here with you. Next thing you know, you'll be jumping in the mud, too. Maybe that's what *really* happened to Lois. She was out here and got depressed and went for a dive in the mud. She ate the poisoned berries just to make sure."

Peggy shivered, but his words had broken her morbid mood. "You're right. Let's get out of here and do something fun."

"What did you have in mind?"

"I have to go to Lois's funeral this afternoon. How's that for fun?"

21

Barberry

Botanical: *Berberis vulgaris*

Medicinal use of barberry dates back to ancient Egypt. It has been used to treat diarrhea and fever, and is said to improve appetite and relieve upset stomach. Folklore even says it will give a sense of well-being. It is still widely used today for gall-bladder disease and heartburn. In the language of flowers, barberry means sharpness.

A GROUP OF SCOTSMEN WEARING kilts and *skean dhu* played the bagpipes at the funeral home. The wailing music reverberated through the old house on Morehead Street. Several mourners from other family groups came to the door to complain, but apparently the Mullis family had paid the funeral director well to allow the music.

Next came all of the members of the Shamrock Historical Society. They were dressed in black garments from the eighteenth and nineteenth centuries. Grace wore a full, black bonnet that obscured her face. She tripped on her gown but was rescued by Geneva's helping hand. Mrs. Waynewright's black taffeta gown looked like it was something she wore every day. Annabelle smiled at Peggy who joined them.

Peggy nodded solemnly to her mother, who was wearing her grandmother's black silk evening gown. She knew it well, having played "dress up" many times in it in the attic on rainy days. The large, stylish black hat had a dyed ostrich feather that lent it an air of elegance.

In traditional Southern fashion, the women laid a wreath of flowers intertwined with strands of Lois's hair. The flowers, dyed black for the event, were significant. There was cyclamen for resignation and good-bye, oleander for beauty and grace, and hellebore for peace and tranquillity. Usually this was easily done because the women bathed and dressed the dead. But those days were long gone, and Peggy knew from her mother that Geneva had taken strands of hair from Lois's brush when they'd been in her house.

Hired mourners cried loudly as they followed the procession of women to the gray coffin. The bottom half of the coffin was closed, but the top half remained open, revealing Lois's gray face in repose. The mourners were unneeded in this case because there were plenty of people there who were sorry to see her go. Still, as Lilla had explained, better to have too many mourners than not enough.

Peggy sat close to the coffin, wearing what she'd come to think of as her funeral outfit: a crushed black felt hat and an older Ann Klein suit. Her black pumps hurt her feet as the procession to the coffin continued and everyone stood. The Mullises had two children, a boy and a girl. Chief Mullis walked behind them with a woman Peggy assumed was his wife. She was rather drab and ordinary in her gray suit when compared to the flamboyant historical society members and the mourners.

Peggy couldn't help but notice that Lois's son seemed to be angry with Chief Mullis, his cousin. No doubt upset not to inherit the estate, just as she was angry sometimes that Paul wouldn't live on the Lee estate. It worked for families to pass the property down in this way; there was no favoritism about who inherited. But it was still hard.

As the family stood near the coffin, paying their last respects to Lois, Chief Mullis put his hand on the younger man's shoulder. Lois's son violently shrugged it off, and glared at him for good measure.

The woman pointed out to Peggy as Lois's daughter seemed to be inspecting her mother rather carefully. She pointed something out to her brother at the same time that a small child beside her began to cry. The daughter picked up the child and mouthed *Where's the ring?* to her brother.

Peggy wondered if she was talking about the carnelian ring. She glanced at Lois's folded hands as the family went by. There was only a plain gold wedding band on Lois's hand. There might be something more to this.

The procession continued following the family, down to the fourth and fifth cousins, before friends and neighbors were allowed to view the dead woman. In many ways, Peggy was glad Steve had been called away on an emergency when they got back from the lake. She felt sure he'd been happy as well. It took a true Southerner to appreciate a Southern funeral.

The daggerlike glances continued between the Mullis family members as Peggy sat back and watched them. She wished they'd say something more about the ring. Of course, it could be a completely different ring. There was no way of knowing. But she glanced up from her program from time to time and kept her ears open.

The preacher was charming and very ordinary for a funeral speaker. He said all the right things about Lois without the fire and brimstone many there probably expected. It started raining before the preacher and family members were finished eulogizing the dead woman. The rain added an appropriate air of sadness to the event.

Peggy stayed close to the family as they left the funeral service before the rest of the crowd. If she was mistaken for a member of the family, she was willing to play along. The group might never have words about whatever was bothering them, but it was possible. Many family feuds were begun while standing on the steps of the funeral home after the service.

She was beginning to think the family was too civilized to exchange words in public. Lord knows, hers would've been. But as the brother and sister reached the car that had brought them to the service, Chief Mullis pulled them aside.

At first, their words were heated but quiet. The little boy started crying again, and it seemed to aggravate the situation. "You've got everything now," Lois's daughter charged, looking pathetic as the rain plastered her thin brown hair to her head. "Leave us alone. I hope you rot with it."

"I can't help the way things are set up," the chief said. "Honestly, I wouldn't if I could. It's served our family well for more than a hundred years. Your children will have their turn. My kids will be left out then."

"You know there's more to it than the estate," the young man declared. "You weren't supposed to keep her personal effects. Her jewelry—"

"Most of which goes with the estate," the chief reminded him. "Look, I'll let you go through her stuff that isn't part of the estate."

"You know what we want. Mother brought Uncle Silas's ring with her to the marriage. You have no right to claim it." Lois's daughter stood her ground. "We'll take you to court over this, Cousin. Make no mistake about it."

Chief Mullis smiled in a gloating sort of way that turned Peggy's stomach. "And who do you think a judge and jury are likely to find in favor of? Hell, I probably have lunch on a regular basis with whoever the probate judge is. Good luck, Cousins. I guess I'll see you in court."

He stalked away from the long, black car, ignoring everything else. Peggy had held her program to her face, but she hadn't needed the disguise. As soon as the chief was gone, she walked over to the brother and sister, ignoring the quickening pace of the rain.

"I'm so sorry for your loss," she told them. "Lois was a wonderful woman. I know you must miss her. We all do."

At first they looked at her with something like suspicion in their eyes. Then the son's face lit up and he hugged her. "Aunt Matilda! I haven't seen you in years. I'm glad you could come for Mother's funeral. How's the rheumatism?"

"Not too bad right now." Peggy played along. "I'm glad I could be here, too. You seem to be at odds with Arnold."

"That's putting it nicely," Lois's daughter said. "He's cheating us out of everything. He's taking the house and land, of course. We expected that. But we wanted her jewelry and the art she'd collected, along with some other personal effects. I don't think we'll get them without a fight."

"Are you talking about the carnelian ring?"

Both children stared at her. "Not that we know of," Lois's son replied with a meaningful glance at his sister. "The most valuable piece is Uncle Silas's diamond pinky ring. You know, it was handed down from your side of the family. The Mullises have no excuse for keeping it."

Peggy's hopes were dashed. She hadn't found a diamond pinky ring. "What about the carved carnelian ring? That has historical family value."

"We're not sure about that piece," the daughter said, "although now that you mention it, Mother did talk about an heirloom ring from the Civil War. I don't know if she had it at the house. If so, Cousin Arnold has that, too."

"We'll add that to our list," Lois's son said. "Thanks for your help, Aunt Matilda. Do you need a ride to the cemetery?"

"Oh, no. I'm here with the historical society. We'll all ride over together."

"Mother loved them like family." The woman wiped away tears that mingled with the rain on her thin face. "I know they'll miss her."

Peggy agreed, then hugged both adult children and the little boy before leaving them at the limousine. It wasn't such a terrible masquerade after all. Nothing to report on as far as the ring was concerned. Why was it such a mystery? If Lois knew it was hers, why had it been in the museum? And if it had been that valuable, why didn't her children know about it?

There was one missed call on her cell phone, which had been turned off during the funeral service. It was from Mai, no doubt wondering where the yew branches were. Peggy didn't bother answering. She'd just stop in and give her a progress report.

Glad she had driven to the funeral, Peggy made her way out of the procession headed for the cemetery. Lois's coffin had been taken to the hearse waiting to receive it. She was glad this part was over for the family. It probably wouldn't have helped the ME's office to keep her any longer. The family needed closure.

She remembered how terrible the wait had been after John had been killed. She didn't know if they were ever going to finish their work on his body. It was stupid, really. What had made John Lee special was gone forever. Burying him was just an afterthought. Yet it was all she could think of in the days that followed his death. The relief the phone call from Al brought when he'd called to say the funeral home had picked up John's body was like spring after winter. The details of observing life and death rituals could go on.

Peggy had never looked at the terrible marks left behind by the autopsy they'd done on John. She'd gone through the motions of laying him to rest without asking for more information than she could process. She'd known he'd been shot twice in the chest, one bullet nicking his heart, causing him to bleed to death before they could get him to the hospital. She didn't need to know more than that. Even that information had kept her from sleeping for weeks after he was gone.

Peggy decided to call Hunter, Sam's sister, and suggest

Lois's children might be in need of a good lawyer. Hunter was on the attack as soon as she saw Peggy's number on her cell phone. "You know the police are railroading that poor man," Hunter complained. "I can't believe you'd be a part of that."

"I'm not part of anything except the botanical part of the investigation into what happened to Lois at the lake. I was there when they questioned your client because I knew some information about what had happened."

"That makes you part of the problem, Peggy."

"Hunter, that man has gone to jail several times for stealing historic artifacts, including skulls he dug up in cemeteries. That's about as low-down as someone can get. You can't blame the police for thinking he could hurt Lois."

"But I can tell from your voice you don't believe it," Hunter said. "So, what gives? Tell me the superawful secret waiting to be discovered."

"If there is one, I haven't found it." Peggy considered Chief Mullis's behavior at the funeral. "Or at least I don't think I've found it."

"And you're not going to tell me any more than that?"

"No, not right now. Maybe when I know a little more. But I have another case you might be interested in." She told her about Lois's children. "Maybe you could help them."

"I think that might be a conflict of interest, since I'm representing the man the police believe killed their mother. But thanks for looking out for me. How's Sam doing with those rainwater things he's making? He's really enthusiastic about them."

"He seems to be doing very well. I suppose it's one way of looking positively at the drought."

"You mean there's always money to be made from any misfortune." Hunter laughed. "Spoken like a true capitalist."

Peggy had another call waiting, and told Hunter she'd

talk to her later. She looked at the number on her cell phone and almost didn't answer. It was her mother, doubtless complaining about her not going into the chief's house to look for historic artifacts. Finally she relented and pressed Talk.

"Margaret? This is your mother. I need your help." Lilla's voice was a frightened whisper on the phone.

"What's wrong? Where are you?"

"I'm at Lois Mullis's house. And before you start lecturing me about not being here, it's too late. I'm here, and there's no way to change that."

Peggy took a deep breath and caught hold of her temper. "All right. You're there, and there's nothing I can do about it. I've done some stupid things myself. What do you want me to do?"

"Get me out of here!" Lilla sounded frantic. "I'm stuck in a closet in Lois's bedroom. The ladies were supposed to distract Chief Mullis in case he came here, but we thought it would be unlikely, since he should be at the cemetery right now. I mean, who wouldn't be there for the rest of the service? She was his aunt. He shouldn't be here at all."

Peggy closed her eyes. Even though her mother was obviously scared and worried, her voice stayed low and modulated. "Okay. Calm down. Take a deep breath."

"Is that how you got through being trapped in a coffin that time? Your father told me all about it."

"You're not making this any easier, Mom. Why are you in the closet?"

"I heard someone come in the house, and thought I should hide. I think whoever it is might still be here. But it doesn't matter, because the door to the closet is stuck, and I can't push it open."

"It might be better if someone *is* still there," Peggy said. "I can't break into the house. You have the key and the alarm code. There's not a lot I can do besides calling the police."

"Well, for heaven's sake, call Paul if you have to call

someone. At least we can trust him to keep this a secret. I don't want your father to know, either. He's always going on about the historical society being a bad influence."

"In this case, I don't blame him." Peggy had started her truck and was turning toward Central Avenue. "But we can't call Paul."

"Why not? He's my grandson. I know he wouldn't mind coming over and getting me out."

"Because he's on duty and he'd have to log the call. We don't want him to get into any more trouble with the chief, do we?"

There was silence on the other end for a long moment before Lilla agreed she didn't want Paul to get into trouble. "But there has to be another way out."

Peggy frowned, thinking about it. If the chief was still there, he could charge her mother with trespassing, but that wouldn't be so bad. If he was gone, that option left with him. She could call the police and hope that during the confusion, she'd be able to sneak in and get her mother out of the house. But that was a long shot. "Start yelling and pounding on the door. If the chief is still there, he'll come and get you out."

"And arrest me!" Lilla was quite huffy on that matter. "Is something wrong with your brain today, Margaret? I don't want to go to jail."

"The most it would be is a misdemeanor. You can explain it to the judge, who'll probably be lenient since it's your first time."

"I'm attempting to be a good, upstanding member of my new community," her mother said. "I don't think a trespassing charge, even if it is a misdemeanor, will contribute to that."

"You should've thought of that before you did something so crazy!" Peggy almost bit her tongue talking to her mother that way, even if it was the truth. "I'm sorry, Mom. I'll see what I can do. But this is why I wouldn't do it myself. The ladies didn't want to get their hands dirty with it, either. Maybe Dad is right."

There was no answer, and an instant later her phone said the call had been dropped. Peggy closed her cell phone and put her foot down a little harder on the accelerator. Unfortunately, one of the problems with an electric truck was that it didn't take off the way an internal combustion engine would have. She had to poke down the Charlotte streets until she reached Central Avenue and the Plaza.

Anything could've happened, she considered as she wound her way to Lois's estate. Chief Mullis might've found her mother. That would be the best thing. Maybe Lilla finally managed to get out of the closet by herself. That would be equally good.

Peggy hoped her mother didn't call her father after talking to her, and she'd have to face him at the house as well. Ranson wasn't known for being subtle. He might get riled if he knew Chief Mullis was going to arrest his wife. It was almost enough to make her call Paul and take her chances. But she didn't want him involved unless there wasn't any other option.

Come on, Peggy, she urged her reluctant brain. *Think!*

She turned onto Lois's street and scanned the large house and drive for any signs of someone being there, but she didn't see even her mother's car. Lilla must've parked elsewhere and walked in. She was surprised her mother could be so devious.

But who had Lilla heard in the house? Peggy didn't think Chief Mullis would park up the street and walk back to check for intruders. The garage door was closed, but she knew the garage was filled with Lois's vehicles. Where *was* everyone?

She crept past the curve of the road. She could still see the house without being seen behind some barberry trees. It was unusual to find them in the city. Someone had to know their medicinal value. She tried again to call her mother.

There was no answer. Frustrated, Peggy considered that maybe her mother got out by herself and left. But that notion went away quickly as she saw her mother's car parked about two blocks down.

She tried her mother's number again. Still no response. As a possibility, she called her father and asked him if he'd heard from her mother.

"No. She's at that woman's funeral today, Sweet Pea," he replied. "I'm at the senior center playing chess. Is there a problem?"

"No, Dad. I was just going to ask her if she wanted Thai food for dinner on Tuesday. Steve and I found this great new place over on South Boulevard."

"You know your mother, Margaret Ann. She likes her rice and beans with a little Tabasco, but she's not much for Asian food."

"That's what I thought. I'll talk to you later, Dad." Peggy was eager to get off the phone with him. "Say hi to Mom if she calls."

"I will," Ranson began. "You know, something funny happened this morning . . ."

Peggy hated to do it, but she hung up. She clutched the cell phone in her hand as she tried to think what she should do next. Her mother still seemed to be trapped in the house, even though whoever had been there was gone. Maybe she had her phone turned off for fear the ring would give her away. There seemed to be no solution except to break into the house and get her mother out. She'd have to take her chances on getting caught.

Then something else came to mind. Just last week, someone had reported seeing a fire in the house two doors down from her. The older couple who lived there were in Barbados, and couldn't be reached. The fire department had to break in and make sure everything was all right.

Even as she was thinking about it, Peggy was dialing 911. She gave the woman the information about Lois's

house, then parked her car near her mother's and walked
back to the estate. With any luck, she'd be able to slip inside
while the fire department was checking for the fire, and get
her mother out. Without any luck, her mother would have to
be rescued by the fire department. She waited at the end of
the driveway and hoped her luck was good that day.

Less than five minutes later, a fire department truck and a
smaller vehicle came racing down the street, sirens and lights
flashing. Peggy moved out of the way for them and directed
the firemen to the spot in the house where she said she saw
smoke. The firemen walked around the house, frowning
when they couldn't find any sign of fire.

"Where did you say you saw smoke?" the department
commander asked.

"It was coming from the top and back of the house," she
told him. "Shouldn't you hurry in there? There are a lot of
valuable antiques in the house. I'd hate to see anything happen to them."

"The house has an alarm system," he continued. "If anything was wrong, it should've registered with the monitoring station."

She tapped her foot impatiently. Why was this so difficult? They hadn't stopped to ask so many questions at the
Misenheimers' house.

Before the commander could make a decision, Chief
Mullis pulled up in his truck, demanding to know what was
going on. The commander explained that Peggy had seen
smoke coming from the house.

"Really?" The chief glared at her. "And what, exactly,
are you doing here, Dr. Lee? It's a little far from your neigh-
borhood, isn't it?"

22

Goatsbeard

Botanical: *Aruncus dioicus*

The Roman philosopher Pliny named this shrub. It is a member of the rose family and related to spirea and meadowsweet. Goatsbeard blooms early in warmer climates, later during summer in cooler ones. The plant has thick spikes of white flowers, four to six feet tall, that rise above the leaves.

PEGGY LOOKED HIM IN THE eye. "I have friends all over Charlotte. I was driving by to visit one of them when I thought I saw smoke coming from the house. I did what any citizen would, and called 911. Better safe than sorry, that's what I always say."

Chief Mullis looked at her as though he wanted to call her a liar, but had no proof to base the accusation on. "You're a very good little citizen, aren't you, Dr. Lee?"

The commander stepped in. "We appreciate citizens like you," he told Peggy. "I don't see anything out here, but it would be a good idea to go through the house to be certain."

"That's probably what she wants," Mullis accused. "I caught her here once before with some friends of my aunt's."

"I don't think she's going to try anything with all of us here." The commander's words dripped with sarcasm. "In the meantime, if something *is* wrong in there, we're wasting time."

"I don't want her inside."

"That's up to you, Chief. I just need you to open the door so we can go inside." The commander shrugged beneath his heavy gear. "Or we can do it the hard way and I can have my boys break in the door."

The chief moved to unlock the door without any further prodding from the fire department. He glanced at the alarm. "I thought that was on."

Peggy started into the house behind the commander and two of the firefighters. Chief Mullis extended an arm to keep her out of the foyer. "I don't think they need your help. And I'd feel better if you stay out here."

"That's fine. I was just curious. No need to be hostile."

He rolled his eyes. "Hostile? You don't know the half of it. Someone from that stupid historical group has called me fifty times a day since Aunt Lois died. They've accused me of everything from killing her to inherit the property to purposely stealing their little historical things. Like they matter to me."

"You *do* inherit the property, Chief," she reminded him. "It wouldn't be the first time someone got anxious and didn't want to wait for their inheritance."

"Check with my cousins, if you like. Aunt Lois was all set up to move to a retirement community on the other side of town. There wasn't any reason for me to get impatient. If she hadn't died, we would've wrapped the whole thing up by now. Ask her kids. They hate me enough because of the estate. But they can't deny the whole thing was about to change anyway."

Maybe it was the way he was glaring at her. Maybe it was her involvement with the police that made her feel he was telling the truth. It would be easy enough to check. "What about the jewelry you're keeping from Lois's children? What about the historical artifacts that belong to the group?" She was surprised he'd bothered explaining at all. He didn't have to. "Why are you being so stubborn about giving her friends and relatives what should rightfully be theirs?"

"Not that it's any of your business," he rasped, "but I loved Aunt Lois. I made a mistake taking her out to the lake like that, but you notice who she turned to when she needed a ride. Her kids were never around for her. I don't think it'll hurt them to wonder if they'll get anything from her now that she's dead."

She nodded. "And the historical society?"

"Those ladies are *crazy*. Who can believe what they say belongs to them? I want someone responsible from the museum to come out and tell me what's supposed to be theirs."

Unfortunately, all of that sounded reasonable to her. Part of her brain was still concentrating on finding her mother and getting her out of the house. Maybe that was why it made sense. She didn't like the chief's attitude, but if what he said about Lois's children was true, she could understand the hard feelings between them.

"I really believe someone killed your aunt out at the lake." She shook her head as he began mentioning Snook. "Not him. He's a convenient scapegoat. But I think what happened had something to do with a carnelian ring."

She described the ring and finding the empty box in his aunt's purse. He listened intently without throwing out wisecracks every few seconds. "And where's this ring right now?"

"The ME's office gave it back to the museum. It technically has no value in the case against Snook. There were no unusual fingerprints on it. It seems harmless enough. But I think we're missing the bigger picture that involved it and may have been what made your aunt agree to the early morning excursion to the lake."

"You mean she was going to meet someone there and give them the ring?"

"Maybe. She definitely had the ring with her. It somehow ended up in the mud, just as she did. I think whoever met her there, someone she knew and trusted, killed her by giving her yew berries to eat."

The chief seemed to consider her words as he sat down on the concrete step outside the front door. "It seems like you have it all worked out. How do you know it wasn't me? I know that's what some people are saying."

"As far as I can tell, you have no interest in antiquities. You're also the kind of person who would've jumped in the mud after the ring. Whoever did this to your aunt left it in the mud. It obviously had value to him or her. Why didn't they go after it?"

"Like you did." He looked up at her. "Any suspects?"

"Not yet. I'm almost too busy running out to the lake and collecting yew branches to be able to formulate any possibilities."

"Have you considered Lois's son or daughter?"

"No. But I suppose you could check that out and see if they have alibis for that morning. It strikes me that one of them would've simply taken her out there if that were the case, but anything is possible."

The chief got to his feet as the commander and his men approached the open door. "We can't find any sign of smoke or fire in the house," the commander said. "I guess it's a false alarm. Sorry for the inconvenience."

"That's okay." Chief Mullis shook the commander's hand. "I got to hear a few things I needed to hear. Thanks for checking up on it."

"Sure thing." The commander frowned at Peggy. "I hope this isn't something you go around doing all the time."

"Not at all. I really thought there was an emergency situation in the house."

The commander nodded, and left without saying anything else. Chief Mullis turned to Peggy as the fire trucks were leaving. "What's this all about, Dr. Lee? Did you do this just to get me out here and tell me about this ring?"

"No. Actually, there's an emergency in your house, Chief. It's just not a fire emergency. I hope our new understanding is strong enough to weather what I have to tell you."

Peggy explained about the ladies from the historical society. Then she explained about her mother. "As far as I know, she's still trapped in your aunt's bedroom closet."

"I don't know whether to laugh or shoot both of you and all those other crazy women." He stared into the old house and took a deep breath. "Aunt Lois loved that group. I guess she was as crazy as the rest of them. Let's go save your mother."

Peggy followed him up the stairs in the huge old house. She could tell from the neglect in its care that Lois wasn't interested in it. Chief Mullis would probably get more use from the labyrinth of parlors and bedrooms than the previous owner.

"When I was a kid and my uncle was still alive, they had big parties here." The chief looked around the hall and touched the hand-carved banister with obvious pride. "I'd like the place to shine like that again. I still have two kids at home who'll have a blast exploring this old place."

He showed Peggy the large second-floor bedroom his aunt had occupied. Everything was done in a shade of rose, with roses on furniture, rugs, and drapes. The red was reflected from the light coming through the drapes into the room.

Peggy found the closet and tugged hard on the door until it opened. The space was nearly as big as many people's whole bedroom, and loaded with clothes, blankets, and other interesting paraphernalia. She didn't see any sign of her mother until she looked a little closer and saw size 5 feet to the left.

"Mom," she whispered, "it's me, Margaret. It's safe to come out now."

Her mother took a hesitant step forward and peeked between two large fur coats. "Is that really *you*, Margaret?"

"It's me, Mom. Let's go home before Dad misses you."

"How did you do it?" Lilla wondered as she stepped out of the closet. "How did you get in to let me out?"

"He helped me." Peggy nodded toward the chief, who was waiting outside the bedroom door.

"Have you lost your mind?" Lilla hissed. "He'll have us both arrested."

"I don't think so. It's okay. Let's just go."

Lilla watched Chief Mullis like a mouse watching a cat who's ready to pounce. She walked carefully around him to the stairs, the heels of her feet barely touching the carpet.

The chief smirked as he watched her head down the stairs and out the front door. "You owe me for this one, Dr. Lee. Make sure she didn't take anything. And tell the crazy ladies what I said about someone, *besides* one of them, coming over here to identify the artifacts they say are theirs. I'll hand them over to that representative."

"Chief Mullis, that's my mother you're accusing of stealing from you," she reminded him. "But I'll tell the ladies what you said. I'd expect to hear from the museum pretty quickly."

"I'll check on those alibis, ma'am. Let me know if you get any closer to formulating a theory on anyone else you think could be involved."

"I'll do that." She shook his hand and smiled at him. "But if those children aren't guilty of anything bad that happened to Lois, you should think about giving them what you know she'd want them to have, whether you believe they did right by her or not."

He nodded. "Yes, ma'am. I'll think about it."

LILLA WAS GONE WITHOUT A word by the time Peggy reached the area where their cars had been parked. It didn't matter, she thought as she drove away. It wasn't like she needed to be thanked for saving her own mother.

With no particular hurry about getting the yew branches to the university, she called Mai and told her she'd take the new bunch out to UNCC on Monday morning. Then she went home. Her feet were killing her even though her shoes were usually comfortable. She threw off her black suit, swearing she'd buy another. She promised the same thing after every funeral, but somehow it never happened.

She stepped into the shower. The hot water felt good, and her thoughts turned to calling Steve about dinner. Tomorrow was Sunday, and there was nothing pressing that had to be done. They could have a lazy morning together, and then she could go to the Potting Shed for a few hours. It would be nice to have a day off. At least what amounted to a day off for her.

She thought about what Chief Mullis had told her. Despite his family problems and his hard edge about his aunt, she believed he was a decent man. The ladies of the Shamrock Historical Society had already accused Jonathon and Snook of killing Lois. The chief was just another name to add to the list. Most of their ideas on the matter came more from emotion than fact.

Jonathon had been under suspicion because of his argument with Lois, which Peggy now knew to be valid. For whatever reason, Lois had taken the carnelian ring from the museum. If Jonathon was correct, she'd taken other items as well. That hardly seemed a killing offense to Peggy.

Snook could be a suspect. He had motive and opportunity, as well as Lois's pocketbook. She could understand why the police had taken him into custody for what happened to her. But the ring and the poison berries didn't make sense with him. No matter what, he'd be charged again with the theft of human remains and historical artifacts. But that didn't mean he was guilty of murder.

Chief Mullis was another good suspect. His trip out to the lake that morning with Lois was unusual and made his action suspicious. His aunt would've taken poison berries from him. But Peggy believed that if the chief had killed his aunt, they would never have found her body. She didn't believe a veteran police officer would be so sloppy. And she felt his remorse over leaving his aunt at the lake was sincere.

Who was left? If she didn't like any of the three of them for the crime, she wasn't sure where else to look. Jonathon or Chief Mullis could've given the old lady poison berries without her being suspicious. But she couldn't imagine either one of them choosing that as a way to get rid of her. Why not simply push her into the mud? Lois couldn't have fought either one of them.

There was also the ring to consider, as she had from the beginning. Now she felt certain Lois had expressly gone to the lake early to hand over that prize to someone. Snook could fit the bill for that act, although she couldn't imagine the history-proud grande dame doing that. Maybe she was returning it to Jonathon. Peggy couldn't see where the museum director could've threatened Lois to make her return the ring, but maybe she was missing something.

She looked at herself thoughtfully in the steamy mirror after she'd finished her shower. Her mostly white hair was down around her shoulders when it was wet. The marks of age and a life well lived were obvious on her face. She was lucky to have her mother's cheekbones and a good sense of humor. Sometimes she felt they were the only things that got her through life.

Now she was about to enter yet another unplanned phase of her life: getting engaged, and possibly married, again. Steve was wonderful. She loved him. She couldn't imagine anyone else fitting into her life the way he had for the past year.

She looked closer into her green eyes. Was it fair to offer Steve only half of the love she'd given John? She couldn't give more than that since the other half would always belong to John. A part of her would always love him, always need him. He had completed her in ways Steve would never understand.

There was a spark in her eyes that she'd thought was gone forever. She'd been wrong. Steve was going to be there for the next half of her life. She wasn't offering Steve less than she'd given John. There was still a heart full of love that beat inside of her. There was still warmth that met his, and times to be shared.

Being a botanist, she knew plants destroyed in a fire come back, sometimes fuller and richer. They have spores and tendrils that bring new life after they've cushioned their roots in the warm, soft ground.

I'm getting maudlin in my old age. She drew her hand across the mirror in front of her. No doubt it came from too much reflection and self-examination. She wasn't a plant, as much as she loved them. She was human. She lay in bed questioning if she would see the morning many times, as many other humans did. Sharing her life with Steve, despite all the difficulties she'd put in front of her, was going to be the next adventure in her life. They'd be happy together.

Peggy stepped out of the bathroom clutching a big purple towel to her. She gasped when she saw a hundred candles lit in the bedroom and her grandmother's silver tea tray filled with chocolate and strawberries on the bed. "I know you're here somewhere." She laughed and looked around the shadowed room.

Steve stepped close and kissed her. "I was wondering if

you were going to come out of there before all the candles melted away."

"You're a fast worker to get all this set up while I took a shower."

"Let's just leave it at I'm a fast worker." He took a small blue box out of his pocket and got down on one knee before her. "I love you, Peggy. Will you marry me?"

Tears sprang to her eyes as she opened the box and found a flower-shaped diamond engagement ring. The stone in the middle was a yellow diamond, and it was surrounded by petal-shaped pink diamonds. "I love you, too, Steve. And yes, I'll marry you. But maybe we should talk about the house . . ."

He got to his feet and smiled at her. "We probably should. But not right now."

Shakespeare whined outside the closed bedroom door and put his head down on his paws.

PEGGY AND STEVE SLEPT LATE the next morning and enjoyed a leisurely breakfast on the back patio. Despite the rain, the weather was still mild even as Halloween approached. It was as though they had skipped fall, and summer still clung to the misty tree branches.

Steve was reading an article about horse farms in the *Weekly Post* while Peggy looked through some textbooks on drought gardening that a friend had sent her. Shakespeare pranced like a puppy in the garden, looking for butterflies and daring frogs that crossed his path. He attacked a goatsbeard shrub that seemed to get his attention. Peggy called him away from it. The poor thing was having enough trouble surviving without a big dog jumping on it.

"It looks like you might be finished gathering yew branches," Steve said. "The police officially charged Snook Holt with second-degree murder. Apparently they feel it was unplanned."

"I don't know if they can make that stick," she remarked, "although violating his parole by stealing human bones can't look good on his record."

"He seems suspicious to me. They had a history together since she testified against him. I'd think he was guilty of hurting her, too."

There were a dozen reasons why Peggy disagreed, and she would've launched into them, but the phone rang. "Let me get this, and we'll talk."

Steve laughed as she walked away. Peggy answered the phone, surprised to hear Professor Burris on the other end of the line. "I hope I'm not disturbing you," he said. "I was wondering if you could meet with me this evening. I found a few interesting things about that ring you told me about."

"That sounds fine. Would you like to meet at the university?"

"No, I was thinking about the museum. Around seven? I have a friend you should meet."

Peggy agreed to the meeting, curious about Burris bringing a friend along. After going back out to the patio, she asked Steve if he'd like to go with her. "It might be boring. History people can run on sometimes."

"History people, huh? What about plant people?"

She nudged him hard with her foot. "Plant people? What about animal people? They can run on worse than anyone."

"I want to go, anyway. I don't have anything to do today except spend the day with you. What else do you have planned?"

"Maybe I'm planning to sit here in the sun all day."

"Not likely. I'm sure you must be planning some time at the Potting Shed." He smiled at her. "That's okay. I want to do that, too. Maybe Sam left some big, heavy bags of fertilizer or whatever else you stock there that I can move around. That way I'll feel useful."

"If I were you, I'd value my life too much to mess with

Sam's inventory. He knows where everything is in that store."

"Well, then, I'll have to think of something else to do. Maybe I can distract you from counting seeds and talking to your plants while you're there."

"I don't talk to my plants," she protested. "But maybe I can be distracted from counting seeds."

He laughed. "That's saying Sofia and Emil aren't at the Kozy Kettle. Because God knows there's some disaster story they can tell about a couple who spend too much time at their shop."

"No doubt." She took his hand. "We'll have to be very quiet."

Shakespeare whined and pranced around the patio. "I think he wants to go, too," Steve said. "That takes care of the quiet part."

23

Gourds

Botanical: *Cucurbita, lagenaria, luffa*

Gourds have been grown for thousands of years across the world. They are related to squash, melons, and pumpkins. They have been used for everything from cooking utensils to storage containers and in ornamental functions. The cucurbita are the colorful, ornamental gourds. These plants are distinguished by large orange or yellow blossoms that bloom during the day. The lagenaria group includes the birdhouse and dipper gourds. Lagenaria put forth white blossoms that bloom at night. Luffas have a tough, fibrous interior that is used as a sponge. They have vines with yellow blossoms and require a long growing season.

PEGGY TOOK STEVE WITH HER to meet Professor Burris at the history museum. They'd had a wonderful day together, uninterrupted by emergency vet phone calls or Emil and Sofia. Shakespeare had even been good while they were at the Potting Shed. These golden days were too rare not to be greatly appreciated.

Now she pointed out the box-cut yew bushes that lined one side of the museum building near the driveway. The evening shadows made it difficult to tell the difference between them and the boxwoods for many people, but Peggy had noticed them earlier.

"And they have them right out here in a public place even though they're poisonous?" Steve was amazed. "Why don't places like this have only safe plants?"

"People don't really think of plants as being safe or unsafe," she told him. "We plant them because they look good in a spot or because it's a sunny plant or a shade plant. Most people don't even realize a yew is poisonous."

"I guess I should know that from the number of animals I treat that are accidentally poisoned by chewing on some plant they shouldn't get into."

"Exactly. Children are the next most likely group to be poisoned by plants. But plant poisonings are high on the adult list as well."

They stopped talking about the yew as Professor Burris and a short, thin man with glasses that seemed to be too large for his face opened the front doors of the museum.

"Dr. Lee, you haven't met Stanly Hawkins." Professor Burris introduced the two. "Mr. Hawkins is the retired director of the museum."

Hawkins reached out to shake Peggy's hand. His grip was cold and weak. He pushed his glasses back on his nose to take a better look at her. "It's a pleasure to meet you, Dr. Lee. I've heard your name so many times from my friend here. Won't you come in?"

Peggy introduced the two men to Steve. She stumbled over naming him as her fiancé even though the flower-shaped ring gleamed on her finger. It would take some doing to get used to calling Steve the man she was going to marry.

The four of them sat down at a huge conference table that seemed to be little used. The conference room was almost pristine with its pale blue carpet and matching upholstery on the chairs. Good housekeeping, Peggy considered, not seeing a speck of dust anywhere in the room. Even more impressive, a tall ficus by the window was very well cared for. The soil looked as though it had been recently replaced, and the tree leaves were bright green and shiny.

"To bring the discussion up to where we are this evening," Professor Burris began, "let me begin where Dr. Lee and I met at her shop."

Peggy knew a lecture when she heard one. Not surprising, since Professor Burris had been teaching for a long time. Many of her colleagues knew only one way to relate information—lecturing as though it were a seminar. She interrupted as he took a breath to describe the plants she helped him purchase.

"What Professor Burris is trying to say is that I asked him about his experience with local historical artifacts." She withdrew a photo of the carnelian ring from her pocketbook. "This is the ring in question. No one seems to know what it is or where it came from. It's listed in the museum catalog as a carnelian ring circa 1863. I was hoping he would be able to tell me something about it."

Professor Burris cleared his throat to speak, but Hawkins had already picked up the photo. He exclaimed, "Of course! I know this ring very well. That teenager they hired to take my place at the museum would recognize it, too, if he'd ever taken the time to read my notes. I left specific notes behind on *every* artifact cataloged during my time here."

"Is it from the Civil War?" Peggy asked.

"Yes. It was one of four rings made with the emblem of one of the more prestigious companies to fight for the South. It was one of the last great efforts to commend the soldiers and their officers. The Confederacy ran out of money shortly after. It's the only such ring left, as far as I know."

"I don't know if you've been keeping up with Lois Mullis's death in the newspapers," Peggy said, "but I believe this ring may have played an important part in what happened to her."

"How is that possible? The ring has been here in the case for the last ten years." Hawkins peered at the photo again. "I thought Mrs. Mullis died at the lake."

Peggy explained how she'd come to have possession of the ring. "We're fairly sure Mrs. Mullis took the ring out of the case and, for whatever reason, transported it to the lake. She may have been killed for it."

"Oh, my goodness!" Hawkins took out a large white handkerchief and mopped his brow with it. "That's terrible! What is that new director thinking of, allowing artifacts to be checked out like this is the public library?"

"It wasn't exactly his fault. Jonathon accused Mrs. Mullis of stealing that ring and a few other pieces. His accusation was ignored, possibly because she sat on the board of directors. He was accused in turn of leaving the museum door unlocked and facilitating thefts from the museum."

"Yes. I suppose I could understand that. I wouldn't have allowed it in my time here, but things change." Hawkins shrugged. "I don't know what else I can tell you, Dr. Lee. I'm glad the ring was found."

"Did you know Mrs. Mullis?"

"Very well. She was an upstanding patron. Her husband was also a pillar of the museum. They both sat on the board for many years. It's difficult for me to imagine Mrs. Mullis doing anything of this nature." He paused and glanced at the three other people at the table. "Except, of course, for the feud."

"Feud?" Professor Burris leaned forward on his elbows. "That sounds interesting, Stanly. What feud is that?"

"Well, it started when we received the ring and several other artifacts, which were supposedly owned by the same officer in that regiment I mentioned. Unfortunately, the artifacts were unearthed in a field in South Carolina, where this group fought their final battle. Because of that, there's always been some question of which officer the artifacts, and the ring, belonged to."

"You mean all four families of the officers who received the matching rings all claimed it?" Peggy took out a pad of paper, preparing to write their names.

"Not exactly." Hawkins smiled in the quick, rabbitlike fashion of a man who's used to appeasing others. "There are only two remaining families of the four officers. The other two died in the 1900s. Our question came into play when another family, who also sat on the museum board, challenged the ownership of the ring."

"Only one?" Professor Burris shook his head. "Many fine Southern families were lost after the war."

"Yes," Hawkins continued. "The Waynewright family, Thomas and Agnes, were the other family. There was some debate between the families as to which officer the artifacts belonged to. Of course, since both families were heavy donors and important to the museum, we had to come up with a solution that would appease the Waynewrights and the Mullises."

"So there was a feud between these two families about the ring?" Steve summed up.

"Maybe not so much a feud," the retired museum director backtracked. "Perhaps that was the wrong terminology. It was more that both families believed they could claim ownership of the pieces, so neither would allow the ring to bear any name. We agreed to keep the artifacts and the ring anonymous."

"And did that help?" Peggy's mind was racing forward with the information.

"For the most part," Hawkins said. "There were occasional flare-ups. You have to understand and appreciate how important historical significance is to some families in this area. We can be very history-proud, and these pieces would've meant a great deal to either family if it could claim them."

"So Lois took the ring out of the case and had it in her pocketbook at the lake," Peggy thought out loud. "But Mrs.

Waynewright believed that ring was hers as well. She may have known from Jonathon that Lois had taken it."

"But certainly you aren't thinking that Agnes Waynewright would hurt Lois Mullis because of the ring, are you?" Hawkins asked with a nervous twitch near his eye. "I-I didn't realize what I had to tell you would be repeated."

"I'll try not to repeat it if I can help it," Peggy promised. "But this could be the missing information I've been looking for." She thanked the two men, and Steve got to his feet beside her. "I appreciate your time, Mr. Hawkins."

He stood quickly and came around the table to her. "Dr. Lee, you simply can't tell anyone about this disagreement between the two families. It could ruin the museum. That young pup they have running it won't know how to handle it."

"I'm sure Dr. Lee will do what's right with what you've told her," Professor Burris assured him. "No matter what, you could be an anonymous source, Stanly. Don't be so nervous. You aren't the director anymore."

Peggy asked to see the other artifacts claimed by both families. They weren't as impressive as the carnelian ring: an old canteen, a compass, and a belt in another case. As with the ring, there was no identification beyond that the artifacts had been found in South Carolina and had belonged to a Confederate officer.

Hawkins pointed out some hollow gourds in the case that had been found on the battlefield. "The same men probably used these, too. Their survival equipment was as important as their trappings of wealth and society."

When they had finished looking at the exhibit, Peggy thanked both men for meeting her there. Hawkins asked again about protecting what he'd told her. She promised nothing, but told him she'd do the best she could to keep him out of the fray.

When she and Steve were back in the truck, she tapped

her fingers on the steering wheel and thought about the possibilities. "Mrs. Waynewright still drives. But if she wanted the ring so badly, why didn't she go in the mud and get it?"

"Maybe she killed Lois, Lois dropped the ring, and Mrs. Waynewright thought it was lost in all that muck."

"But why kill her now?" Peggy started the truck. "They'd been at peace over it for some time, according to Mr. Hawkins. Why now?"

"Maybe because Lois stole the ring from the case." He shrugged and yawned. "How about if we talk about this over dinner? I'm starving."

They talked about the ring as they ate pizza and watched a rerun of an old movie they both liked. Peggy's mind was too busy with connecting all the dots for her to go right to bed at eleven, after the news. She went downstairs and spent some time on her experiments with Shakespeare at her feet.

She realized by two a.m. that she was going to have to pay Mrs. Waynewright a visit. She looked up the old lady's address on the Internet, recalling what Jonathon had said about picking her up last that fateful morning, then managed to go to bed and close her eyes until the alarm went off at six.

PEGGY GOT THROUGH BREAKFAST, eating as she bustled around the kitchen. She was bristling with anticipation of what she'd learn that day. The night had brought some clarity as she considered what role Mrs. Waynewright could've played in Lois's death.

"I hope you're going to call Paul or Mai to go with you," Steve said as he put his plate in the dishwasher. "I don't think you should go by yourself, in case this woman really poisoned someone over some old stuff."

"I'm just going over to talk to her, not accuse her. She's

at least eighty. She can't convince me to eat poison berries, so I think I'm safe."

Steve kissed her. "For my sake, and to keep me on schedule with my patients so I don't have to go with you, call a buddy. Okay?"

"Okay," she agreed. "I think Paul is off this morning. I'll give him a call. But honestly, if this attitude continues, I might have to find another fiancé who doesn't worry so much."

"If that's what you need to do"—he grinned wickedly—"be sure to put my ring in the mail."

"Is that all I mean to you—this ring?"

"That and all the hours of worry I didn't have before I met you. Look at my hair. I'm going gray."

She hugged him and kissed him again. "I promise not to do anything that will worry you. I love you."

"I love you, too. Just to be on the safe side, call me when you leave the Waynewright house."

She promised to call him, and waved as he pulled out of the drive. Fortunately, what he didn't know wouldn't hurt him or make him go gray. She knew Mrs. Waynewright was basically harmless. Besides, all she planned to do was talk to her about the family feud. Where was the harm in that?

As she was leaving, her mother pulled up to the house and jumped out of her car. "Margaret! Geneva got the most astonishing phone call late last night. The old museum director—his name escapes me right now—told her Mrs. Waynewright might be responsible for what happened to Lois. Can you believe it?"

"No." Peggy really couldn't believe it. This made matters much worse. There was no doubt in her mind that Geneva had called Mrs. Waynewright as well. How was she supposed to go in and talk to her?

"Are you on your way to the Potting Shed?" her mother asked.

"No. Not exactly. At least, not until later. Selena is opening this morning. I have some business I have to take care of."

"Great! Would you mind if I ride along with you? Your father wants to teach me to play some new game he's learned. It sounds like peanut butter."

"Pinochle," Peggy supplied. "You play other games. What's wrong with pinochle?"

"Ranson is becoming obsessed with games," Lilla complained. "He's at that senior center eight hours a day, playing one thing or another. Honestly, who thought he even liked playing games?"

Peggy didn't particularly want to hear her mother complain about her father. But Lilla might be just the ticket for talking to Mrs. Waynewright without arousing her suspicion. "Okay. I'm on my over to the Waynewright house. I have a few questions I want to ask Mrs. Waynewright."

"Oh, no! You aren't going after her about this thing with Lois, are you?"

"No, of course not." Lying to her mother was so much easier than lying to Steve. It might be because she'd had so much more practice at it. "I just need to know what she remembers from that day."

Lilla went along despite her misgivings. The ride between the two houses was short even in Monday morning traffic. The first thing Peggy noticed as she got out of the truck was the yew bushes on the east side of the house.

A lot of people had them, she told herself. That in itself wasn't cause for suspicion. If Mrs. Waynewright had wanted to use yew berries on Lois, she could've gotten them from the museum as well.

While she looked at the bushes, her mother was already at the front door of the impressive, redbrick, two-story house, ringing the bell. Peggy took a look around the yard, but everything was as it should be. The flower beds were perfectly mulched, though not a thing was blooming. The white trim on the house had recently been painted.

What was she looking for, anyway? Was she expecting a neon sign with an arrow pointing to Mrs. Waynewright's house that said I'M GUILTY? She shook her head and quickly joined her mother as the front door opened.

A young Hispanic woman ushered them inside. The foyer was dark and a little dreary, but in good shape. It smelled wonderful thanks to a huge vase filled with star lilies. A dour man with a white wig stared out from his portrait near the entrance to the front sitting room. Peggy felt his eyes on her, and shivered. Was this the mysterious Civil War ancestor who may or may not have owned the carnelian ring?

"Mrs. Waynewright!" her mother gushed when she saw the older woman. "Margaret and I wanted to pay you a visit after hearing that terrible gossip being spread about you. Geneva told me what that man had to say. Can you imagine the nerve?"

Peggy suppressed a smile, now actually glad she'd brought her mother along. There was no ice to break or tiptoeing around the subject. "Yes, Mrs. Waynewright. This is a terrible thing."

Agnes Waynewright sat stiffly in a nineteenth-century pecan rocking chair with excellent handwrought scrollwork on the arms and back. Her lap was covered by a blue crocheted blanket. She didn't acknowledge them until they'd stood before her for several long moments. Finally she looked up. Her gray eyes were distant and foggy.

"Are you all right?" Lilla asked her.

"I'm quite all right," she replied in a cold voice. She brought the biggest pistol Peggy had ever seen from under the blanket. "It's you who should look to your own well-being."

"That's interesting. An 1851 Colt revolver. Thirty-six caliber, if I'm not mistaken. I've never seen one in person." Lilla took a quick step back and threw up her hands. "I can leave if that's better for you. I didn't mean to cause you any anxiety."

"I think you should both sit down over there on the settee." Agnes Waynewright waved the gun at them.

Peggy realized this wasn't a game—and, worse, just because the pistol was old didn't mean it wouldn't kill one of them. There was no doubt in her mind that the old lady couldn't shoot both of them, but she really didn't want to make a choice on which one that would be. "Mrs. Waynewright, this won't help. If you're responsible for Lois's death—"

"Responsible?" The old lady cackled, near hysteria. "I *killed* Lois Mullis. I did what was necessary for the family honor. It was the least I could do for my great-great grandfather. All this time I've let it go that Lois had taken what was rightfully mine. And those men at the museum didn't understand. They know nothing of honor and pride."

"But why kill her now?" Peggy pushed, then bit her lip. This might not be the best time for answers. She glanced around the room, hoping the young Hispanic woman was watching, but she didn't see her.

"You're right, of course. I should've done it years ago. It seemed the best for all involved if my great-great-grandfather's ring was kept locked away at the museum, even if it didn't bear his name. Then Lois took it and began taunting me with it. She told me she'd meet me early at the lake and let me see it. It was simple to put the yew berries into a plastic bag and offer her some. How was I to know she'd fall into the mud with the ring?"

Lilla choked. "So you *really* did kill her? I can't believe it."

"It doesn't matter. Everyone will know now, since that fool of a museum director can't keep his mouth shut. My name will be in the newspaper. My mother would die of shame. A lady *never* has her name in the newspaper."

"Did you get the yew berries from your bushes outside?" Peggy asked as she saw Mrs. Waynewright was complacent about being caught.

"Yes. Seeing them that morning inspired me. I almost didn't go through with it. Then Lois didn't want me to touch the ring. Imagine! My own ancestor's ring. Like her great-great-grandfather would've been awarded such a prize. He had to *buy* his commission, you know. What kind of gentleman does that?"

She went very quiet then, and the gun drifted into her lap. Lilla looked at her daughter. "What do we do now?" she whispered. "You do this kind of thing all the time. Should we take the gun from her or call 911?"

"I think we should do both." Peggy got to her feet. "We may need an ambulance as well."

"I'll make the phone call. You take the gun."

Peggy went over and put her hand on the old gun. She thought it probably wasn't loaded, but she was wrong. The bullets were of a size that would've done some serious damage.

The old lady's hand was like ice. She looked up as Peggy gently took the gun. "People don't understand about honor anymore. If we'd been men, we could've dueled for the artifacts and the ring. It would've been so much more glorious. Honor would've been satisfied."

Peggy didn't know what to say. She took the gun and walked away.

Epilogue

PEGGY AND STEVE WERE THE last ones to arrive at Sir Edmund Halley's Restaurant and Freehouse behind the Park Road Shopping Center. Steve had come from a last-minute emergency involving a guinea pig stuck in his food bowl, and Peggy had come from her first drought workshop. They'd met in the parking lot.

"How'd it go?" Steve asked her.

"Great! We had a packed house. All those nice ladies from the Shamrock Historical Society brought their friends and neighbors. They listened to what I had to say, then bought everything I had that related to plants and dry weather. Sam sold five new water reclamation units."

"Excellent!" Steve took her hand. "Are we ready for this?"

"Yes. I've thought of almost nothing else the last few days. I'm ready."

"I'm amazed you could squeeze me in between drought perennials and catching killers. You must really care about me."

She kissed him right there in the parking lot. "I care a lot, sir."

"Then let's face the music." He smiled as they began walking toward the restaurant.

A sizable crowd had gathered by the time they walked through the front door. Peggy's father jumped to his feet and raised his glass of Guinness to the couple when he saw them. "To Margaret and Steve!"

The rest of the group joined him in the toast that brought tears to Peggy's eyes. Everyone who mattered had managed to be there. Paul had his arm around Mai. Jonathon raised his glass with his left hand, his right hand captured by a pretty brunette.

The Shamrock Historical Society was trying to teach Al and his wife, Mary, how to dance the way they had a hundred years ago. There was even a bagpiper whose music contrasted sharply with the background sounds.

"We thought you'd decided to elope," Peggy's mother said. "Where were you?"

"Don't answer that," her father advised. "No more personal questions. You two go off and do whatever you feel like doing. You're adults. You've earned it."

Steve's friend Skipper introduced his wife, Barbara, to Peggy. "Don't pay any attention to whatever she tells you I do wrong," he said. "Steve will back me up that I'm nearly perfect."

Barbara shook Peggy's hand and kissed Steve's cheek. "You're not, but Steve is. Congratulations, Peggy. I know the two of you will be very happy together."

A few of the women coaxed their male escorts out on the dance floor and convinced the bagpiper to play something romantic. Steve took Peggy's hand and drew her to the dance floor, not needing to be coaxed. "This looks pretty good, huh? Is there some old Southern folklore about a good engagement party leading to a good marriage?"

"I think there is. Especially for us." She smiled up at him and closed her eyes. It was going to be all right, she realized, accepting the wishes for future happiness. She had turned the page.

Peggy's
Garden Journal

✹

Fall / drought

All of North Carolina has been stuck in a drought for more
than a year. Historically, it was too soon for another drought
for us, since we just had one in 2002. The weather patterns
seem to be changing, not just here but in other places across
the world. Water is becoming a much more valuable resource than any of us had ever thought. The days of taking
it for granted are over.

As gardeners, we're aware that planting in our yards
may not be as important as farmers' food crops and drink-
ing water. But that doesn't mean we want to give up what
we love. We have to be smarter, and choose vegetables,
fruits, and ornamentals that will weather drier conditions.
Many times, this is only a matter of planting natives that
are used to changes our areas have seen for many years.
These plants are tough and have seen droughts before.

We can help them by using better soils and mulching to
protect them from the sun and help them to better use the
water we give them.

I hope you'll find the information in this journal useful for your own gardens.

Happy gardening!

Drought-resistant perennials

Perennials are a favorite in any garden. They are hardier than annuals in most cases, and they come back year after year.

Some drought-resistant perennials that sip water and still keep going are yucca, asters, geraniums, daylilies, and Shasta daisies. Most herbs don't require much moisture so long as they are mulched well. Liatris, black-eyed Susan, sunflowers, and poppies are all drought-hardy plants.

Increase your chances of success

To increase your chances of a successful summer garden, despite a lack of rain, try these suggestions:

- Apply water slowly to the bases of plants. This will reduce water usage by half.

- Check soil moisture regularly. If soil clumps together, it is moist and doesn't need water.

- Water in the morning, when temperatures are cool, for less moisture loss. Evaporation accounts for 75 percent of moisture loss in the afternoon.

- Mulch your garden to minimize moisture loss from the soil surface. Use an organic mulch at least one inch deep. Grass clippings make a great mulch for your garden. Apply fresh clippings in thin layers (up to 1/4 inch thick) and allow each layer to dry before adding more.

- Black or colored plastic will conserve moisture and increase soil temperature. Lay down plastic early in the season.

- Avoid vegetables like beans, sweet corn, melons, squash, and cucumbers. They are heavy water users.

- Grow only what you need. One or two tomato plants can yield enough tomatoes for a family.

- Consider planting a couple of containers with vegetables. Containers are easier to water by hand if that becomes necessary.

- Buy prepared soil with hydrogel crystals to conserve water in the soil.

- Grass is not always the best ground cover during dry spells. Try ivy, periwinkle, or clover. These plants and others will cover your yard and are able to survive drought times.

- Talk to local agriculture officials to learn about plants that are native to your area. Be sure to buy them from garden centers rather than rip them out from alongside the road, so the plant continues in the wild.

Be creative!

Catch water in a barrel or trash can when it rains. Save water that runs while you're waiting for hot water from the tap. Save water from showers that would otherwise go down the drain. Check to see if your area allows "gray water" from baths and dishwater to be used on plants during droughts.

Links to help get you through the drought

www.eartheasy.com/grow_xeriscape.htm
http://landscaping.about.com/cs/cheaplandscaping1/a/
    xeriscaping.htm
www.arts4all.com/elca/page3.html
www.thisoldhouse.com/toh/photos/0,,1213573,00.html

A nice place to visit: The Creative Little Garden

The Creative Little Garden is a great place to visit if you're
in New York City and looking for a nice green spot in the
midst of all that concrete. It's located on East Sixth Street,
between Avenues A and B. The garden has been here in the
East Village for twenty-five years. It is a community garden
tended by volunteers who collaborate on the landscaping.
Take a peek at www.creativelittlegarden.org.

Turn the page for a preview of the next book
in the Renaissance Faire Mysteries
by Joyce and Jim Lavene . . .

Ghastly Glass

Coming soon from Berkley Prime Crime!

"HEAR YE! HEAR YE! DEATH stalks the streets of Renaissance Village. Run for your lives."

"Would it hurt him to add some inflection?" A fairy, waiting in the costume line ahead of me, rolled her eyes and watched the Village crier go by on the cobblestone street.

"I'll add some inflection, Dearie," the little man in the dwarf costume responded as he walked by, "when *you* take some acting lessons."

Standing between them was making me nervous. The Black Dwarf, alias Marcus Fleck, was holding a long pole with a swinging lantern on one end. It was pointed at me instead of the fairy.

"Acting lessons?" the fairy shot back, her translucent wings quivering. "I've been in dinner theaters across the South."

He snorted. "So has roast beef. What's your point?"

The fairy (I'm not sure if I know her. Fairies all look the same to me) made a noise somewhere between a screech and a howl. "I'll show you my point, little man!" She threatened the dwarf, long, red fingernails poised in his direction.

I was still standing between them. "Could you take this somewhere else?" I was hoping for a quick resolution to the problem since it looked like rain and I was still a good twenty minutes from the inside of the costume shop.

This was the first year that Renaissance Village in Myrtle Beach was decking itself out for Halloween. I'd wrangled and made promises to everyone but the devil to be here for an eight-week sabbatical to continue my research on Renaissance crafts. Of course, I could've done it next summer, and probably still will, but I *really* wanted to be there for Halloween. I'd heard terrible tales of all the fantastic stuff the Village theme makers had lined up for the season. I couldn't wait!

"Jessie!" A former student of mine at the University of South Carolina at Columbia, where I was teaching and working on my PhD, hailed me. Debby had dropped out during the last semester to work here full-time. Some people came to the Village and couldn't go home again. "I was wondering when you were going to get here. We're roomies!"

She hugged me, and I absently patted her shoulder. I looked around at the crowds of actors and students ready to trade in their traditional Renaissance Village garb of knaves, varlets, wenches, and ladies for their special Halloween costumes.

I'd hoped to see Chase here. Actually, I'd hoped he'd be waiting at the gate with breathless anticipation for my arrival. He was the Village bailiff but also my main man since July. I hadn't seen him in a few weeks. Those promises and commitments to be here for the next two months had really dragged me down for awhile. But I was firm in my determination that he was probably, *hopefully*, still my man. You never know for sure. A few weeks can be a lifetime.

I was hoping not to need a roomie or Village housing because I'd be staying with Chase. But maybe not. I wouldn't know for sure until I saw him, hopefully not wrapped around some smug little fairy or one of the storybook characters that inhabited this full-time Renaissance Village.

"I'm glad to see you, too." I smiled at Debby. The line for costumes had moved closer to the shop and the Black Dwarf had moved on with his cheery message.

But in fact, the Village crier was right about Death stalking the Village. I was looking right at him. He seemed to be following the Black Dwarf, complete with black robe and huge scythe. He was Death incarnate. He was tall, too. Or on stilts.

Debby laughed at me as I couldn't take my eyes from the character. "You just got here, right? Let me introduce Ross, or as we like to call him, Mr. Big." She turned to the spectacularly frightening figure of Death. "Ross DeMilo, meet my good friend, Jessie Morton, of late apprenticed to Mary Shift at Wicked Weaves. Jessie, this is Ross. And he's gonna get you if you don't watch out."

Ross pulled back his black hood, frowning at me. His brown hair was greased back from his narrow, skull-shaped face. He wasn't on stilts. He was just tall and thin, his ribs showing beneath his black Renaissance Village T-shirt.

"Welcome to Renaissance Village, a horrible place to live but a worse place to die. I am Death, the original dark stalker. My scythe will separate your body from your soul."

As terrifying speeches went, it was pretty good. He had a deep, John Carradine voice that added a certain monster charm that worked even in the bright September sunshine. I didn't want to think what it would do after dark.

"Hi. That's a great costume." I smiled at him. He scowled at me. Then he moved away, mingling with the crowd. I turned to Debby, who was in a red wench's costume. "Where's your scary outfit? I thought everyone was dressing up."

"Today's the last day to turn in your non-Halloween costume for the scary one." She shrugged. "I figure why do anything right away when you can wait until the last minute? There are plenty of people who say they aren't dressing up for Halloween. Robin Hood and the Merry Men aren't into it, and some of the Craft Guild. They want the dancing girls at the Caravan Stage to dress up like witches. Kind of corny, huh?"

I should mention that a lot of people here take their roles at Renaissance Village very seriously. They live and work here full-time, and sometimes get a little weird. Robin and his Merry Men tend to be that way more than most, since they hang out in Sherwood Forest together, dispatching brigands and stealing toaster ovens from the rich to give to the poor.

"How do the people from Adventure Land feel about people *not* dressing up?" I looked around at the milling crowd of residents and visitors. Adventure Land is the owner of the Village, and supposedly dictates the rules and regulations. "Has Robin told Livy and Harry about this?"

"You are behind the times, I fear, Good Lady. Queen Olivia and King Harold are on the royal outs. Neither one is taking visitors or problems. It looks as though they're leaving that to our good bailiff, Chase Manhattan. Methinks you know of him. Tall fellow who has shoulders like a Viking and tends to be good at most sporting events?"

Yeah. I know him. I glanced around as the crowd continued to form outside the costume keeper's shop, hoping to see his handsome, smiling face. No such luck.

I stood in line behind the fairy, talking to Debby about her full-time life at the Village. I was surprised she wasn't living with Fred, the red dragon, but she laughed when I mentioned it. "You were so right about not getting involved with any of these guys on a permanent basis, Jessie. I'm over Fred. Now I'm seeing the new blacksmith. His name is Hans von Rupp. He's from Latvaria or Germany. Somewhere in Europe. He's *big*, too." She giggled. "All over. He can lift me with one arm and . . ."

"Sounds like fun." I cut her off, not wanting to hear so much that my ears started bleeding. Why do people always feel like they have to give you more information than you need?

I wished I could just ask if she'd seen Chase with Little Miss Muffet or one of the underdressed woodland creatures. I couldn't. I wasn't willing to sound that needy. I was really sure everything was fine, anyway. It was only a few weeks. No reason to panic just because I'd been here an hour already, and hadn't seen him.

The fairy in front of me was at the window where Portia the costume keeper handed out apparel to those of us who didn't own the costumes we wore every day. "I hope I'm not going to be one of those dead people walking around," the fairy told Portia. "I didn't come all the way from Texas to be a zombie."

Portia put a gauzy, gray garment in front of her. "All fairies are wraiths for the duration of the Halloween season. Please turn in your wings when you exchange costumes. Wraiths do *not* fly in the Village."

"What? This is big and long," the fairy complained. "My legs are my best feature. I can't work like this."

"Then go back to Texas," Portia recommended, sounding tired, as always. "Next?"

Debby smiled at the unhappy fairy-wraith. "Look at it this way, wraiths don't have to wash their hair or dye it. You'll save time and money during the next few weeks."

The fairy, about to turn wraith, hissed at Debby. "Stay out of my way, or I'll take you straight to hell."

Like I said, an intense group of people. While Debby and the fairy-wraith argued about what the other deserved, I stepped up to the window and smiled at Portia. "This is exciting, huh? The first Halloween in Renaissance Village. I've really looked forward to it."

She glanced at me. "Where are you working, Julie?"

"Jessie." I smiled again. It hadn't been *that* long. What was wrong with everyone? How could they all just forget me? "I'm apprenticing at The Glass Gryphon until Halloween. What kind of costume do you have cooked up for me?"

Portia yawned. Her graying black hair was pulled starkly away from her thin face. "Craft Guild has a choice between ghosts and witches."

Ghosts and witches? Neither one sounded appealing. "What does the ghost costume look like?"

"If I take it out, it's yours for the duration. I'm not dragging costumes out for everyone to look over at this point. Ghost or witch?"

I tried to imagine which one would be less likely to catch on fire, since, as an apprentice glassblower, I'd be working with flame. I tend to have a little bad luck when it comes to my apprenticeships. I didn't want to catch on fire, no matter how memorable that might seem to some diehard Ren-Faire visitors.

"Ghost. I look better in white."

Portia lifted a black costume complete with pointed hat. "Sorry. Fresh out. Try back the beginning of the week. Good to have you back. Enjoy your stay."

Was it just me, or did everyone seem to have a bad attitude about this venture? Where was the spirit? Where was the excitement?

"Next." Portia looked past me at Debby. "All bawdy wenches are the undead."

"The undead what?" Debby demanded. "You mean vampires? Or zombies?"

"I'll see you later." I tactfully sneaked away before it got any worse. This visit to Renaissance Village wasn't turning out the way I'd envisioned. No Chase. No excitement. I was disappointed, to say the least.

"Greetings, Good Lady!" A handsome lord doffed his

large, feathered hat in a deep bow. "Might you be the apprentice for The Glass Gryphon?"

My heart sped up a little when I took in the excellent attributes that even his lordly apparel couldn't hide. His hair was thick, chestnut brown, gleaming with red highlights in the sun. His smiling blue eyes looked me over from the tight jeans to the low-neck green sweater I'd worn for Chase, who wasn't around to appreciate me. All in all, a sweet welcome package.

"I'm Jessie Morton, Good Sir. Who might you be?" I dropped him a little curtsy that showed off a couple of my attributes.

"I am Henry Trent, nephew of Roger Trent, owner of The Glass Gryphon. My uncle sent me to meet you and escort you through the Village to the shop. Are you ready to go?"

I knew I should get my bag from the car and settle in with Debby, but this seemed a good opportunity to meet Roger again and go over my responsibilities as an apprentice. You had to be careful in the Village, or the craftsman you served would have you running errands and picking up his laundry from the lovely washer women instead of learning the craft. Since I'm already working on my dissertation, which I hope will become a book someday, my research here has become very important to me. I've titled my dissertation "Proliferation of Renaissance Crafts in Modern Times."

I've already apprenticed with a Gullah basket weaver at Wicked Weaves and Master Archer Simmons at The Feathered Shaft. This time it's glassblowing. Who knows what it will be next summer? I've talked to a few other Craft Guild members, including The Hands of Time clock shop and Pope's Pots pottery. I'm ready for anything.

Especially if a good-looking man comes along with the project. It can't hurt. "Lead on, Good Sir."

Henry swept me another elegant bow, then took my hand

and laid it on his forearm as we started walking through
Renaissance Village.

The Village is situated where the Myrtle Beach Air
Force Base was before it closed down. Most of the shops
have living quarters above them for the full-time merchants.
The rest of the space is filled with part-timers like me,
about three hundred of them at any given time.

Unlike most Renaissance faires, this one goes on every
day except Christmas. It's open from morning to evening
seven days a week with the King's Feast held at the castle
every Sunday night. Hundreds of thousands of visitors
come through the main gate every year to be delighted and
swept back in time with Shakespeare walking the cobblestone streets reciting odes, King Arthur retrieving Excali-
bur from the stone every two hours, and fantasy creatures
ready to have their picture taken. The experience is nonstop
fun, excitement, and good food. Adventure Land, the parent company, says it will be so, and it is.

"How was your trip to the Village, My Lady?" Henry
asked as we walked past the first fountain toward the hatchet-
throwing contest.

"It went well, thank you. How is your uncle?" The monks
were chanting in the Monastery Bakery, usually a good
sign because it meant they were baking instead of getting
into various kinds of trouble. Their bread is to die for, but
their quasi religion of the Brotherhood of the Sheaf is a little strange.

"My uncle is quite well. I am here visiting him because I
am opening another shop for him outside the Village."
Henry smiled at me, his big blue eyes crinkling at the corners. I *love* men with crinkly eyes.

We were passing the elegant houses on Squire's Lane,
which are eclipsed only by the sight of the castle rising
above Mirror Lake, where the pirates live. There was loud
laughter from Peter's Pub, a favorite of Village residents
after hours. It was a good crowd for a Monday.

Lady Godiva rode by with her bodysuit and butt-length blond wig. I didn't have to look closely to see that Arlene, the last Lady Godiva, had been replaced. Everything here was transitory. People came and went all the time. Even shops and restaurants changed from time to time. Nothing like a real Renaissance village, where the same families lived and died for generations.

"Hail to thee, Mistress Jessica!" Alex, one of Robin Hood's Merry Men (and a former summer love) walked by us quickly. "I see you have selected a new gentleman friend."

I knew this was a jab at the many years I had been coming to the Village and seemed to find a new love interest each time. I wanted to set that rumor to rest before he spread it everywhere. "I'm working with Henry and Roger during the Halloween season. That's it."

Alex laughed, nearly unsettling his forest green hat from his blond head. "Of course, Good Lady. Who would think otherwise?"

I was about to protest when Henry swept me into his arms and planted his mouth on mine. It was only an instant before he set me back on my feet. *All right.* I said he was interesting. But not *that* interesting. At least not within the first twenty minutes of meeting him.

I was about to wipe the grin from both their faces when someone behind me cleared their throat. I didn't have to look. It was Chase, of course. He might not have been there to greet me in the first hour, when I didn't do anything but look for him. But he managed to be there for the split second I got into trouble. Why do things like this always happen to me?

All four of us stood there like time really had stopped, as they say in the ads for the Village. I guess Alex and Henry were waiting to see what would happen next. It suddenly occurred to me that Henry may have been in the Village long enough to know about me and Chase. Had he seen

Chase coming as I spoke to Alex and purposely tried to break us up? I didn't want to judge him right away, but my relationship with Chase could be on the line.

Without hesitating (any further), I hauled back and slapped Henry. His head jerked back, and he looked at me with real hurt in his eyes. "Sorry, My Lady. I could not resist your tempting lips a moment longer."

I glared at Alex. He laughed, and trotted off toward Sherwood Forest. I turned my attention back to Henry who was still standing there. "I'll meet you and your uncle at The Glass Gryphon shortly. Please give him my regards while I take care of another matter."

Henry bowed, seemingly chastened, but the evil little smile on his face told me otherwise. "I will take your message to my uncle." He nodded at Chase. "Good day to you, Bailiff."

When we were finally alone (except for the hundreds of visitors, wandering knaves, and a few serfs), I turned to Chase. "Hi, there."

"Hi." He was staring at me in an un-Chaselike way. Normally he'd be running up, throwing me in the air (not a small task, since I'm six feet tall and not at all waiflike). There was no big grin on his handsome face, no big kiss coming my way.

I couldn't decide which course would be better. You know how sometimes when you defend yourself it makes you seem guiltier than when you keep your mouth shut? I didn't know which way to go with this. No matter what, it was only a stupid kiss. How upset could he be?

Before I could really ascertain if he was upset or not, a varlet, now dressed all in black instead of varlet brown, came running up breathlessly. "Bailiff! It's happened again! Except this time it's Death."

Chase frowned. "What are you talking about, Lonnie? Did another visitor collapse?"

"No. It's Death. Really."

"You mean another one died?"

"No. Really, Chase. Death died."

"I think he's talking about Ross." I pushed into the conversation before I had to hit either one of them. "You know, the tall guy with the scythe."

Chase glanced at me like he'd forgotten I was there. "Oh, yeah. Where is he?"

"In the Village Square. One minute he was threatening a few visitors and telling them he'd take their souls, and the next minute, boom! He was on the cobblestones for the count."

"Let's go," Chase said.

"Me, too." I started running after him. "Have visitors died in the Village? How did I miss that?"

"Too busy, I guess," Chase returned as we cut through the alleyway between Squire's Lane and Harriet's Hat House. "Too busy to watch CNN, or call anyone."

"CNN was down here covering visitor deaths?" How did I miss that?

"Yep." Lonnie's little ratlike face twisted up as we ran across the cobblestones. "That's why I left Sir Latte's Beanery. Chase needs all the help he can get."

"So what killed them? It was probably the heat, right? Lots of visitors wear those heavy clothes and get heat stroke during the summer." I looked from Chase to Lonnie.

"We don't know for sure yet," Chase finally answered.

A large crowd of visitors and residents had gathered near the Good Luck Fountain right in the middle of the Village Square. I stayed with Chase, almost having to push Lonnie out of the way, as we broke through the crowd to take a look at the man on the ground.

Ross's black robe had fallen open around his bony body, but his hood covered his face. The scythe lay beside him, not far from his reach. There was blood everywhere and something sticking out of his chest. Everyone was whispering around us as Chase knelt beside the giant's form.

"Call the police," Chase said finally. "He's dead. And I don't think it's heat stroke."